PRAISE FOR *MAIDEN VOYAGE*:

"Bass gracefully blends the coming-of-age tale of one boy with that of an entire society."
—*Publishers Weekly*

"Refreshing . . . I longed to know more about the fate of some of its characters even as I chewed over the moral."
—*Contra Costa Times*

"Cynthia Bass is exceptionally skilled at . . . converting historical backdrops into stunning fiction."
—*Between the Lines*

"Reflects the glamour of the luxury liner and has all the suspense and harrowing detail expected in a first-person account of the shipwreck . . ."
—*School Library Journal*

ALSO BY CYNTHIA BASS

Sherman's March

BANTAM BOOKS

New York   Toronto   London   Sydney   Auckland

MAIDEN VOYAGE

CYNTHIA BASS

MAIDEN VOYAGE

A Bantam Book

PUBLISHING HISTORY

Previously published in hardcover by Villard Books 1996

Bantam trade paperback edition / June 1997

BOOK DESIGN BY GLEN M. EDELSTEIN

Library of Congress Cataloging-in-Publication Data

Bass, Cynthia.

Maiden voyage / Cynthia Bass. — 1st ed.

p.   cm.

ISBN 0-553-37889-9 (pbk.)

1. Titanic (Steamship)—Fiction.   I. Title.

PS3552.A816M35   1997

813'.54—dc20   96-44921

CIP

Published simultaneously in the United States and Canada

Bantam Books are published by Bantam Books, a division of Bantam Doubleday Dell Publishing
Group, Inc. Its trademark, consisting of the words "Bantam Books" and the portrayal of a
rooster, is Registered in U.S. Patent and Trademark Office and in other countries. Marca Regis-
trada. Bantam Books, 1540 Broadway, New York, New York 10036.

PRINTED IN THE UNITED STATES OF AMERICA

BVG   10 9 8 7 6 5 4 3 2 1

FOR

STEVE

The many men, so beautiful!
And they all dead did lie:
And a thousand thousand slimy things
Lived on; and so did I.

The Rime of the Ancient Mariner

PROLOGUE

OTHER BELIEVED STORIES FROM HISTORY WERE IMPORTANT. I grew up with fables of heroes and martyrs—of people who never bargained with fate or argued with God, people who did the right thing without qualm or question, scruple or doubt. She told me about Leonidas, the perfect death for a soldier; Joan of Arc, the perfect death for a saint; she told me about the great American patriots—John Paul Jones, Harriet Tubman, Charles Sumner—scorning danger and capture, hazard and pain. They were stories she loved to tell me, stories I loved to hear—powerful stories, stories of valor and honor, of conscience rewarded and moral strength. And they always seemed, even though they were stories from history, also to be, in a secret and special and wonderful way, stories about me.

But this habit of seeing myself in historical sagas of grandeur and courage proved, in the end, a hellish and woeful mistake. For my personal story from history is very different from those I grew up with. It is the story of my journey across the Atlantic on the maiden voyage of the *Titanic*. And unlike Leonidas at the pass, Saint Joan in flames, the great abolitionist Sumner on the floor of the U.S. Senate, I cringed. I flinched, I faltered, I ran. The truth is, I *survived*.

Of all of those stories whose heroes I failed to live up to, it was the Sumner story which hurt the worst. Because Senator Sumner embodied everything—conscience, conspicuous virtue, honor, and public martyrdom—that I yearned for. Plus we both were American, we both were men of the modern era, we both came from Boston, had the same sort of families, the same sort of interests, the same sort of politics . . . we shared so much.

I first discovered the full story of Senator Sumner in a history book in the family library. I was just eight years old. My mother and older sisters were holding a suffragists' meeting in the parlor, and, as usual, I had been greeted by everyone, smiled at vaguely, and then forgotten. I wandered into the library, plucked a book from an upper shelf, and began skimming its crowded pages. I was listening to the women's voices, wishing I were with them, trying to overhear them—not really concentrating. Then, suddenly, I came across something I had never known about Senator Charles Sumner. I remember sitting up very straight, very stiff, in the high hard-backed chair, reading and rereading, word after word, very slowly.

According to this book—Franklin's *Annotated Documents of the War Between the States, Volume One*—on the nineteenth of May, 1856, Charles Sumner of the Commonwealth of Massachusetts had risen before the U.S. Senate to deliver what historians still consider the single most stunning oration of the antebellum period. In that speech Sumner had railed for *three solid hours* against slavery, calling it a "Harlot"—a word I didn't recognize, but sensed was forbidden and thrilling. Two days later, in response to that metaphor, he was attacked, brutally, with a cane, by a Southern congressman named Preston Brooks. He was carried, bleeding and unconscious, from the Senate floor.

I read on, uncomprehending but fascinated. Behind me, the voices of my mother and sisters and their suffragist friends rose and fell, bobbing between the paragraphs of Sumner's imagined roar. Slavery. Justice. The Harlot. Then the final, bloody assault.

I finished the chapter and closed the book. I felt dizzy, excited, ignited—I longed for more. Finding, eventually, a slender official biography, I flipped through its early pages, ignoring the senator's ancestry, childhood, college, seeking only that single exalted moment—that shocking detail in this American hero's life. Again I read slowly, memorizing each particular, picturing every aspect: the light in the room, the creaking of Brooks's boots as he approached, the tone of his voice, tight with hatred and violence. The crack of the cane as it slammed against Sumner's skull. And I pictured Sumner, too, not resisting, not reacting, just absorbing the blows, one after another, never uttering a sound, never calling out. Completely silent, completely resigned, while blood like salty roses trickled down his forehead and into his uncomplaining mouth.

In that quiet library, on that quiet Boston morning of early boyhood, I held this vision before my dazzled eyes. I held it and I waited, willing myself to *become* Charles Sumner. I wanted to be there, standing just as he had—perfect, stoic, triumphant, almost enjoying the pain, as blow after blow rained on my head. I too would not resist, would not flinch or respond—just take it, all of it, every inch of suffering, wood against bone, cane against skull, sustained by the knowledge that I was right, good was possible, evil is wrong, I am against it. I had first imagined the room filled with shocked senators, all in their waistcoats and top hats, too stunned to move, gaping at this dreadful spectacle. But now, as I replaced Charles Sumner with myself, I replaced the senators with Mother and my three sisters. They all were watching, too appalled, too horrified to stop it, yet each secretly proud that Sumner, *their* Sumner, was so strong, so heroic, so brave, so able to protect them.

I stood up and walked to the hall. From the parlor I still could hear the cool hum of women's voices. Everything they stood for I believed in passionately, and I longed for some way to burst through that door, through that thick double bulwark of maleness and youth, and tell them how much I loved them, how

I was ready to suffer for them, how I wanted to help their cause the way Sumner had helped the Negro, a public martyr to what was Right.

I opened the closet and found a large wooden cane with a silver handle. I ran my fingers along its length. I imagined that hard shiny wood striking, striking. The pain would be excruciating. No one could possibly bear it. No one but me.

It would be four years later that I received my own shot at public martyrdom. In April 1912—three months before my thirteenth birthday, two years before the onset of the First World War—I was a passenger on the maiden voyage of the most beautiful ship ever built. On our fifth night at sea, she hit an iceberg and rapidly started to sink. It was "Women and children first." A more perfect setting for an admiring student of Charles Sumner to prove his manhood— to be a hero, to be a martyr, to be an adult—could not be imagined.

But manhood is one thing when merely imagined, another when actually called for; and eyeing a cane in your mother's hallway is not the same as choosing whether to drown. On the deck of that ruptured liner I made a decision—a decision whose outcome has haunted me ever since. It can never be changed— not by time, not by tears, not by prayers or regrets, not even by dreams in which everything turns out differently. I can never become Pierce Andrews, ready to die; I can never save Ivy; I can never look into that ice-ridden darkness, counting those lifeboats and thinking of Senator Sumner. All I can do is remember— remember with absolute clarity—who I was when it happened, and who I was afterward. And how everything, everything, changed forever.

MAIDEN VOYAGE

CHAPTER ONE

MY PRESENCE ON BOARD THE *TITANIC* ON HER MAIDEN (AND only) voyage across the Atlantic was due to the un-likely intersection of two distinct histories, hers and mine. For whether we think so or not, ships do have histories, much the way people do, and both the *Titanic* and I became who we were in the present by what we had been in the past.

Unlike my own history, though (or anyone else's), the *Ti-tanic*'s story begins on a single, specific day—not her birthday, exactly, and certainly not her christening, but more like the moment of her conception. It wasn't a quiet conception, either, as mine probably was; nor was it private, as mine definitely was, or in any sense of the word spontaneous: thousands of people knew it was going on; millions more were about to; three years later, almost to the day, the whole world would know. Still, it was, like many conceptions, a moment of passion, of zealous romance and fevered grace, and it had both the nervy faith and the pure audacity of any belief in a hopeful future.

Hull 390904 (the number was published after she sank) was sired on March 31, 1909, in a Belfast shipyard—no, *the* Belfast shipyard, Harland & Wolff, builders of, among others, such great ocean liners as the *Titanic*'s own sister, the *Olympic,* who was later to ferry so many soldiers to horror and glory in the

First World War. The hull, once completed, would be enormous, almost one sixth of a mile long, and nearly 100 feet wide at its widest, held together with 3 million customized iron rivets: the backbone of what, when completed, would weigh 46,000 tons—steel, wood, silver, and glass—and displace more than 60,000 tons of water. Not yet born, still officially nameless, her name was already a legend; little more, at that time, than a dream and a blueprint, she already was thrilling beyond belief. For everyone knew, on that Belfast morning when her keel was laid, who she was, and what was her destiny: to become not just the loveliest ship ever built, or the safest, or one of the fastest, but to become, over the next three years, the largest moving man-made object on the face of the planet.

Why was she, even when fetal—prefetal, really—already so famous? How was it that someone like me—a nine-year-old boy on this day of gestation, totally cold to technology, on the opposite side of the only ocean that mattered, and gifted with no intuition whatever that she and I ever would meet—how did I know she existed? The answer is simple. She was *expected*. A ship like the *Titanic* was expected before a ship like the *Titanic* ever was built. All of us knew that our beautiful, brilliant, unstoppable twentieth century could do anything: end poverty, abolish ignorance, cure any disease. Surely we could create the perfect, the flawless ship.

And we did. Two years and two months after Hull 390904 leapt from her builder's imagination, her century's expectations were answered in full. The *Titanic* was christened. Not with champagne—that was old-fashioned, that was for ships that needed luck—but with that most typical, useful of modern devices, a simple button. J. Bruce Ismay, president of the White Star Line, just stood up, nodded, happily smiled, and pushed a knob which activated a massive hydraulic ram. Silence, more silence, more silence still, and then she started to move, slip-

ping out of her womb with the tentative instincts ℧
born, curious, cautious, and eager to breathe. Cheers bro
all through the harbor as she glided down the slipway, trailı̣
chains and timbers; whistles shrilled, eyes filled with tears of
pride and delight. She was huger than anyone ever expected,
even expecting the truth—huger, steadier, sounder, and more
refined. And of course she wasn't a warship, like a dreadnought
or cruiser, which, while large and impressive themselves, were
always daunting—somber predictors of battle, sober reminders
of death. *She* was a vessel of life—of harmony, happiness, pleasure; of energy, commerce, and peace.

She still wasn't finished, of course. The stream of reporters
—French, English, German, American, Russian—attending this
bright celebration told us that. This was merely a christening of
her hull. She still awaited what all of us wanted: her transformation from a nautical triumph whose details none of us really
could fathom into an actual ship—into the living and breathing
wonder we had been promised. She still wasn't really a miracle
—that took almost another year. And that took journalism.

Over the next ten months the *Titanic* became the most
talked-about, written-up, filmed, painted, and photographed
ship in the world. Every aspect of her being was discussed and
dissected; not to know who she was became nearly impossible;
not to know how she was coming along required more effort
than knowing did. Superlatives faded as the descriptions
mounted: a floating city, a buoyant skyscraper, a seaborne
heaven. The pomp of her First Class compartments, we heard,
made Versailles look like Calcutta; the food would match
Maxim's; the service, Delmonico's; the wines, those served at
the court of the greatest king. The stairways were marble; the
panels the finest oak. Even the blankets were praised; even the
plumbing. She was the single most lavish creation on earth,
though her home was the sea.

In time, everything becomes boring, even perfection; after a while the stories about the *Titanic*'s luxury and unmatched elegance became somewhat repetitive, somewhat less interesting. It was right about then that her greatest feature was fully revealed. Not only was she the safest ship ever built (this we already knew), but she had gone beyond safety: she wasn't just safe, she was *unsinkable*. A series of watertight compartments and electric doors would, in the unlikely event of collision, keep her afloat virtually indefinitely. This was perfection on a truly unthinkable level. She could outwit the ocean itself—she could almost hoodwink death. She was more than the work of man—she was an act of God.

By the time I was finally on board, I knew her history almost as well as I did my own.

Five days and an iceberg later, our histories merged.

Unlike the *Titanic*'s international pedigree—conceived in Belfast, financed in New York, envied in Paris, and imitated in Hamburg—my background is strictly and wholly American. It is, in fact, a striking peculiarity of my family that our history runs in a definite parallel to the history of this country. We didn't *make* history, exactly—no more than anyone does just by being alive—but we certainly never failed to react to it. The result of this was, among other things, my grandfather's misogyny, my mother's feminism, and my father's moving to the other side of the Atlantic to get away from them both. I came home on a ship who made history as a result of how history shaped my family, then ripped it apart.

It was in several houses on Beacon Hill, that gentle Bostonian jewel of privilege, decorum, and charm, that my family's tumultuous history played itself out. Father's family, the Jordans —extremely nice people, by the way, much easier to get on with than most of my mother's relations—purchased a house there in 1853. The Jordans were very wealthy, having made money first in shipping, then tea, then railroads, then, finally, in money itself, becoming bankers. Their dollars helped sponsor the Union Army during the War, and afterward financed the cream of late-nineteenth-century technology. In 1880, however, a Jordan made an uncharacteristically disastrous technological decision. One day my paternal grandfather's brother—"a delightful gentleman," as Father described him, "but hardly the sharpest tool in the shed"—decided all twelve of their banks needed telephones and he would install them himself. He shorted out Cambridge and burned down two banks, neither one his. His brothers, embarrassed, sent him abroad. Here he discovered Art, Wine, Women, and, well, *Europe*.

Great-uncle Harry loved Europe and vice versa, for though the Europeans were careful never to let him anywhere near their telephone boxes, they did allow him to buy their paintings and back their horses and bankroll their plays—he was the first Jordan ever to *see* a play—and in general have a much better time than he'd ever had at home. One day, when quite an old man, and bedded with double pneumonia, he had written his nephew —my father—and told him that dying in Europe beat living in Boston. Father kept it in mind.

It was my maternal great-grandfather who, in 1831, built the house that was later to be my home on Pinckney Street. My grandfather Jeremiah was born there in 1839. Like the Jordans, the Fairclifts were wealthy: insurance, the Fairclift actuarial table. Unlike the Jordans, however, though like many other Bostonians of that time, the Fairclifts were very politically active, especially in the abolitionist movement. And Sumner—*my* Sumner, *the* Senator Sumner—was a frequent visitor to this very house.

Now, in antebellum Boston, as you might imagine, Senator

Sumner was a lion, almost a god. My grandfather became a spellbound acolyte. The senator was forty-five. My grandfather was sixteen.

"Up until then," my grandfather later told me, "I held no specific political beliefs; I was a child, with a child's political interests, which is to say none whatsoever. But Senator Sumner changed all that. He used to hold teas—abolitionist teas—and I was invited, almost as a servant, there just to open doors and take coats and pass sugar and cream and lemon to the great man's friends. And he used to invite Negroes to those teas, and I used to look at these well-dressed and well-spoken black people and wonder, How can these people look like this and ninety-eight percent of their brothers and sisters be slaves?"

Grandfather's exposure to Charles Sumner reached its zenith in the spring of 1856, when the Kansas Territory applied for statehood and the question arose as to how she should enter the Union—slave state or free. Grandfather was one of the senator's many invited guests in the gallery on that morning when Sumner gave his famous speech, "The Crime Against Kansas."

"It was dazzling," Grandfather reported. "A brilliant speech: citations from English common law and the Napoleonic Code, huge chunks of Cato and Cicero, plus the purest American rhetoric. And all perfectly, impeccably, flawlessly committed to memory. Not just the language—the technique had been memorized too. Every gesture, every glare, every empty pause when outrage appeared to render him spontaneously speechless —all rigidly rehearsed. The single most prodigious feat of memory I have ever witnessed."

Two days later, Charles Sumner lay bleeding on the Senate floor, while everyone watched and nobody helped. Grandfather hardened his heart against the incredible animal immorality of the Southern third of his country and waited for the inevitable war.

Three days after Fort Sumter, my grandfather enlisted as a captain in the 5th Massachusetts; three months later, his father died. Thus Grandfather, attending the funeral, was not present at the Union's disastrous First Battle of Bull Run. It was the only major action of the Army of the Potomac he missed.

Grandfather fought at Fair Oaks. He fought at the Battle of Malvern Hill. He fought at Second Bull Run, Antietam, Fredericksburg, Chancellorsville, Gettysburg, Petersburg ("the 'burgs," he called them), White Oaks, Five Forks, and Appomattox. He was shot at and into, and he lost more horses than Stuart and Sheridan. He fought with astounding courage and continual bravery, and was mentioned often in dispatches—his great friend, Senator Charles Sumner, praised him before the United States Senate and Lincoln himself. My grandfather was one of the few Northern soldiers of the Civil War who was actually fighting for what we now know almost nobody was. Grandfather was *not* fighting to preserve the Union. He was fighting to ensure the liberation of the black man.

The War ended. Grandfather, filled with Sumnerian idealism and commitment, journeyed south, into that maelstrom of distrust, institutionalized humiliation, and misguided forgiveness known as Reconstruction. He became a carpetbag congressman for Alabama.

It was at this point that Grandfather began to undergo a surprising and ugly transformation. Exposed for the first time to black people who were neither "political" nor educated nor professionally charming—who were, in fact, incredibly poor, almost universally uneducated, and caught in the nasty crossfire between a vindictive North and an unreconstructed South—he was revolted. Not by the poverty, not by the ignorance—that would be understandable, forgivable, even laudable. But that, I'm afraid, wasn't it. Grandfather was revolted by the people themselves.

They just weren't what he'd expected. They didn't talk like Frederick Douglass. They didn't orate like Sojourner Truth. They weren't impressed by his friendship with Charles Sumner, of whom they had never heard. Worst of all, they didn't appear grateful to him for the wounds and years and dedication he had offered on their behalf. They seemed to my grandfather—they seemed, more and more, to be "they." "They" were ignorant. "They" were illiterate. They were—or, rather, they *weren't*— they simply didn't have the godgiven talents and drive of people like . . . oh, say, the Fairclifts of Beacon Hill.

By 1870 Grandfather had had it with Reconstruction and was ready to come back home. Though not directly: first, he decided, he should tour America—see what the rest of his country, not only the South, was up to. And what he saw filled him with horror. For the entire nation was flooded with— swarming with—"they"s! Inferior peoples everywhere: Swedes in Minnesota, Portuguese in Rhode Island, Poles all over Chicago, Indians on reservations, Chinese in Seattle and San Francisco, Greeks and Italians in New York City. Even his beloved Boston—though not Beacon Hill—had been overrun by the Irish.

Grandfather was an educated man. He used his education to interpret his observations. He read Darwin, Galton, and Herbert Spencer, while all around him "they" lurked and huddled —unrestrainedly breeding, celebrating odd holidays, practicing strange religions: threatening the very fiber of American life. It drove my grandfather into, then rapidly out of, despair; and as he watched with growing disdain and loathing, he harnessed his education to hack out a theory of why everything Charles Sumner had stood for—equality—was wrong.

His theory was cruelly simple. The world, he contended, was divided: superior over inferior; white over nonwhite; man over woman. And nothing could change it.

He lived very much as a freelance writer after that, traveling extensively and specializing in stories about the threat to America and Europe from various Backward Societies: Russia, Persia, Siam. He called for stiff racial immigration laws and a total reexamination of the politics of the Civil War. But he saved his strongest anger, his greatest, blackest bitterness, for his ex-mentor, Senator Charles Sumner.

In 1873 Grandfather produced his still-famous, still-quoted pamphlet, *In Refutation of Charles Sumner: A New Look at Reconstruction*. It was self-published: no editor, at least for the first printing, would touch it. The *Refutation* sold over fifty thousand copies—phenomenal in those days: a postwar *Uncle Tom's Cabin*. Apparently thousands of Americans shared Grandfather's disillusionment with the dated politics of moral purpose.

Three months after the *Refutation,* he went to England. There he met and married Cassandra Wheeler, a beautiful purple-eyed innocent young woman who loved children but suffered a terrible fear of childbirth: her mother and two of her aunts had died within three weeks of delivery. Grandfather took Cassandra back to Beacon Hill, where she soon became anxiously pregnant. She delivered a perfectly healthy baby girl and then, within the month, proved the prophetic power of her name and the accuracy of her fears by dying of puerperal septicemia. Grandfather foisted the child, Rebecca Cassandra Fairclift, onto one of his aunts, and returned to Europe. He retrieved her when he came back to Boston eight years later, to set up a gloomy household on Pinckney Street.

Rebecca Cassandra was, of course, Mother.

During the 1880s, as the suffrage movement gained momentum, Grandfather became one of its most virulent and articulate opponents. As he saw it, it was imperative that the country not make the same horrifying mistake with women it had made with the black man. Not surprisingly, Grandfather, after all those adolescent hours in the rhetorical service of Charles Sumner, was quite adept at public debate; his specialty was skewering his suffragist opponents with a flurry of Spencer, Latin, and bewildering wit. He delighted in denigrating women, both in print and in person: always frigidly polite, and pretty damn funny, he was a terribly dangerous, difficult, fast-on-the-uptake opponent.

Revelation comes at surprising times. For Rebecca Cassandra it came during a dessert course of ice cream and gingered honeydew, on a hot summer evening in 1890, after her freshman (and only) year at Radcliffe, then known as the Harvard Annex. She was sitting in her father's dining room with her spanking new husband—my father, William Barrington Jordan —by her side. Father was extremely good-looking in those days, and so was my mother; eyeing them both, Grandfather realized he was likely to have a number of grandchildren, probably in the not-very-distant future. Pondering how best to provide for this predicted brood, he turned—as he usually did whenever the conversation concerned anything much weightier than yesterday's weather—to the man in the family, my father, William.

"I imagine you'll be a father before too long," he rumbled.

His new son-in-law squirmed. "A father?" he repeated.

"God, nature, and Darwin willing," my grandfather said.

Neither my father nor my mother was a prude, exactly, but who wants to discuss sex with your father—or, worse yet, your father-in-law? Both of my parents gazed at the floor.

"Rebecca has her mother's fortune, as you of course know," Grandfather continued. "And when I die—"

"Oh, Daddy," said Rebecca.

"And when I die—" Grandfather repeated.

"Oh, Daddy," said Rebecca again.

"When I die, she'll get my money, too," Grandfather finally finished. "Plus this house and some legacies her grandfather set up. They'll commence when she's twenty-five. Now, William, what I would suggest you do—"

My father leaned forward. "Yes, sir?"

"What I want you to do—"

"Wait a minute here," said Rebecca.

Both men looked at her with expectant toleration, her interruption assumed to be an announcement of her imminent departure from this boring financial conversation. How proper! thought my doting father. How typical! thought my grandfather.

"If this is *my* money," said Rebecca Fairclift Jordan, "then why are you telling *him* how to spend it?"

The sun erupted. Stars reeled, moons exploded, galaxies bubbled, and the earth emitted a mighty roar. My mother stood like an Amazon on the edge of a flaming precipice, fire behind her, only empty space below. Tides rushed forward, rivers sped to the sea. Then the world righted itself: three very surprised people staring at one another in the late Boston twilight.

My bright, sharp, vituperative, literate, quick-thinking grandfather said, "Huh?"

"I said," Mother repeated, "if this is *my* money, then why are you telling *him* how to spend it?"

"Well, if you really must know," Grandfather answered, "I'm afraid you don't have the brains of a goose in heat."

"That doesn't seem to deter you," said Mother, "from hoping I lay some golden eggs."

Grandfather blinked. How sharper than a serpent's tooth, et cetera. All these years he had been nurturing not only a viper, but an *intelligent* one. And now it had chosen to bite.

As for Mother, who selected that moment of her very recent marriage to despise her husband forever for not supporting her in this first clumsy lurch toward independence, all was suddenly, horrifyingly clear. Men had everything. They wrote the rules, umpired the action, ran the scoreboard, and never would let you hit. Women had nothing. She became a feminist.

That fall, Grandfather was invited to Radcliffe to participate in a debate on women's suffrage. Mother, no longer a student and already pregnant with my eldest sister, went to the Debating Society sponsors and asked who would be facing her father. The Society admitted that they had nobody lined up yet—people kept coming up with the oddest excuses. It was the perfect opportunity—one my mother, fast becoming a reverse Electra, couldn't possibly pass up. She convinced the Society to allow her to represent the college. Then she marched off to the Annex library at Fay House, rubbing her swollen stomach, and began to read.

At first, Mother found her textbooks—Mill's *On Liberty,* Darwin's *Origin of Species,* Grandfather's *In Refutation of Charles Sumner*—almost indigestible, following as they did a previous diet of romances, lightweight poetry, and *Godey's Lady's Book.* But eventually certain points and assertions began to form first suggestions, then patterns, then total worldviews. It was, in fact, in the preparation for this debate that Mother came up with the ideas which remained the cornerstone of her thinking most of her life.

Some families mythologize their happiness. My family mythologizes acrimony. The eventual debate between Rebecca Fairclift Jordan and Jeremiah Fairclift has become legend in my family. Actually, it became *two* legends, each with completely different heroes, events, symbols, settings, and outcomes. And like all receivers of legends, I learned both versions by heart.

According to my grandfather, the debate took place during a snowstorm, in an auditorium packed to overflowing with "cat-like women" who "hissed disapproval" whenever he tried to make a point. "Obviously," he always would say, his voice still phlegmy with rage after all these years, "I was unable, under such circumstances, to frame my arguments as cogently as I otherwise might. As if a woman would appreciate cogency anyway! However, I felt it my duty to at least try to educate them, if not in logic, at least in manners, and in their biological role"—here his voice would smooth into pedantic flatness—"as the meeker and weaker side of the human dialectic. And I assured them that although God had not given them the tools to protect themselves, He had not abandoned them. 'If a woman is in a burning building, if she is drowning, if she is any danger whatsoever,' I told them, 'it is the duty of a man—a true man—to save her, even at the price of his own life. Just as one would save a child,' I said. 'A cat saves her kittens. A man protects women.'

"Naturally," he continued, "they would have none of it. They behaved like wild Indians ready to hit the warpath. They chanted and clamored and shouted me down like a tribe of Hottentots."

That's Version A. Version B—"Rebecca's interpretation"—differs considerably. Though I tend to think Version B is the accurate story, mainly since Father—certainly no friend of the suffrage movement—has verified most of my mother's memories. In fact, I believe that Father, rather ironically, took considerable pride in Mother's performance that day: he always had enormous respect for people who took risks—for art, for politics, whatever. And Mother certainly was taking a risk by facing one of Boston's most prominent thinkers on his favorite hate.

According to Mother, the debate occurred on a sunny day, not during a snowstorm; in a classroom, not in an auditorium; and before a small and well-behaved audience, not all female at all but half men, half women, and with pro- and anti-suffrage sentiment scattered equally through the sexes. When Grandfather rose to speak, Mother says, he was greeted with recognition, smiles, and polite applause. The only hissing in the room came from a samovar.

Grandfather began by contrasting the histories of men and women, white and black, colonizer versus colonized. He brought up all his usual points. Why is there no civilization in Africa? Why is there no science in India? Why are there no women painters? He kept hammering away at the same conclusion: natural selection. Nature favors the strong and axes the weak. Darwin has proved that the fit inevitably triumph over the unfit. It stands to reason, and history demonstrates, that in the human world, as in the natural world, some cultures, some races, some *sexes* have been naturally selected over others. Obviously, the position of men in our world today proves that nature has selected men to be its artists, its manufacturers, its generals, its geniuses. And, most important, its rulers. Therefore men, and only they, should vote.

He concluded by offering a bit of modest contrition. "I was once the disciple of a very great, but very mistaken, gentleman. That man was Charles Sumner. He claimed all races are equal. However, a simple observation of the different peoples of the world shows they are *not* equal. Some races are meant to lead; others, to follow. So it is with the sexes. The weaker sex is made to nurture. The stronger sex is made to protect and to rule. There is nothing 'wrong' or 'right' about this; it simply *is*. And there is nothing any of us can do to change it."

Grandfather sat down to enthusiastic applause: Darwinism was considered a daring, enlightened theory. Then Mother rose. She was, by her own admission, extremely nervous (something I find hard to picture). She began with a world history of her own, but her notes became jumbled and she started to stammer. It was then that my grandfather—slavering caveman sensing kill —made a fatal error. He began mocking his enemy as she stood fumbling with her note cards.

"My beloved daughter," he said from his seat, "seems bent on proving my thesis for me."

This was too much for Mother. As she rather formally tells it, "I saw, not red, but white—a total blotting out of filial obligation. I became so angry I completely forsook my notes and spoke extemporaneously. 'Certainly,' I began, 'certainly I would never claim to be anything other than a biologically weak and intellectually inferior female, selected by nature—or, perhaps, *abandoned* by it—to be forever inferior to man. The Lord knows I am not as physically powerful as a man—although how brute force helps in voting I'm not sure. Nor could I ever have harnessed so remarkable a force as fire—although how Mr. Fairclift knows it was a man who did that is beyond me, unless he is considerably older than he claims. Besides, one has only to watch a man in a kitchen to know that even if man did discover fire, he has yet to master its usage.

" 'However, we are getting far afield. I submit to you that the question before us today is not one of natural selection but natural rights—those rights of human beings so cherished by our forebears that they fought a revolution over them. These rights belong to each person, no matter how high- or low-born, how rich, how poor, how intelligent, how simple. In our country, all men possess equal access to the ballot because each possesses an equal quotient of inalienable rights. I believe no man should be deprived of those rights, whether he be as gifted as Charles Darwin or as . . . less gifted as my beloved father. You both deserve to vote. As do I.' "

It was laying the golden egg all over again. The logic of the argument may not have been perfect (later she refined it so that it *was* perfect), but you couldn't beat it for impact. Mother had managed a triple her first time up.

Five months after the debate, she gave birth to my sister Marcella. By now doctors knew enough about sepsis to wash off the blood from one delivery before proceeding to the next; mother and child were healthily home in ten days. Mother was delighted to have a daughter, because she knew it meant one more woman on earth to bedevil my grandfather; but to her surprise, Grandfather did not rise to the bait. He very properly set up a trust fund for Marcella and donated five thousand dollars in her name to Massachusetts General Hospital; he did the same for Cornelia, four years later, and Julia, two years afterward. He dutifully attended birthday parties and Christmases (usually for less than an hour), and he did his best not to alienate his daughter's daughters. Mother watched with suspicion.

When she became pregnant the fourth time, Grandfather told my parents he hoped this time they had a son, if only because they were starting to run out of feminine Latin names. Father mumbled something vaguely appropriate; Mother just smiled. And she did have a son. She had me.

Grandfather visited my mother three times while she was still in the hospital. He visited me (I'm told) in the nursery; he even came over to the house and bullied my father into sharing two bottles of brandy with him. He happened to be in the hallway when mother and infant arrived home from the hospital. Grandfather peered at me with what he claims was mystic delight.

"It was as if I could see my father," he told me, "and *his* father, and his father's father, and back further and further in time—all these achievers, all these good, strong, hardworking men with the natural morals and goodness with which nature had endowed them. And I saw your sons and your grandsons— damn it, it was as if I could see forwards and backwards into history, just by looking into your face."

I have often tried to imagine that scene: all of them crunched into the narrow hallway of my parents' house, me squalling, Mother soothing, Father making some ineffectual patting motions, and Grandfather standing there reading the history of the Western world in my squinched-up infant's eyes. My sisters, I'm told, were there as well, adorably woven around my mother's skirts so that she could not take a step in any direction. According to Marcella, Grandfather even held out his hands to my mother, in an unprecedented attempt to cuddle one of his grandchildren.

"You are a very handsome baby," he told me. "You will go far."

He was probably about to tell me exactly how far, when it dawned on him that he did not know my name. Brandied and jocular, he asked my mother after what famous Roman she intended to name her son.

"No Romans," Mother unhesitatingly answered. "Just Americans this time."

"Excellent," Grandfather said.

Father reached down and absentmindedly touched Julia's coppery head. I think he wanted to be attached to something warm when the bomb fell.

"Well?" Grandfather said. "What have you named him?"

"His middle name is my maiden name," Mother said. "Because I want to be certain that when people hear his name, they associate him with you."

Eight-year-old Marcella and my father both sighed.

"And his first name is Sumner," Mother said. "Sumner Fairclift Jordan is your grandson's full name."

Julia later claimed that Grandfather did not utter a sound for over two minutes. His face turned red, then white, then—Julia swore—green. He was still holding me, gazing at me, while God knows how many reactions offered themselves: anger, disappointment, humiliation, helplessness. Finally he spoke.

"You poor baby," he said to me. "Better for you to have been born a bastard."

Mother smiled. "Better for *you*," she said. "But unfortunately he's perfectly legitimate."

Grandfather handed me over to Marcella. To my mother he said, "I've treated the girls well. I shall do the same for him. If you think by naming my only grandson after Senator Sumner you'll keep me away from him, you're wrong. If I have to hire a lawyer to show you how wrong—well, then, my beloved daughter, I shall."

"Nobody wants to keep you away from him," Mother said. "I *want* people to see you and Sumner together."

Just hearing my name made Grandfather wince. He walked out without another word.

Three days later Mother received a letter from Barton Pugh, the only lawyer in Boston who still called himself a barrister. The letter informed her that her father was moving to New York City. He was deeding her his house on Pinckney Street— "for her to live in or sell, just as she chooses"—and was arranging for me the same trust fund and endowment he had bestowed on my sisters. He requested in return that when I was old enough to travel, either with servant or paid companion, I be allowed to visit him in Manhattan at least once a year.

"I ask for no other favors than this," Grandfather's letter said, "for fear that you will take too much pleasure in granting them. You, my beloved daughter, have succeeded all too easily in breaking my heart. But you did not do it when you named my grandson after Charles Sumner. That was a petty hurt. My heart was broken years earlier, when your mother died—not in a war, not in an accident, not in the deserved tranquillity of old age, but in the boring and wasteful sacrifice of giving birth to a daughter."

Mother memorized that letter, burned it, then recited it to me nearly five years later, the first time I went to Manhattan, accompanied by Melville, our butler, to visit Grandfather. She repeated it before every trip which followed. But she did not try to prevent the trips, and she did move into her father's home. And the house where Charles Sumner had demanded war or liberty continued to war for liberation.

And where in this hothouse of struggle did Father fit? He didn't, that's all. Father had no interest whatsoever in social change. By the time my mother was one of the six most important women in American suffrage and well on her way to international prominence, Father had clearly become, by anyone's standards, including his own, a failure: he even had failed at being a Jordan—that is, making money and behaving himself. Instead he had become the reincarnation of Great-uncle Harry—a sweet-tempered, dreamy-eyed bumbler who liked hanging around artists. I was crazy about Father, but nobody else was; they didn't even bother to hate him. "What's the point?" asked my grandfather. "It's like not liking custard. You don't make a speech about it—you simply avoid it."

My parents separated right after my second birthday, though they never divorced—too many financial complications, for one thing, plus it just wasn't done. Mother continued her suffrage work; my sisters flourished; I flourished too. In time Father moved, first to Paris, then to Venice, and finally to London, where he wrote to me weekly, always on colorful stationery with contrasting inks. As with my grandfather, I was put on a visitation schedule, one which allowed me to see Father in England every two years. This—1912—was one of those years.

CHAPTER TWO

WHEN I LOOK BACK AT MY CHILDHOOD AND YOUNG ADOLES-cence, it's like looking at a well-preserved tapestry. Everything is connected, everything flows: the senator, suffrage, my mother; my grandfather's bigotry; my father's living in London; the *Titanic* awaiting her iceberg. Since it's my tapestry, I figure in most of the panels, doing what everyone does growing up, which is dealing with everyday life while longing to grow up faster, to get on with the show—to move to the right on the time line. Which eventually happened, though not in a way I could have predicted, but, perhaps, should have. Because it was thanks to Senator Sumner and Mother's involvement in women's suffrage that I did what I did at the poetry contest, and what I did at the poetry contest is the reason I came home from London on the *Titanic,* and lost my youth.

This poetry contest—the Greater and Metropolitan Boston Fine Arts and Poetry Fair—was an annual competition, now in its seventy-fifth year. It was, like all public contests, ostensibly open to everyone, though by "everyone" the organizers really meant anyone of, at a minimum, high-school age, most of the participants traditionally being quite a bit older; I therefore was making history by my presence. For I was, at that moment—

Valentine's Day, 1912—exactly twelve years, seven months, and fourteen days old, which made me the competition's youngest entrant ever. Thanks, however, to a growth spurt begun in the middle of last September, at least I wasn't the shortest. Thank You, God, for Your mercies of physiology!

The mercies of physiology, however, were not completely unstrained. I was extremely nervous—so chilly with perspiration I felt as though I had just stepped out of a bathtub, and crawling with so many butterflies I could hardly sit still. Though it wasn't the act of reciting itself which was making me feel so invaded. I had done recitations before; done dozens of them, in fact, although only in contests with fellow students—foes my own size, literarily speaking, against whom, in general, I was triumphant: the truth is, the only occasion I didn't get a First Place with Merit was after I'd already bagged it so often they had made me a judge, just to give somebody else a crack at the shiver of victory. So, no, it wasn't the prospect of reading a poem in public which was causing this heart-slinging, hand-wringing tension: it was *this* public reading of one of my poems. This poem, and this audience.

It was also this competition. They were all so much *older* than I. And with age had come all of the usual benefits: they were cool, they were calm, they were poised, they were casual. And they all were able to *write*. For the first time in my life, I respected and feared my opponents.

Well, most of them, anyway. The senior representing Thayer Academy was, I recognized early on, easy pickings. An obvious devotee of the New Poetry, he had presented a dreadful free-verse exposition on the death of the frontier at the hands of ravaging capitalism ("Adieu, adieu, O Daniel Boone! struck down / By the Small Pox of Big Business"). Even had the poem been good—and it wasn't, it wasn't—it would have been a disaster, for the Greater and Metropolitan Boston Fine Arts and Poetry judges were not yet ready for unrhymed poetry, let alone anything involving monetary-philosophical puns on Marx and marks, Hegel and The Hague. By the time he had finished, I was, if not breathing normally, at least no longer panting. I could demolish this guy with a decent limerick.

But his, unfortunately, was the only truly terrible offering. He was followed—after sullen applause—by a police inspector from the North End who presented a surprisingly excellent poem on Gettysburg. "Gettysburg, thou hallowed word," it began—perking me up immediately by its sheer awfulness—but then it rallied and became quite moving, bodies strewn on the steaming rocks, blood clotting the stalks in the drooping wheat field, unfinished letters to mothers and weeping lovers, the stiffening limbs of young men who would run no longer, et cetera, et cetera. Sure it was corny, but it was *touching*—all that mattered. I felt apprehension, unwelcome as winter, stalk back to my side.

The next poem was so good I almost vomited. The author was Mrs. Eleanor Rantis Dixon, my oldest sister Marcella's (and practically half of Boston's) beloved former Latin instructor. Frail and white-haired and almost seventy, Mrs. Dixon always had struck me as a typically lovable aging schoolmarm given to lost glasses, misplaced gloves, and extreme generosity in the saltwater taffy department. But not any longer. Now I could see what she *really* was: a most dangerous foe, a trickster, a vixen who had lain low in her lair all these years, biding her time and patiently cooking her taffy while awaiting this chance to humiliate the brother of her former student.

Her poem was wonderful! A gentle exploration of the soul of an elderly female American tourist sadly observing the fading heather on a lonely Scottish moor, and written in a deceptively simple Emily Dickinsonian style, it had it all: poignancy, evocation, frighteningly universal comprehensibility. And frightening brevity as well. For everyone seemed to admire the fact that it was short, and my own offering was at least six times longer!

Mrs. Dixon sat down to sparkling applause. I joined in, palms wet with envy.

Creative jealousy. What a draining emotion. How low, how un-Greek, how noncommunal. All I had to do was look into the faces of the other contestants to see how disgustingly different I was from everyone else. They were all beaming at one another's offerings, whispering good luck as each of them rose, clutching hands and patting shoulders when they returned, wishing only the best for one another. They were obviously here solely because they loved poetry—loved writing it, loved sharing it, loved the Little Voice which gave them the little gift. Whereas I was here only to win.

It was not that I didn't like writing. I did; to some extent I liked it better than anything else I could think of. When I was writing and it worked, when that little click bounced off my brain and onto paper, I felt the same sharp shudder of bliss I imagined the great love poets were talking about. When an image appeared to me, coming, as images always seemed to, from outer space, from nothing I could predict or control, I knew a contentment and satisfaction that turned my whole being inside out with pride and gratitude. And it wasn't that I didn't enjoy helping out fellow poets, either; I had spent hours with classmates, offering—when asked—endless enthused suggestions, and taking true pleasure in my friends' creations. Indeed, had this been any other poem, and any other contest, I could have been as good-natured and neighborly as Mrs. Dixon and as noncompetitive as a sheep. But this was *not* any other poem and any other contest. This was my opus and I was performing before my mother. It was hard to be kind and smiling when I knew in my soul I was prepared to strangle the competition for the sake of victory.

Part of it was just having sweated the details for so very long. I had dashed off "The Martyrdom of Charles Sumner" (surprised by the title? the subject?) nearly four years ago, just after that moment of staggering revelation in Mother's library, and since then had written and devised and assembled dozens of variations—at least five a year, so that by now there were over twenty individual versions, each simultaneously far better and much worse than the sincere and spontaneous original. Four years is a long time by anyone's reckoning, and things change: wars become treaties, seeds become saplings, children become adolescents. And poems become epics. What had begun as sixteen heartfelt and childish lines had evolved, under the light and warmth of benign exposure to Byron and Pope and the Cult of the Iamb in English poetry, into twenty stanzas of blood, patriotism, historical minutiae, and forced rhymes. Whether the poem was still any good at all—whether, indeed, it ever had been, and I hadn't been wasting all this time feverishly trying to save what had been meant from conception to be aborted—I really couldn't say.

I also really couldn't say whether, technically, I was still the legitimate author. Over the years I had solicited and wheedled and incorporated so much advice from so many people I could barely remember which lines were mine and which had come from somebody else. Father, for instance, had sent countless instructive missives from London, urging me to relax about the historical plotline and "dig into that imagery," enclosing as examples several beautiful, meaningless jumbles of words. Then there was my best friend, Mitchell: "Couldn't you show more of the beating?" My sisters—Marcella: "Make sure it's symbolic, but not so symbolic no one can tell what you're talking about." Cornelia: "Wouldn't it be more interesting to do that terrible scandal about Senator Sumner's marriage?" Julia: "What'll you do if your mind goes blank in front of so many people?" And Grandfather: "Can't you find anything more worthwhile to write about than that self-serving moralizing maniac?" Even Melville the butler had chimed in: "Enunciate, Sumner, enunciate!"

And, finally, my mother's continued counsel. Naturally, she advocated exactly what Father deplored: "Make sure it's clear what the issues in Kansas were . . . make sure it's clear who Preston Brooks was," and so on. Mother's prescription was always for absolute clarity; she loathed allusion, distrusted illusion, and considered lyrical effect injurious to content—content, the heart of, the only point to, her own clear-cut speeches and brilliant essays on feminism, freedom, and female suffrage.

I looked at my family now, surrounded by friends and well-wishers: it was like looking at almost every human I ever had loved, and who loved me back. Mother, regal in olive velvet, headed the row; Mr. Bannister, the first teacher to expose me to the sinew and bone of Middle English, sat at the foot. Next to Mother was our minister; next to Mr. Bannister was our family doctor. In between them sat George, Marcella's fiancé, a committed socialist and writer (though *not,* he was always saying, a socialist writer). Next to George, naturally, was Marcella, then Julia, Cornelia, and Mitchell.

I stared at them all with envy. How safe they all were, each and every one, there in their chairs! No pressure, no looming future, not a care in the world: the fleshy pinch of impending performance meant nothing to them. Mother, listening politely to the current reciter; Mr. Bannister, wearing his wince in response to excessive dactyls; George, sitting with one arm around the back of Marcella's chair; Julia, frantically trying to catch the eye of a handsome college student in the next row. As for Cornelia and Mitchell, they simply looked bored.

Bored! Consumed by my showman's majesty, I nearly sneered. My God, what wouldn't I give for a chance to replace terror with boredom!

"Our youngest contestant, his family and friends here to support him . . . Mr. Sumner Jordan!"

My head jerked at the call. Was it already over—had I already risen, recited, been tabulated, applauded, and won? Father once wrote me he'd had occasional days when at sunset he found he had absolutely no idea what he'd been doing since dawn. Now I didn't seem to remember either.

"Thank you," I mumbled.

Kindly Mrs. Dixon jabbed me in the ribs. "It's your turn, dear," she whispered.

"Oh. Oh, yes. Of course. I know that. Thank you."

"You're very welcome. And the best of luck!"

I walked to the lectern, queasy with guilt: it had never occurred to me, all that time she had been sitting beside me awaiting her turn, to have wished her good fortune, or even good day.

"Hello," I said, staring down at the podium. My voice, out of control, seemed to soar and flutter; "hello" lasted six syllables. "My poem is entitled—"

I heard a hiss in the audience and looked up. An act of God, an exploding water heater? Leaking gas? Snakes? It was Julia, holding up her program; on the back she had scrawled, "Don't worry! Yours is best!"

"My poem is entitled"—I swallowed, my voice still unsteady—" 'The Martyrdom of Charles Sumner. A poetic history.' "

The room grew warm with expectancy. No enemies here, I

told myself. . . . And then I remembered the alteration I had made three days ago—that change, that minor twist in the final stanza, that deviation nobody knew about, not even Mother, that switch I could still back out of. No enemies *yet*, I amended.

I began to recite.

"He sits aloof, his noble brow
   Reflection of his noble thought,
   He contemplates in sorrow how
   Men still are cattle, sold and bought."

There! First stanza out, flung at the world, and the world still ticking. I sneaked my first evaluative glance. The audience and judges (five shadowy figures taking notes in the back row) looked polite and interested, obviously pleased with the singsong rhythm and impressed by those nervy twin "noble"s. I felt a flutter of hope. Everyone who had heard the opening, I remembered, also had liked it—even George, in spite of some trouble with the fourth line. "Shouldn't that be 'bought and sold'?" he had asked. "I mean, that's the usual order one does it in. Unless maybe you're Vanderbilt, shortselling railroads." To which I had replied with the professional rhymester's traditional comeback. "Poetic license," I'd told him loftily. "If you'd read more poetry you'd recognize it. 'Bought and sold' doesn't rhyme."

Mother flashed me a smile, and I waded farther in.

"His pen before his restless hand,
   The words before his stormy eyes,
   The blight upon his native land,
   He lifts his voice to criticize

"The pain of those enchained, the crime
   Of those enchaining, in the face

Of all the Western world, where time
Has come to free the Negro race.

"The world he knows, of trees and snows,
A scholar's world, of bookish bravery,
He throws to foes to bold oppose
The Whore, the Harlot Slavery."

The audience remained alert, attentive, locked upright by
the bolt of my poem's cradle-rocking rhythms. "Go slower,"
Marcella mouthed. "Slow-er." I nodded.

"Outside, the air, virescent, clear,
Columbia! Thou fair metropolis,
Inside, the case: embrace a race,
Or fall, like Heliopolis."

I smothered a smile. I wished that Father were here; it was
he who had supplied both "virescent" and a rhyme for "metropolis."

"He rises from his Senate seat,
His face impassive, as he picks
His Southern foe. Their eyes do meet.
The date is May in fifty-six.

"His speech describes the pain, the wail,
The breaking-up of mother and child,
The whip, the dog, the chain, the jail,
The crime by night and orgy wild."

I paused. That last line—that is, that "orgy wild"—had
created quite a stir during the poem's pre-performance trial

runs. Mother felt "orgy" was not a word to be used in public, and she suggested replacing it with "party," at which George had swallowed a choking spasm of laughter. Marcella had defended me—"they *were* orgies, Mother"—causing Julia to ask, "What's an orgy, what's an orgy?" Cornelia had leaned over and whispered something; Julia's eyes had turned round with excitement. Grandfather complained from Manhattan that "it was Senator Sumner, not the Southern foe, who was the wild one."

Actually it was Father who had given the best advice on the orgy question. "I personally prefer the line above it," he had written. "Those pounding iambs, that dispassionate listing of atrocities. The 'orgy wild' image seems in comparison unoriginal and bland, and I would tend to agree with Marcella's young man that an orgy is by definition somewhat wild, or otherwise it's a tea party on the verandah. Your poor mother does not understand this, and your grandfather has as usual missed the entire point.

"For the point, Sumner," his letter had continued, "is this: this is both *a* poem, and *your* poem. It both stands alone and is inextricably bound to your very soul. It was from your soul that the image emerged; it is to your soul that such questions as propriety and poetic impact must be addressed.

"I say, have at it!"

Well, I had and I hadn't. " '. . . and orgy wild,' " I said defiantly. But not very loudly.

The audience looked impassive. Probably most of them hadn't even heard me. Or perhaps Melville had been right; his contribution to *cette affaire du mot juste* had been to acidly comment that most of "that Fine Arts crowd wouldn't be able to recognize an orgy if they stumbled over one in the middle of Boston Common"—an observation which had surprised me, as

I wouldn't have thought Melville would, either. Yet another example of how even those we know best, we really don't know at all.

> "Three hours he speaks, cajoles, entreats,
> Threatens, demands, decries, denounces
> The evil that eats the heart. At last,
> Exhausted, he sighs and then announces,

> " 'We cannot run away from pain,
> And not for moral reasons alone,
> We cannot run away from pain,
> For others' torment is our own.
> Their blow our blood, their fear our terror,
> The pain of others is our own pain,
> mirrored.' "

I hazarded another outward glance. That jump from four lines to six had obviously snagged the judges' attention. And the listeners', too: I heard a hum of approval, like the warm, happy buzz of pollinating bees.

"Excellent, my dear!" Mrs. Dixon murmured. "Yes, indeed," rumbled the police inspector.

I almost gurgled with joy. Sumner, I said to myself, you are definitely cooking.

> "A balmy morning finds our man,
> His pen again against the night
> That dims his sunny country where
> All men are equal, but not quite.

> "Both new and old, his thesis bold,
> Allusions Greek, with Latin tossed in:

'To own a soul enchains a soul.'
(True everywhere, not just in Boston.)

"A shadow blights his wooden desk!
A stranger breaks his scholar's spell!
He glances up, his mild gaze
Meets eyes of madness, bred in hell!

"He tries to rise, to organize
A second's flash of manly fear!
A cane strikes out! Wood ripping bone!!
A cry of hatred rends the air!!!"

"Oh! Goodness!" gasped Mrs. Dixon.

"The crying is not Sumner's, no—
It is his foe who weeps with rage,
Who knows as throws his grievous blows
How men will spit upon his page

"In History. For all the pain
Of Charles Sumner, blind with blood
Will transfer into glory by
The bootless troop through conquered mud,

"From Fredericksburg to Gettysburg
To Petersburg. The Keys, the Hallecks,
The Popes, McClellans, Frémonts, Banks,
Then Grant and peace at Appomattox."

The audience was my personal toy. "Appomattox," I
thought gleefully: even harder to rhyme than "metropolis."
Thank God General Henry Halleck had briefly been made com-
mander of the Union Army!

"The triumph of the Union sealed,
  Five years before the War, by terror,
  By broken skull of martyr's blood,
  By Charles Sumner, standard-bearer.

"By Charles Sumner, foe of wrong,
  Of other's pain, inflicted sorrows,
  Infected inequality,
  His own day's struggle, now tomorrow's."

Well, here goes, I thought to myself: here it is. I am *not* chickening out, even though no one would ever know if I did. I am setting myself up for failure, Mother, because of you, and what you have taught me to know is right.

And looking straight at her, I recited:

"His own bold cry must never die,
  Even in face of forecast doom,
  Even that caste who cries, 'Too fast!' "

—I looked at the audience—

"Even by others in this room.

"For we cannot run away from pain,
  And not for moral reasons alone,
  We cannot run away from pain,
  For others' torment is our own.
    Their blow our blood, their fear our terror,
    Injustice to our sisters is our own slavery, mirrored."

End of poem. End of spell. Adieu, assured victory!—nice while you lasted. The audience exploded. "Votes for women!" Marcella screamed. "Votes for women!" She leapt to her feet,

George, Cornelia, and Julia applauding wildly. So did Mother. So did Mrs. Dixon; so did the policeman; so did maybe twenty others. The rest began booing. I saw one of the judges slash a long vertical line through his evaluation sheet; another didn't even bother, just balled his up and threw it over his shoulder.

I stood there blushing, approved and excoriated. Catcalls mingled with acclaiming hands. "Injustice to our sisters" had hit its mark as accurately as that cane had slammed into Charles Sumner's eagerly offered skull.

I lost the Greater and Metropolitan Boston Fine Arts and Poetry Fair, of course. A poem on Bunker Hill ("Brave lads! Red coats / Spilling our patriots' blood / On precious Massachusetts mud") won instead. Mrs. Dixon placed second. "Gettysburg" got third. I got Honorable Mention. It felt honorable, too.

It felt especially honorable two days later, when Mother, face still aglow, took me aside and told me how much she knew winning had meant to me, and how proud she was of my sacrifice. To show her appreciation, she said, she had arranged a present—a marvelous gift made possible through her many friends, her connections on two continents, a lot of favors, a lot of influence, a lot of money, a lot of badgering, and a flurry of frenzied telegrams. When my trip to see Father in London was over, she said, I could come home on that brand-new ship everyone was talking about.

I was delighted. So it's true, I thought: life really does work out the way it's supposed to. For sacrificing my art on the altar of women's suffrage, I was receiving a reward far greater than winning a contest. I couldn't imagine a gift in the world more exciting than passage on board the *Titanic*.

CHAPTER THREE

THE FIRST SIX DAYS OF MY VISIT TO LONDON WERE MUCH LIKE my previous visits: instructive, enjoyable, busy—a little bit boring. Father, with much fanfare, took time off from his usual life—whatever that was—to show me the standard attractions: the Thames, the bridges, the theaters, the National Gallery; Johnson's home, Dickens's home; the Tower, the Tate. Dozens of churches; acres of parks; hundreds of statues. It was fun, because being with Father was fun, but we'd done it before, all of it—we'd done it, in fact, each time I'd come over, and each time we did, it became slightly less interesting. I longed for my father to come up with something different, something which might explain—or better yet, demonstrate—the allure and seduction of living abroad. But I didn't want to hurt his feelings by asking for anything special.

It was at tea on the seventh day that Father announced he was hosting, that very evening, one of his "little parties." But not just a party, he said—a *literary* party. And not just literature as I knew it, either, but *artistic* literature—that hazy subspecies of brilliance and slag known as Bohemia. I was delighted; it was, I instantly realized, Father's peculiar and charming way of both recognizing my restlessness and acknowledging my approaching adulthood. A party! An authors' party, a party of freaks and geniuses: a *grown-ups'* party. Just what I'd wanted, and had been too polite to request.

Dressing for such an occasion turned out to be somewhat confusing. Father had been singularly vague: "Anything you want, Sumner—walking shorts, sandals, a suit. *Express* yourself. But nothing formal." Huh? I had studied my clothes for an hour, pondering which combination of garments best expressed me, before settling on gray cotton slacks and an Irish fisherman's sweater my mother had given me last Christmas. I slipped on the pants and sweater and looked in the mirror.

As usual, I was a shock. Sometime during the last eight months I had leapt from boyhood to adolescence, losing in the process almost every physical trait I had learned to recognize as my own. I used to be short, blond, round, and happy; now I was tall, my hair had darkened, I was bruisingly skinny, and no matter how I felt or what I was thinking, I looked perpetually anxious. Even my eyes, once a bright, cheerful blue, now were purple and brooding, so that even when I wasn't worried, I looked it. I felt like a fraud, presenting a gravity I was not really experiencing: that *did* worry me, and then the circle was complete. I looked like a terribly serious, seriously gawky young man.

I studied my unfamiliar reflection. The Irish sweater was definitely much too casual for Mayfair; it was also too short, my wrists and neck both popping out long before its knitter had ever intended. My new dark hair needed cutting. My new sad face needed joy. I looked horrifying; I looked like the type of boy who was sweet as a child but later grew up to bludgeon a senator. I was starting to peel off the sweater when Father entered.

"Sumner!" he smiled. "What a . . . what an original getup!"

"I was just taking it off."

"No, no, it's perfect. You look like an anarchist."

That was good? I started to wonder about this party. Father nudged me aside to peer at his own reflection. He was wearing a perfectly fitted gray-striped suit, matching vest, gray handkerchief, ink-black shoes, and a shirt as crisp as a doily. Around his throat was a black silk scarf, dotted with little yellow and green palm trees and orange crescent moons.

I stared at his tropical neckwear.

"Oh, just a little affectation," he said. "Some of the people who'll be showing up tonight go in for this sort of thing. Appearance a mirror of the inner soul and all that, you know. 'His outer self, himself within—' "

He stopped reciting and began pacing my little room. "You wouldn't have anything to drink in here, would you?" he asked. "No, of course not. Just joking. We could go downstairs and have something there. That is, I could, and you could watch. Or you could too, if you like. Brace yourself for the evening, as it were. Does your mother let you imbibe on special occasions?"

"No, sir," I said.

"Quite right," said Father. "America is baffling enough to intoxicate the perfectly sober." He stopped in front of the mirror again and readjusted the scarf.

"I must confess," he said, "I'm a tiny bit nervous tonight. I've finally decided to read some of my own work—just a little poem, nothing special. But I've seen this audience get unbelievably hostile when they don't like something. And I'm a tad uneasy what they might do to me."

"Do to you?"

"Hurt me," my father said.

I joined him at the mirror. Bursting from both ends of the sweater, I looked even more apprehensive than usual. I gazed at both our uncertain faces.

"These people," I said, "they're all your friends, aren't they?"

"Yes, of course. I also support them. Literature unfortunately is almost always its only reward."

"Yes, but—I mean, how could they hurt you if they like you? Nobody's that rude."

"Don't be so sure. Besides," he added, fluffing his knot, "I don't want them cheering because they *have* to. I want them cheering because they *want* to."

I was surprised—I'd wondered myself, on occasion, if people who told me they liked my poetry really meant they liked *me*. But I'd always assumed that such worries were part of the special preserve of childhood, where perception of talent is so tightly linked with perception of personality. Now, hearing Father express my own fears, I felt liberated and also depressed: liberated to know that my feelings were shared, depressed since it meant they would not disappear with adulthood. Also, his use of the word "cheering" was interesting—embarrassingly frank, perfectly appropriate. For the last thing an artist—even a child artist—wants is polite applause. Cheers or else the most bitter and yapping criticism, which you always can blame on an idiot audience's missing your point.

Father darted one final glance at the mirror. So did I— hopeless—and we went downstairs.

The drawing room, during my hour of angst-driven primping, had been transformed. The silk wall hangings had been rolled down, the Flemish carpets had been rolled up; the tranquil gaslit oasis where Father and I had spent six nights of peaceful musings now looked ready to entertain a high-ranking diplomat, or a circus. Every corner was crammed with extra chairs and tables and large black vases I'd never seen before. Armfuls of sprightly jonquils spilled yellow nuggets of pollen over the shiny wood. In the center of the room an enormous amount of edibles beckoned: round seeded rye breads, wheels of leaky Camembert, mounds of berries and apples, piles of meat. Bottles of wine and decanters of peppered vodka lined every table.

"Now, Sumner," my father said, "I need to warn you about some of tonight's guests. They may not be quite what you're used to. When people say 'avant-garde,' they usually mean—"

Just then there was a rumble outside of footsteps and laughter; the door was flung open, no one having knocked, and people began flooding in, kissing each other, tossing their hats onto the floor, bumping into planters and umbrella stands. A woman kissed Fischer, my father's butler, on the mouth, for what seemed to me a very long time; Fischer stood impassive, arms stiff with a dozen furs. Guests streamed through on either side, flashes of color and laughter exploding as they headed into the drawing room. Some men, and most of the women, sparkled, their jackets and suits and gowns hours ahead of the latest fashion. A few wore each other's clothes; I stared at a woman in a skintight uniform from the Boer War, and a man in the lace-collared mourning robes of Queen Victoria.

Heads and names bobbed around me like Halloween apples. The lady who had kissed Fischer admired my sweater. The man in the dress asked if I thought Roosevelt could defeat Taft. The Boer soldier gave me her autograph, signed on a napkin with disappearing ink; before I could read it, it was gone. I was entranced and enchanted and fascinated; never had I felt so much energy, sensed so much vigor—seen so much glitter and zing.

I was hoping to perch in an empty corner, to attend in private absorption this public play with no secondary characters, when I saw Father waving at me, proudly pointing me out to a bulky, bearded gentleman. I waved back, waiting for the man's lips to part in the expected smile. No smile came. Suddenly I was afraid: not for me, but for Father, his arm intertwined with a guest too boorish to be bothered to smile at his host's own son. I hurried over to protect him.

Father slapped my hand into the bearded man's unenthused fingers.

"Sumner, this is Gordon Marsh, the famous playwright and politician. Gordon, my son."

"How do you do, young sir?" said Mr. Marsh, pummeling my hand.

"Fine, sir, and you?" I answered, trying to recollect what he had written: imitation Ibsen and bad Shaw, Mother had once said. "Are you working on a new play?" I asked brightly.

"Always, always." His voice was gravelly and his breath smelled of rum. "And how is your mother's work coming along? The suffragette movement?"

"Suffra*gist*, sir," I corrected without thinking. "Very well, thank you. Are you interested in voting rights for women?"

"I," he said, after a pompous, annoying pause, "am interested in human rights. For everyone. That's why I can't support people like your mother. They see women's rights only as women's rights, not in terms of the overall oppression of the working masses by the ruling class. They don't understand that real equality is possible only in a truly egalitarian society." He prodded me with a stubby finger. "Do you follow me?"

Suddenly I remembered one of his plays: the women did nothing but cook and have children, then later one of them died delivering a message which allowed her brother to become a hero during the Paris Commune. I looked at Father, but he refused to look back, torn between his trinary duties as host, parent, and totally apolitical *artiste*. I was about to compose what I hoped would come out as a blistering comeback when the front door opened again. Two more men entered, one very cautiously, one with the force of a packet of dynamite.

"Oh, Christ," Marsh muttered, "not him," and he withdrew so quickly that I immediately decided I liked both new men enormously.

The cautious man was dressed plainly, with a black wool suit like a rural schoolmaster's, black-framed spectacles, and a black crumpled hat, which he obviously didn't know he ought to remove. His glasses were horrifying, as chunky and thick as telescope lenses, and his eyes behind all that refraction were distorted, enormous, almost monstrous—yet, for all that, very kind-looking. His companion outshone him at every step: red hair, ruddy features, veined nose, bloodshot eyes. He wore a yellow shirt, and, unbelievably, purple trousers, and a purple-and-white-striped jacket. He looked like a gypsy, a clown without makeup. He spotted Father and rushed over, clutching Father's shoulders with both manicured hands.

"They burned his goddamn book, Jordan!" he shouted. "They burned every copy!"

My father showed no shock at the man's clothes, only dismay at his words. "A pity, a pity," he murmured. The man in the black suit glided up. "I'm very sorry," Father said. The man nodded.

"Sumner," my father said, "I want you to meet two very close friends. Mr. Ezra Pound and Mr. James Joyce. My son, Sumner."

Mr. Joyce, the man with the glasses, smiled slightly. Mr. Pound grabbed my hand and shook it fervently.

"The Bostonian!" he cried. "Good to see someone from the States around here! How are things in *patria mia?*"

I blushed. "Fine, I guess."

" 'A boyish young Brahmin from Beantown,' " Mr. Pound

bellowed, " 'Found Cambridge too much of a mean town. / He preferred joining swords / With the angels at Lourdes'—give me a hand here, somebody—"

"Sumner's a poet himself," Father said. "He's even won awards for his work. However, he writes—well, let's say in the classic mode, inspired by the Greeks . . ."

"The greatest poets," Mr. Joyce said shyly. "Excellent models to work from."

"Damn right!" Mr. Pound echoed. "Jordan, where's the victuals, as we say in America. I'm starved!"

Father pointed toward the rapidly disappearing food.

"Sumner," rasped Mr. Pound, slapping my back, "if you want to feed your soul, become a poet; your body, a politician. Poets starve, or they would if it weren't for folks like your pop. J.J., come!"

I watched them walk to one of the tables. Gordon Marsh was hunched in a corner, glaring; I was surprised it was the sweet Mr. Joyce, not the fiery Mr. Pound, he was snarling at. I turned around to ask Father why, but he had gone to join Fischer at the doorway, where a short, striking woman was removing her chalky ermine.

I think she was beautiful, though I really couldn't tell. She was so different—even in that crowd, even with people like Mr. Pound and the male Victoria, she stood out. Her hair was blond and so closely cropped that it was shorter than mine; it clung to her small head like a tiny feathery cap. She wore a silk dress in a disturbing green: not green like grass, not green like jade— green like the bottom of a swamp, a thick, mottled, dirty, enticing green. On her face was something I never had seen on a woman, ever—powder. And not just powder, but something red over the powder that glistened like gel; and the same gel was on her lips. Her eyes were heavily shadowed and her lashes looked like absurdly tiny black bones. Her whole face seemed like a mask, painted and dried and lying perfectly over her own flesh.

She didn't wait for Father's formal introduction; she stepped right by him and swooped up my hand.

"And this must be Sumner!" she said, as if declaiming. "I've heard so much about you from your papa. It's a pleasure, my dear, truly a pleasure."

I found myself staring at her eyelashes, entranced by their color and imagined weight. "It's a pleasure for me, too, miss," I said. I started helplessly blinking.

"What lashes!" the woman said to my father. She turned to him, smiling. "And I see where he got them," she added.

"Sumner, this is Miss Evelyn Manning," Father said. "One of the best-known actresses in British theater today. A Shavian interpretess of the first order."

"You have a very handsome son," Miss Manning told him.

Father looked at me, suddenly curious. "Would you mind if he and I spoke a little?" she asked him.

"Please do. Of course, if it's all right with you, Sumner?"

"Yes, sir," I said manfully.

With neither discernible look nor gesture she somehow directed me to a small sofa. We both sat down, I stiffly, she with studied grace. I noticed her perfume. It was like nothing I ever had smelled before. It wasn't Mother's rosewater, or my sisters' violets, or my Aunt Grace's pleasantly tart lemon verbena; and it wasn't the candied ginger my cousin Emmy stole from the kitchen and daubed in the crooks of her elbows. Miss Manning's perfume smelled like Europe, like a mixture of votive candles, aged cider, and fallen leaves. It was pleasurable and almost nauseating at the same time.

"I've heard so much about you," she said. "I really hope I can become one of your friends."

"Yes, ma'am," I said. I wondered what she must think the rest of my friends were like—if she really imagined she was but one great actress among my many.

"Your papa tells me you've become quite a good writer. You must have gotten that from him along with the eyelashes."

I felt myself redden. My inherited eyelashes were downcast, as were my eyes; I couldn't stop staring at her hypnotic dress. It seemed to have its own animation, shifting, breathing, living its own life, catching color and light. I tried to look at Miss Manning's face but her features were blurred; only her frock, nestled in at the waist, out at the hips, seemed focused. Her bare right shoulder was less than six inches from my mouth; I felt I either could kiss her or nip her arm.

"I've never read anything Father's written," I said. "Except letters, of course."

"Ah, yes," she said. "I've received some letters myself."

"They're pretty," I said.

Her eyebrows, thin as fresh silk, rose in surprise. "Once he used a different color ink for every letter in my name," I explained.

She smiled, and without my quite seeing how, lifted her shoulder nearer my lips.

"He hasn't done that for me," she said. "At least not yet."

She seemed to be waiting for me to say something, but I was afraid to move my mouth.

"Do you also write multicolored love letters?" she asked.

I knew if I kept looking at her something momentous would happen. Trying frantically to decide whether or not I wanted it to, I looked across the room. Someone was saying something about Mr. Joyce's mentioning real people and real events when he wrote, and that was why his stories were burned.

"Oh, hell!" yelled Mr. Pound, wine dribbling from his lips. "We all know why books are burned! They only get burned when they're about copulation. Copulation! That's what causes book burnings!''

I'd heard the word "copulation" before but what I thought it meant didn't seem to make sense in this context. I looked sheepishly at Miss Manning. Again she arched her silken brows.

"Sounds intriguing," she said.

"Yes, indeed," said someone behind us. "I always come to Jordan's for the latest literary intercourse."

I looked up. A sandy-haired man in his early thirties, wearing wide white pants and a red kimono, stood grinning toothily at us both.

"Evelyn, you mustn't flirt so outrageously or people will talk," he said, ignoring me completely as he leaned over and kissed her shoulder with enviable naturalness. "This youngster will be tempted out of Eden soon enough, without any of us having to play Eve."

"Why, Lord Penbrooke!" Miss Manning exclaimed without sounding offended. "Be serious! How can you say such things?"

"It's easy, madam, I just open my mouth and out they fly. And I'm perfectly serious. There's so little of you to go around, and so much of it's already gone."

I gaped, trying to follow.

"Besides, you already have the senior Jordan," this Penbrooke added. "Let Junior here find someone else."

It was like watching a play in a half-known language; I could make out the words but not the meaning. I knew in a roundabout way Miss Manning was being complimented, Father insulted, and I derided, all at once; but I had no idea why, or exactly how. But I knew where my loyalties lay, and it certainly wasn't with this mean-tongued aristocrat who liked to make fun of people who were too awkward or young or polite to fight back. I mumbled my excuses to Miss Manning and slid off the sofa. She looked hurt—but then, I reminded myself, she was an actress. She could probably look anything.

I took a few steps away from her and saw I was deep in the heart of my father's party.

All seemed successful and under control. Already things had settled into the usual pattern of large gatherings: one master circle ruled by a single loud speaker; several groups of auxiliary listeners, each willing the osmosis of proximity to ooze them into the main cell; three or four soulful couples blind to all but each other; numerous rejects and outcasts; and those who had just come to eat. Without really meaning or wanting to, I found myself starting to eavesdrop. Most of the conversations concerned the arts (somehow always pronounced, by these people, with a capital A), but more than a few, I observed, were about the *Titanic*'s imminent maiden voyage—her existence had managed to catch the attention of even these rarefied people. However, I soon enough noticed, this attention was largely negative: Gordon Marsh was decrying her "egregious extravagance" and "inordinate decadence," while Lord Penbrooke chimed in with a snide little speech about "exhibitionist peacocks displaying their First Class tickets like so many tail feathers." He should talk, I thought.

Then I saw Mr. Joyce. He was sitting all by himself, sipping tea, next to one of my father's fiercest Picassos; the painting seemed to engulf him, its colors absorbing his pale skin and black suit, turning him monochromatic. Of all the fruits and breads and sweets and cheeses set up, he had taken only one scrap of seedcake; he chewed it slowly, his glasses bobbing up and down as he swallowed.

I watched him. He looked—or I felt—a little forlorn, a little lonely; at any rate I sensed a kinship I liked.

"Mr. Joyce, may I join you?" I asked.

"Please do." He put his plate on the floor, brushed off his fingers, and turned to me attentively, in a way few other grown-ups ever had: as an adult settling in for an adult conversation. I was so flattered my mind went empty.

"It's difficult," he suggested, "to get your bearings some-times at these affairs."

"Yes, sir," I said gratefully.

"At least it is for me."

"Oh, me too, sir," I assured him.

"I just always hope there'll be a peaceful little shadow for me to deposit myself into," he said. "Then when I feel more easeful I venture out."

He had a melodic voice, very deep, very pleasant, with only a whisper of childhood lilt.

"I'm sorry they burned your book, sir," I said.

He smiled slightly. "Thank you for your sympathy."

"Why did they do it?"

I'm sure no one had ever asked him; he looked surprised, then amused.

"Let's just say," he replied, "when I mentioned the city of Dublin, I got a bit personal. Said things, and painted images, my fellow countrymen wished not to hear, nor to see. I certainly wasn't shocked at their reaction."

I remembered the response of *my* fellow countrymen to the amended last line of "The Martyrdom of Charles Sumner." But this didn't seem at all like the same thing: that was political, this was personal. "If you knew people weren't going to like it," I said, "then why write it down in the first place?"

His heavy glasses focused on my face before he answered. "There are many ways I can explain," he said after several moments. "However, I want to be sure I do it clearly. Your father said you wrote poetry. Do you find it easy to write?"

"Not exactly, sir."

"Why not?"

Now I was the one without answers. It wasn't exactly easy because . . . well, it just wasn't, that's all.

"I'm not sure," I said slowly. "I guess it's because there's so much going on at once. You have to follow certain rules, and you have to sound good, and you have to look intelligent, and you have to communicate—and all at the same time. You feel something, or you see something, and it's so real to you, but to make it real to somebody else and still play by the rules—well, it's just really very hard."

Mr. Joyce nodded. "Your answer is very thoughtful, and I think correct. Writing as you describe it is very difficult. Now those rules you referred to—the rules of poetry, correct? Meter, line, et cetera."

"Yes, sir."

"Now, suppose to all those literary rules," he said, "I added a thousand others. Not rules of language but rules of limitation. Rules which determine the nature of your visions, and rules which determine how you express what you've envisioned. Wouldn't those rules make it more difficult—almost impossible—to write?"

"Yes, sir," I said. "It's hard enough as it is."

"Well, that's why I wrote what I did. To write, truly write, you have to discard as many rules as possible. The literary rules if you can dream up something better. The other rules even if you can't."

He leaned forward, his eyes flashing and misting behind their thick lenses.

"Permit me to give some unsolicited advice, Mr. Jordan," he said. "If you wish to continue as a writer you must resign yourself to living without rules. You must learn to survive without the clutching solace of your family, your community, your church. You must discard all their comforting, stifling instructions, and in the resulting loneliness you will have plenty of time, plenty of energy, plenty of freedom to write."

I felt puzzled, a little cowardly: I wasn't sure that I wanted to live—let alone write—in so lawless a world. But before I had time to ask for more details, Miss Manning joined us.

Mr. Joyce gazed sightlessly as she took my hand.

"Sumner, I'm sorry," she whispered, her voice warm, confidential. "Lord Penbrooke and I are old friends, that's all. I certainly didn't mean to hurt your father's son's feelings. It's just an ongoing joke, really."

"I don't appreciate being the subject of ongoing jokes," I said coldly. "Nor do I appreciate being twitted simply because I happen to be twelve years old and you happen not to. And saying you're both old friends doesn't make it any better. I'd rather be alone than play by your rules."

Beside me I saw Mr. Joyce smile, then rise. Miss Manning, flustered, repeated her apology, this time more entreatingly.

"Please, Sumner," she said, "please. I'm really sorry. Don't tell your father. Please."

With Mr. Joyce gone, my stance as the lonely outcast left too. "Of course I won't tell him," I said loftily. "It's none of his affair."

"And we can be friends?"

"Naturally," I said in my most gracious voice.

"Thank you, Sumner."

"You're welcome, Evelyn."

She allowed that to pass and surveyed the room, where people were gulping the last of the food and wine and looking for places to sit. "The readings are ready to start," she whispered. "Will you join me?"

I looked at my father, patiently urging those still eating to finish up; he spotted me and Miss Manning and pointed to three empty chairs. I took her elbow and coolly—I hoped—

walked her over. Father nervously joined us, and the readings began.

It was nothing like the Greater and Metropolitan Boston Fine Arts and Poetry Fair. There were no introductions. There was no applause. There was no *order:* people just stood up, opened their mouths, and started to read. They mostly recited poems; a few, bits of stories. I couldn't tell whether what Mr. Pound read was a poem or not, only that it somehow came out both sweetly delicate and massively cruel at the same time. Most of what I heard I didn't understand; what I *did* understand, I mostly didn't like. Everything seemed messy, and weirdly vague, the poetry full of language which sounded wonderful but really never evoked an image, or stories which started off in one direction and then ended up not in that direction or even in another direction, but with no direction at all that I could perceive.

If the content was vague, the critiques were not. Everybody was attacked, sometimes viciously, always loudly, and often with a verve the attacker's own offering itself had lacked. The male Victoria, after shooting down a short story about a Kenyan coffee plantation, read a poem which rhymed the words "chasm" and "spasm," "Tasso" and "lasso," "schism" and "jism"; Mr. Pound laughed so hard he started spitting up. Gordon Marsh presented a scene from his latest play: five voluble socialist prostitutes discussing the Corn Laws. More shrieks and catcalls. An earnest-looking girl with curly red hair read something tender and springlike, then trembled as Lord Penbrooke shouted, "Pretty words, but it's got no guts, no passion! It's like hearing your goddamn report card!"

"You don't care, you don't feel it, you don't love it!" Pound howled in agreement.

"You're writing a poem about coming!" sneered the Boer woman. "I want to come when I read it!"

I looked at Mr. Joyce. He had removed his glasses and now sat looking puzzled and overwhelmed, like a student in the wrong math class. He put his glasses back on only when Father's turn came, smiling sweetly as Father twisted his fingers, mumbled a greeting no one could hear, swallowed a few times, and withdrew a piece of paper from his pocket. I felt instant recognition: all Father's behavior patterns were mine exactly, and I wondered how many stalls and mumbles I would try shuffling through before reading my poem to Ezra Pound. I hoped with heart-quickening fervency that my father would be a success.

"Well," Father said. "The title of my work is 'Images of Life and Death.' " He swallowed again and cleared his throat. His voice cracking—God, exactly like me!—he read, " 'Sunrise . . . bobbing gems in the golden light, / Moonrise . . . sobbing Thames in the . . .' "

Nobody moved.

" '. . . olden blight,' " Father whispered. " 'Like the chords from Pan's lyre, plucked from visions of youth and love' —uh—that is, 'love and youth, plucked from visions of love and'—uh—'youth . . .' "

And this went on, Father losing his place, swallowing, then choking out another line while everyone listened in perfect silence. I felt a gnawing in my stomach, just as though it were my poem—me—being injected into this stillness. I studied each face, trying to read what anyone thought. Pass? Fail? I couldn't tell.

When he finally finished, I braced myself for the inevitable hatchet. But no one said anything.

"Comments?" Father anxiously asked.

Silence.

I couldn't believe it. They'd been so nasty, so plain and happily brutal, with everyone else! I felt relieved and very, very surprised: these people hadn't struck me as this polite. But Father looked crestfallen.

"Nothing?" he said.

Mr. Pound reached for an apple. "Fine, Jordan, fine," he belched.

"Yes, very nice," said the Victoria. "Nice in a nice way, that is. Very imagistic."

Miss Manning, on my right, sighed.

What I didn't understand was why everyone seemed so uncomfortable. No one had acted like this with anyone else—even the redheaded girl looked embarrassed. Mr. Pound finished his apple and tossed the core across the room.

"J.J.!" he shouted. "It's your turn! Let's hear some *real* writing!"

So there it was. These people—my father's friends—had not found his work good enough even to criticize. They just liked him because he had money and gave parties, and was kind enough to attend to their ill-mannered comments while serving them food. They didn't see, and if they saw they didn't care, that he had a sweetness in him, a deep will to please, and a genuine love and respect for the talent the nucleus of this group represented.

I tugged his arm. "I enjoyed your recitation very much, Father," I said.

He smiled in pain. "Thank you, Sumner."

"I really did. I really liked it."

"Thank you," he said again. He looked sad and wistful, a wallflower at his own party. Then he turned toward Mr. Joyce, who was quietly checking his notes as though preparing a lecture. Watching Father's face change from mournful to rapt, with no pause for envy or resentment, I felt an almost crippling love for this goodhearted man. I took his hand and squeezed it. Across his lap Miss Manning smiled at our little clan.

The others were still talking when Mr. Joyce began. His voice was low, and he made no effort to raise it; it was his audience who had to make accommodations. One by one, like a crowd in a darkening theater, the guests turned silent, expectant.

> "Mr. James Duffy lived in Chapelizoid because he wished to live as far as possible from the city of which he was a citizen and because he found all the other suburbs of Dublin mean, modern and pretentious. He lived in an old somber house and from his windows he could look into the disused distillery or upwards along the shallow river on which Dublin is built. The lofty walls of his uncarpeted room were free from pictures. He had himself bought every article of furniture in the room; a black iron bedstead, an iron washstand, four cane chairs. . . ."

He read without expression or apparent interest, like someone reading somebody else's shopping list. He read for fifteen minutes, a short sad story with very little plot, almost no action, a poignant veer toward the end, and language as simple as water. The story finished with the main character, whom I didn't really like, mourning someone I didn't really know; how this could be wrenching and judgmental and terrifying I couldn't understand, but it was. And how it could sound like poetry at the same time it sounded so simple baffled and delighted me. For the first time in my life I experienced that oddest of cosmic gratitudes: thankfulness I spoke English.

The guests' reaction to Mr. Joyce was the same as to Father. They didn't say a word. They were so still I could hear water hissing in the distant kitchen. They were so quiet I could hear the wood burning in my bedroom fireplace, three stories up. They sat unapplauding, their faces dazed, their eyes passionate, their expressions flickering with pain and wonder. They sat paralyzed, like that Pennsylvania audience almost fifty years earlier, sitting motionless for ten minutes, unwilling to clap or weep, after the oration at Gettysburg.

About ten minutes later I went to my room. I wasn't tired but I undressed anyway, and lay down on the bed. I wanted to think about a subject which several of tonight's guests and a number of their recitations had brought into most sharp focus.

The subject was sex.

Sex was something about which I had heard much and understood little. I knew it was not just one thing, just one act; it was an entire cluster of acts, all leading up to the same baffling conclusion. Dozens, hundreds of distinct phenomena were all sex-related: Sunday-school lectures on concupiscence; Mother's rule about never reading Zola; those off-limits medical texts at the Boston Public Library. That quick hush of voices whenever I walked past a room where someone was newly pregnant. All this had to do with sex, and so did my nearly biting Miss Manning's shoulder, and Mr. Joyce's book being burned, and the male Victoria's poem, and Mr. Pound's shriek about copulation. But how could so many unconnected strictures, experiences, and allusions all be steps up the same stairway?

Reason, our science teachers were always intoning—Reason is the key. What did I know for certain? Like an archaeologist at a meager dig, I surveyed my flimsy data:

1. Sex was related to the birth of children.

2. All animals did it.

2a. So did some plants.

3. It had to do with the genitals.

4. It was dangerous and evil—except this seemed unreasonable in light of Points 1 and 2. For if sex had to do with the

birth of children, if it was the mechanism used by all species to propagate, how could it be dangerous or evil?

The contradiction troubled me. And what troubled me most was how I felt as I tried bringing Reason to this particular riddle. Excitement assailed me; I felt giddy with helpless elation, and I knew I had never been this enthusiastic applying Reason to any subject before. Perhaps it was this excitement, how easily it overcame rational thought, which made sex such a tainted subject.

But something was off in the overall picture. I had Points 1, 2, 3, and 4, but the next step didn't seem like Point 5, it was more like Point 88, or 720—some infinitely distant positive integer. I could fathom procreation, I could fathom evil: nature procreated, and certain actions—murder, violence—were obviously evil. What I couldn't comprehend was the nonbiological, nonmoral aspect of sex. It affected all sorts of components of life—interactions with others, the way we dressed, the books they allowed you to read—far beyond the borders of biology or morality. It was the human side of sex, the way it determined behavior, which I couldn't understand.

Maybe if I just knew what it looked like. I could envision a man and woman standing together doing something or other, but that was about as far as I got. I certainly didn't know what a woman's body looked like, despite living in a house filled with them, and I couldn't make out how a man's would—I don't know—*interact* with one. It all seemed so mysterious.

And exciting. I remained excited. I was still excited until finally I was asleep.

I don't know how long I slept—only that after what felt like hours I awoke with a start as my door creaked open. I saw a man's silhouette peeking in. Then Father called, softly, "Sumner?"

Something made me not answer. He called again, then whispered, "It looks as though he's fast asleep."

I didn't budge. Another voice responded, "I'm certain he is. Children his age sleep so soundly."

It was Miss Manning.

"I'm sure we won't disturb him," she continued. "And besides, I don't know how much longer I can wait for you."

"Yes, darling, I feel just like—"

Father pulled shut the door and blocked out the rest. Strain as I might, I couldn't hear another word.

But I knew this was it. Right here, within my grasp, was the fifth piece in the sex puzzle. I knew I should stay in bed; that was not only reasonable, it was also the only polite, decent, honorable thing to do. But Reason, as I was already discovering, was weaker than my drive to know the unknowable.

I slipped out of bed and tiptoed to the door. If opening it made any noise at all, I resolved, I would go no farther; I would make this door my adviser in what to do next. I knew I needed an adviser because it was obvious I no longer had a conscience.

The door did not make even the slightest sound. I walked into the hall. Light from my father's bedroom splashed the wall. I crept to his door.

What was *wrong* with me? How could I do this? Do what, I didn't know, I just knew it was wrong. And it wasn't wrong like eavesdropping on my sisters, or trying to find hidden Christmas presents: those acts were mischievous; this act was shocking. What would Mother think if she caught me in this corridor? What about all my friends and family back home?

But you're not home, I argued. You're in London with the father who left your mother, and with his strange friends who associate arson with intercourse. No wonder you're behaving this way. You'll be fine when you get back to Boston.

I reached the door and peeked around the corner. I couldn't see into the room, but I did make out a cool shimmer of mirror. And within its center I saw my father.

He was standing next to Miss Manning and kissing her. The kiss seemed to go on endlessly. Finally he lifted his head and I saw his expression: it was pained, desperate, foreign. He was fumbling with something on her dress. Miss Manning gently pushed his hand away and loosened a snap. Her dress fell open. She undid a row of buttons on her corset and removed it. She was completely naked from the waist up.

I couldn't stop watching. Father bent down again and kissed her neck and her shoulders and then her small breasts—kissed them right on the nipples, which stood out like tattoos on her pale flesh. He seemed to spend an inordinate amount of time with each breast, rotating his tongue on her skin like a cat cleaning a kitten. Then he pulled back, gasping, and blew out a candle burning next to the bed. I twisted back into the corridor just as he shut the door.

I stayed there for several minutes, pressed flat to the wall, a gothic carving. I could hear moans and sighs from inside the room. At my wrists, at my neck, inside my temples, behind my eyes, blood rushed about wildly, like a river after a tempest, full to the brim, roiling through banks and flooding the innocent countryside. My heart smashed against my chest. And between my legs pulsed a painful grossness that burned, and throbbed, and fretted, and whispered to me to touch.

I ran back into my room, leapt beneath the blankets, and yanked up my nightshirt. I thrust my hands down to my groin.

Then I hesitated. My hands were coiled but still not touching. For it was too dangerous, too evil. I could not go through with It, whatever It was that I could not go through with.

But then something happened: that short hesitation, that

sole single second of minor resistance, had the effect of convincing me everything was under control—presented, argued, and duly adjudged acceptable. My hands reached down again. It felt better than anyone could imagine. Didn't other people know about this? I yanked, tugged, stroked, and massaged. My heart beat louder, my blood rushed quicker. The bonfire burning my hands burned brighter.

Then came release. Flying, floating, falling, landing. An unseen force soothed me, caressing me into utter bliss. I was whole, perfect, finished. I felt completely justified.

And then I felt a horrible, disgusting, sticky glob crawling over my hands and thighs. Was it blood? Had I horribly injured myself? My hands shuddered, bliss replaced fully by absolute fear. I had done something terrible. I had sinned a great sin. I was now incapable of goodness, of godliness. Unlike my mother. Unlike my sisters, or my namesake. And I was totally alone. There was no one I could turn to. I could never confess to another living soul what I had done. I rolled over and curled up, wet and frightened and far from home, and wondering how everything in my life could have changed so quickly.

The gray scowling light of a London morning awoke me. It took a few moments for everything to come back, and when it did, it wasn't the fear I recalled, it was the ecstasy. I pulled back the covers, expecting blood or, at the very least, gallons of shellac. Everything had felt so sticky. But there was only a slight clotted residue on my legs and stomach. Like all dreams and nightmares, it washed off with water and light.

Father was already eating breakfast when I walked downstairs. He sat alone, with his tea and the London *Times*. No sign whatsoever of Evelyn Manning, or yesterday night.

"Good morning, Sumner," he said cheerfully, bobbing his cup at me. "Did you sleep well?"

"Yes, sir," I answered quietly, taking the opposite chair.

He seemed in the highest of spirits. "A beautiful morning," he said, folding up his newspaper. I looked doubtfully out the window. "Once the fog clears," he added, and buttered some toast. His euphoria was like a third presence in the room.

A servant silently handed me scones and marmalade. But I didn't seem capable of such mundane desires as hunger—I only had room in my mind for last night's memories. I felt that, for a few moments anyway, I truly had gone insane, and was unsure which could have caused it—the pulsing pleasure or the immobilizing fear.

But at least I had settled a piece of the sexual puzzle. I still didn't know exactly what it was that Father and Evelyn Manning had done in the darkness, causing their bed to rattle and them to tremble and moan, but I knew I had witnessed a moment of the *human* side of sex: the behavioral side. Sex was something done by adults when they were in love. It was probably best performed between two people within the bonds of matrimony, but apparently you could do it otherwise, too. Example: my father and Miss Manning.

Suddenly I wondered whether Mother had any lovers. Or my sisters. Or their girlfriends. I was horrified how easy it was to visualize any of them, all of them, exactly as I had seen Miss Manning last night, dress flung open, corset undone, a lover kissing their waiting breasts. I wanted desperately to halt this invasion of images, but I couldn't—I was pressing to picture what each of them looked like naked, even as I was loathing myself for doing so. I could see each of them, even my mother, and myself bent over, kissing their mouths, their throats, their breasts.

I tossed my napkin to the floor and raced upstairs. I barely had time to see Father's surprised face; if he spoke, I didn't hear him. I ran to my room. Slammed the door. Forced myself to wait a few seconds to see whether Father would follow. Then I unfastened my trousers and let them drop to the floor.

Before me beckoned my shocking secret, as enticing as yesterday night. Like candy, like a present, like a most-deserved prize. Again, like last night, I hesitated, and again this hesitation provided the justification to proceed. Besides, this would be the last time, absolutely—*absolutely,* I promised, as I felt my hands, already knowing what to do, reach for myself. A moment later, that warm silent explosion and the deadening calm.

But unlike last night, when I was finished there was no guilt —no paralyzing fear, no confusion. Instead I felt wonderful: very buoyed, very electric, the way I felt when I drank two cups of coffee without eating. My blood was bouncing in every artery; I couldn't stay still. Quickly I dug through my desk till I found my good pens and my journal. I had a great urge to do something creative and energetic: something totally nonsexual. Something to prove to my body my brain still worked.

I started a poem but nothing happened. I thought about writing Mother but that seemed terribly inappropriate at the moment. So I began a story. In my much-praised handwriting I wrote "Sumner Jordan's Trip to London" on the top of the page.

In the early spring of 1912, Sumner Jordan, having rejected all the clutching solace of his Boston upbringing, except his commitment to women's rights, came to London determined to dedicate his life to art and poetry. He also rather hoped a trip abroad might restore his body and spirit, for he had suffered a horrible beating following a poetry contest in which he had defended female suffrage before an ugly and well-armed mob.

While in London he became the darling of the English avant-garde, and was a frequent visitor to the salons of the great poets and dramatists of the day. They befriended him immediately, and soon he was regarded as the finest among them. Although recitation of poetry and short stories was usually followed by harsh criticism, Sumner's words were of such great beauty they were accompanied only by the most rapt silences, and then an endless amount of high praise.

While reading a selection from his book of collected— and later burned—short stories entitled *Bostonians,* a famous and beautiful actress, Miss M——— (discretion forbids me from giving her name!) fell in love with the handsome young invalid. She was fascinated by the story he read, which chroni- cled a young man's trip to a baseball game, since she, being English, had never seen, or even heard of, the Red Sox. She returned with Sumner to his home, and that night, in total darkness, they became

I couldn't write the word. Instead I reread what I had penned. I knew I ought to destroy it. But on a second reading I decided I rather approved of it, in a perverse sort of way. I liked the fantasy Sumner very much; he was doing everything the original was still waiting for, and for a few moments I allowed myself to believe the story Sumner was the real one, and I was only a figment of his imagination.

I heard a knock. My hands and arms smothered the paper.

"Sumner?"

"Yes, sir."

Father opened the door, at once seeing me slumped over my journal. "A letter?" he asked politely.

I was about to say yes when I heard him mumbling, "Sum- ner Jordan's Trip to London." He inflected the last syllable of "London," letting me know he was curious.

"A journal of our time together," he said lightly. "Might I take a look?"

"It's really very bad," I said. "Not what you or your friends are used to. I don't think you'd like it. I really don't think so."

He said nothing. He just looked hurt.

"I thought you'd been having a good time, Sumner. I didn't realize you thought otherwise."

"I'm having a great time!" I pleaded. "There's nothing in the story about me or you. We're having a wonderful time! It's just some dumb made-up story about an imaginary trip!"

He stepped away from my desk. I knew he was certain the story was about him. Still hunched over my journal, I watched him helplessly. The morning shadows made him taller and more gaunt than ever. I always had thought he looked old, but today he looked almost ancient, like somebody's sickly uncle—too close a relative not to love but too frail and feeble to lean on for anything. He must have had, in his life, dreams and fantasies, just as I did, just as everyone does . . . only he had lived long enough to see none of them come to pass. He was alone in a strange land, surrounded by false friends who courted him only for his wallet, and wooed by a lover who flirted with every man available, including his own son. He had left his home, deserted his wife and children to become a writer, and now his writer child had come to punish him. Now his best and only friend had hurt him in the most appropriate, most painful way possible. Through literature.

I jumped up and shoved the journal into his hands.

Reading, he looked as nervous as I felt. Then, about halfway through, his face softened. He finished. He returned the journal and said in a relieved voice, "So you liked Miss Manning?"

"Yes, sir. She's not like anybody I've ever met."

He smiled in a very gentle way. He was, after all, a very

gentle man. "Yes, I like her too. You have excellent taste in women, son."

He never had called me "son" before. The intimacy of the word engaged me like music, sweeter and deeper and more lyrical than anything anyone ever had written or read.

CHAPTER FOUR

FOR THE REST OF MY TIME IN LONDON, FATHER PRETTY MUCH left me alone; I guess that, having bared to me the reality of his existence—his writing career was a farce, his friends were all leeches, he was keeping a mistress— he now felt himself allowed to resume that existence, and as quickly as possible. He went back to attending the opening nights of new and unusual plays by new and unusual playwrights whose rent he was paying; he went back to visiting a half dozen small art galleries at which he was often the only buyer; he even returned to his poetry readings. Miss Manning now dined with us nightly, and often I met her again at breakfast. I adjusted as coolly as possible to these new routines.

One thing that Father's exposure of his real life did for me was to free me from culture. I understood without being told that my presence was not requested when Father went off on his little outings; he understood without being told that I therefore considered my time on my own to be time *of* my own, which meant I alone ought to get to decide what to do with it. For a couple of days I did nothing but go to street markets and cinema-houses, but that quickly grew tiresome; I never was much of a shopper, and cinema was something we had at home.

I began to get restless, and my efforts to hide this restlessness made me more restless yet. Ten days into my trip I decided to stage a minor revolt: I would visit the *only two places* in London which Father and Mother, who rarely agreed on anything, agreed to disdain and despise. The first one was Madame Tussaud's waxworks ("vulgar," said Father; "immoral," said Mother). The second ("unimportant," said Father; "anti-woman," said Mother) was Whitehall and the British Houses of Parliament.

I started with Madame Tussaud's. The moment I entered, I sensed its enormous appeal. This might be my first time at such an establishment, but, I instantly vowed, it would not be my last: there was something perversely alluring about the idea of preserving History, the eternal victim of time, in a substance as seemingly fragile as wax. Not to mention how much I approved of their choices of whom to immortalize, especially the surprisingly large number of outrageously beautiful royal mistresses. I didn't even bother reading their names—just studied their bodies, comparing them to what I had seen of Miss Manning's. They all were taller (but who cared about height?), and with longer hair (but who cared about hair length, either?); they all also were far more bosomy: as a matter of fact, they were so extremely buxom that some of them looked as though the weight of their breasts made up well over fifty percent of the weight of their entire bodies, so that a well-tossed half-penny piece could topple them bodice-first onto the ground. Even the slenderest were wider-hipped than Miss Manning, and even the widest-hipped were more narrow-waisted, giving the expression "hourglass figure" an erotic explicitness I hadn't realized was probably there all along. But none of them, in spite of the jut of their flesh and the arc of their waxen bodies, was attractive the way Evelyn Manning was, because Evelyn Manning breathed, and these wax dolls couldn't, and that simple act of humanity was far more ravishing than all of this deathless perfection.

After some time—a long time—I abandoned the royal mistresses and set off to examine the more important (though less enticing) historical figures: Nelson, Pepys, the young Queen Victoria, various poets and kings. Of these my favorite was the waxen figure of Madame Tussaud herself, beak-nosed and anxious, beadily eyeing this most original empire with the weary contentment of any successful entrepreneur. I gazed at her: it was easy to see why my parents, without ever once being here, hated this place. It wasn't its vulgarity, it wasn't its immorality —it was its *pointlessness*. There was nothing uplifting at Madame Tussaud's; you just had fun. A most successful first act of today's excursion, I thought. I went back outside.

Ah, to be a tourist—especially a tourist who's already toured the major museums. I decided to walk, via Hyde Park, toward Westminster. This turned out to be, although possible, a very indirect route; I didn't remember, until I got there, just how large Hyde Park was, nor quite how distant from Parliament and the river. But it was beautiful there, April-leafy and midweek-quiet, occupied mainly by dozens of deep-asleep babies and gray-caped nannies, each almost as lovely, in her own way, as Madame Tussaud's waxy concubines. I undertook Hyde Park Corner, ambling onward, into the double jewel of Green Park (swollen with crocuses, maddened with spring) and St. James's Park (if possible even lovelier and, oddly enough, more green). Grass merged into paths, paths into sidewalks, sidewalks into the city streets. I bore to my right, still headed, my maps assured me, toward Parliament.

Up ahead, somewhat vague in the misty air, I could make out, although just barely, the shifting outline of some sort of gathering. Hard to say what it was, exactly . . . anarchists, perhaps? A fire, a bomb, a death? Or maybe just traffic—commuters queued up for a bus. But in another country, everything seems exciting: I quickened my glacial pace. I noticed a few other people, mostly men—no, *all* men—also head up toward the crowd.

And I noticed some women, too. Two were walking the other way. They both looked upset. Four more men scurried by, then a good half dozen; they seemed in a hurry, and I wondered about the dynamics of such an assemblage, repelling women, attracting men.

Then it hit me. It was as though I'd been instantly transferred home, back to my mother, back to my house, back to a totally familiar issue and rhetoric.

There were five women and one man, surrounded by at least fifty male onlookers and maybe ten females. Three of the demonstrators were passing out handbills, pressing them into the spread hands of some, jamming them into the clenched fists of others—even from this distance I could see scores of flyers already crumpled and dropped to the ground. A gust of unfriendly wind blew one my way and I gathered it up. It was wet; the ink was already bleeding.

VOTES FOR WOMEN!

TODAY AT NOON A SPECIAL GUEST
SPEAKER FROM AMERICA!!

PLEASE JOIN US——ASK QUESTIONS——
DISCUSS THE MOST IMPORTANT ISSUE
FACING WOMEN TODAY

SUFFRAGE IS A RIGHT, IT IS NOT
A FAVOUR

Three other men joined the crowd. I don't know what made them stand out: certainly they seemed neither more hostile than anyone else, nor less supportive . . . nonetheless they concerned me. They appeared impatient, as though each had an appointment on the other side of this gathering but for some reason couldn't—wouldn't—be bothered to walk the extra few yards it would take to get there. They looked at each other. One of them noticed me watching; he lifted his hat and nodded, as if we were members of the same club.

Then one of them started barking! The noise came out of his mouth like a snort, a short, nasal, ugly, echoing grunt. Another man joined him. Another. Soon at least a dozen men were barking, hands on their hips, lips in a circle, puffy cheeks flushed with the effort of baying. The few women in the audience began seeking one another out, clumping in twos and threes against the yipping. The barking grew louder and shriller—angrier, more derisive, and more of a threat.

More *than* a threat, too. For the barking men, now wedged like a phalanx, were starting to press to the front, and one of the suffragists, seeing them, stepped back, breaking their fragile line. This was a bad mistake, one that my mother would never have allowed: for instead of six allies they had just become six single segments, six individual prey cornered and held by a snarling, encompassing crowd.

The men began closing in. Elbows and arms and raised umbrellas backed the demonstrators into the wet spiked fence; cursing shouts splattered the air. A gloved hand grabbed a bundle of pamphlets and threw them skyward; shredded newsprint rippled to earth. I saw a man shove the lone male demonstrator; he kicked back, a fist smashed his face, he slumped to the ground. A man in a long gray coat reached out and grabbed one of the women demonstrators.

She froze. The crowd froze too. The barking stopped. The man and woman stared like reflections at one another.

Slowly, gently, with deep concentration, as though unwrapping a rare and awaited present, the man loosened the buttoned collar of the woman's jacket. Fur parted, then a scarf, then the neck of a woolen sweater and a patch of white blouse, a white almost as white as the motionless woman's terrified face. The man pulled at another button. Pink and scarlet, like the interior of a peony, the woman's throat emerged.

The pale air turned a little darker. None of us seemed strong enough to move.

The man in the gray coat tugged a third button. I caught a glimpse of some green lacy undergarment I'd never seen before.

The woman gave a quiet moan which reverberated like a drumbeat in our silent circle. The suffrage man, still on the ground, tried to sit up but couldn't. I must do something! I told myself; I must move, act, make something happen! This woman could be my mother, my sister, my cousin, my aunt! But the silence and formality of this public stripping froze me.

The hand reached out for another button. I opened my mouth, forcing down air, gulping it in like water, holding it, resolving to speak the moment I needed breath. I shuddered, dizzy with fear and lack of oxygen. I exhaled, then started to shout.

"Let go of that woman's jacket immediately!" cried a clear, angry voice.

I jumped; the voice was not mine.

"I said, let her go!" it repeated.

I turned to follow the voice. Over the sea of hats I could see nothing: just the crowd, the fence, the man in the long coat, his wide-eyed intended victim. Everyone seemed paralyzed, already resigned to violence, folly, surrender. . . . Then, like glass against steel, the paralysis snapped. That voice—sharp, harsh, *female*—had penetrated the immobile couple with a fencer's precision. The man's hand dropped. At the very same second the woman pushed him away, with no more than mild annoyance, the way she might shoo a cat. She stepped back, briskly fastening blouse and coat, switching within one heartbeat from public tragedy to the offhand fussiness of a matron trying on waists at her dressmaker's. She straightened her collar and leaned over to pick up her fallen pamphlets.

When she moved, I saw the woman who had spoken. I saw Ivy.

She was tall. Taller than the gray-coated ringleader, taller than most of the rest of the men. Like most women, she wore her hair up, with dark curly masses tucked under and back, but her hair seemed too heavy for hats and hairpins: it looked ready to bounce right out from under her wide straw boater. Her eyes from that distance were brown as acorns. She looked long and slender and polished, ignited with the joy of having a cause she both believed in and might profit from. Her mouth was unsettling. It was a little too thin for convention, a little too wide for propriety. It looked like a smiler's mouth.

She was dressed mainly in red, with a yellow flower, symbol of the American suffrage movement, pinned on her jacket. In that pale spring air she was very bright, very vivid—a Gibson Girl gone haywire. I stared at her, trying to catch her eye. I was sure she was drenched in so much color so I would not miss her.

And I did not.

Nor did anyone else, especially when she raised her two gloved, madder-red hands high, high up in the air. Around her wrists were handcuffs, and falling down the length of the gloves were the links of a chain that wound around her arms and was attached behind her to the Parliament fence.

"Who the hell are *you*?" the man in the coat demanded.

Ivy smiled.

"My name," she said, "is the same as your mother's."

The man stared at her, uncomprehending.

"It's also the name of your sister, your wife, and your daughter," she said.

The crowd murmured, slowly catching on.

"And for the record," she added, "it's also Ivy Amanda Earnshaw. I'm twenty-one years old, a United States citizen, legally sane, propertied, and educated. But I can't vote."

She rattled her chains like Marley's ghost, setting off a fine, dramatic clank. I never had seen anyone handcuffed before; the idea of having it done to yourself on purpose, to make an effect, buffaloed me. I tried to compose myself, forcing my mind from those chains—so weirdly alluring—to her voice as she calmly declared the catechism I had grown up with. Bobbing her head at the man in the long gray coat, she started.

"This gentleman seems not to believe in votes for women," she said. "He believes the franchise works fine enough as it is, in the hands of his brothers."

"It has so far!" somebody shouted.

Ivy acknowledged the heckler, then her own small group of pamphleteers, nervously regrouped behind her.

"It's better than no vote whatsoever," she said. "But we're here today to argue that suffrage is *best* when held in the hands of all." She lifted her own cuffed hands. "For as long as a man can strip a woman in public—"

My stomach lurched at this image.

"Hey, I never—" the gray-coated man interrupted.

"—and a woman is not permitted to voice her demand for justice against such activities—" Ivy interrupted right back.

"Look, miss—" another bystander interjected.

"—then every woman granted citizenship at birth," Ivy

said, "has been given a beautifully wrapped box which inside is totally empty. She's been granted a ghastly, terrible joke for which men on both sides of our ocean have died repeatedly, bloodily, heroically, and utterly pointlessly."

The crowd mumbled, uneasy at this vision of fruitless male bravery. They were listening, all right.

"Women desire the ballot," Ivy continued, "to vote on what already concerns us as human beings. We desire the ballot because we have been placed in a logically indefensible position: we have rights, but we have to depend on others to defend them."

She leaned forward a little and seemed to look at every man in the crowd: the man in the coat, his companions, the half dozen bobbies, shifting in boredom—even me, oozing with sympathy. "And every man here," she added, "requires women's suffrage even more than do women. Because votes for women and that alone will free men from their awesome, exhausting, twenty-four-hour-a-day duty to protect us from the powerless situation in which you have placed us."

By now Ivy had the attention of at least eighty people—still mostly men, but women too, with more and more joining as they saw others drawn into the circle. Now one woman stepped forward, smiled at Ivy, and took a pamphlet. So did another. One of the suffrage workers took a step into the crowd, her pamphlets extended politely, like tickets to amateur theater. Hands reached out, accepted them, folded them over and tucked them in pockets and wallets and bags.

I sighed, letting myself relax. So this was not, after all, to be one of those rabidly passionate suffrage rallies London was famous for, with fistfights and bruises and mass arrests! No, this one was decorous, proper—well plotted, well reasoned, well run, well restrained. *And* well concluded. I shrugged, feeling both filled with relief and—forgive me—a little let down.

But Ivy was not quite finished. Perhaps she, too, felt deflated, for, like most visiting suffragists, she surely had come to England, the fierce bloody fulcrum of female suffrage, to learn, not to lead—and perhaps having triumphed in this particular arena, she found nothing else left to learn. Perhaps that's what made her extend the moment's momentum. Or perhaps it was plain curiosity, eagerness simply to test her own power: to see how long it would take for her, chained to a fence, to bait the crowd she had just charmed, coddled, and even begun to convince.

Theatrically she cleared her throat and raised her head with its billowy hair.

"So my position, I hope, is clear," she said. "I require the franchise solely for social justice. I do not require it, any more than the rest of you do, for daily matters, or matters of the heart. I do not, for instance"—and her slitted eyes with their too-late warning locked on the eyes of the gray-coated man—"I do not for instance require the ballot to determine whether a man who attacks a defenseless woman is really a man at all."

"What's that supposed to mean?" the man snarled.

"You know exactly what it means," Ivy answered. "The real question is—what do you intend to do about it?"

The man hesitated, like an animal sniffing a temptingly outfitted trap.

"Ah, you're lucky you're chained, lady," he finally said. "Otherwise I'd teach you a lesson or two."

"I may be chained, but I'm not helpless," Ivy said. "And that's why you won't do anything. We all understand your affliction. Its social label is cowardice. Its physiological—or should I say medical?—name is impotence."

Two men standing next to me chuckled. Three others behind me stepped forward, expressions flickering: amused first, then sullen, then belligerent. Ivy strode to the end of her chains. Eyes bore into eyes less than ten inches apart.

A man in front sprang at her. I shouted but too late; he leapt, she kicked, he jumped on top of her. I could hear Ivy yelling—she didn't scream like a victim, she howled like a witch —and at her strange wail the police started forward, signaling a mob, and the crowd responded, becoming one. Briefcases and walking sticks became weapons, swung wildly, hitting Ivy, her companions, her sympathizers, her enemies.

I saw her face for a second: she looked both exhilarated and terrified, and that combination felt so utterly natural, I realized I felt the same way. Her chained hands fluttered, then she disappeared into a wave of thrashing arms, reappearing like a rock in surf, then submerging again. I shouted her name without opening my mouth; it felt like an explosion inside my head, a prelude to the pain I would feel saving her.

Only I didn't. I tried to, I truly did, but I couldn't: by the time I had pummeled and shoved and pushed myself forward to where I had seen her last, she was gone, and so were the other demonstrators; instead more police had appeared, and the riot, by now a rout, had lost all focus and was now just a matter of banging heads. Somebody elbowed my ribs and a nightstick rattled my arm, jolting the muscles from shoulder to wrist. I retreated. Police whistles skidded in the sodden air.

As I walked back, slowly and hours later, to Father's apartment, I chided myself for my thwarted martyrdom. Now I could see how I should have moved not only *sooner*—when the barking started, for instance, or the stripping, or the baiting— but *faster,* so that when danger threatened I already was there, not just on my way. In fact, there were many things I should have done differently, including punch everyone, from barker to bobby; make my own fervent pitch on behalf of my sisters;

then, finally, fall—brutally, blatantly, bloodily battered—prefer-
ably at Ivy's feet. And I would, too, I promised I would; I'd do
it all, and I'd do it right, and I'd do it right now, if only God in
His goodness or luck at its most erratic would give me another
chance—another shot at becoming a hero.

Hers.

CHAPTER FIVE

THE *TITANIC* LEFT ENGLAND ON WEDNESDAY, THE TENTH OF April. I traveled alone from Victoria Station to Southampton on the boat train. It seemed to take forever, what with all the commotion—the corridor revelry, the outsize baggage, the inevitable missing tickets—to jostle my way to my seat; by the time I was settled, we already were fifteen minutes outside Victoria. I blew on my window and looked outside. The London of charm and fancy, of Father and Ivy, was fast dissolving, replaced by a drab gray city of frozen clotheslines and barren yards. The train passed so close to some houses we seemed to be aimed straight into cellars and kitchens; had we been moving more slowly we could have seen the occupants' faces as we knifed through their dustbin tenements. I kept on staring, "Sumner Jordan's Trip to London" lying unread in my lap. I was suddenly terribly homesick; the approaching Atlantic crossing seemed like an unbearably long separation between myself and Boston.

In the interval since the demonstration, Ivy had visited me several times. Mostly she came at night—not in dreams, nor even in fantasies, but in that vague intermission, that willow world, between dreams. Floating contentedly in gauzy suspension, asleep without losing consciousness, I saw Ivy in image after image after breathtaking image. Each glimpse was nearly identical to the one before, but not quite; it was like holding a strip of film in my hand, parsing each frame. In Frames 1 and 2 she looked the same, in 3 she started to change . . . by Frame 12 she looked different. And each frame, the duplicates, the changes, fed me for what felt like hours, the minute-long hours of sleep.

Ivy had indicated no awareness whatsoever of my presence at her demonstration. Nonetheless she proved totally cognizant in my motion picture. Usually it was just a look, though sometimes she even spoke; I had to lean forward in bed to read her reply.

"Miss Earnshaw," I began, "I wish to apologize for my behavior at the riot. I didn't do enough."

In one scene she smiled and said, "Mr. Jordan. I know how strongly you sympathize. No apology is necessary."

In another she smiled and said, "Mr. Jordan. Your behavior was irreproachable. No apology is necessary."

In a third version she did not smile. Instead she sternly replied, "You can be certain there'll be another time. And with you by my side, all will go peacefully."

Only this was the wrong answer: peace was the *last* thing I wanted. And here I would stop the film, seething with embarrassed frustration. For I could never admit, not even here, in this secret and self-run scenario, what I *really* was hoping for: catastrophe. Disaster, calamity, chaos, despair. This woman endangered, just so I could save her.

She visited less frequently by day. One time it was a cold, sunny morning in Bond Street, a tall, hatted figure across the square; another time, Regent's Park, late afternoon, air the color of lilacs and every path filled with the wrong women in red dresses. A third time we were on opposite sidewalks in Piccadilly; I went to approach her while all around me time and sound stopped; I was so pleased to see her my eyes swelled,

allergic to my own excitement. I started across the street completely blind and deaf, launching my body to where I had seen
her last. What I would do when I reached her I left completely
to chance. I wanted to kiss her, although I had no idea how, and
I wanted to talk to her, although I had no idea what about. I
wanted to impress, I wanted to charm, I wanted more than
anything else to be *older,* so I would know what I wanted, and
how to achieve it. But when I finally reached her she turned out
to be another woman—very pretty, quite beautiful, really, but
not Ivy, and therefore not interesting.

It was in this private state of the siege of my own heart that
I passed my last hours in England. I did more sightseeing in
those three days than I had in the rest of my visits combined,
hastily zipping from park to museum, cathedral to dockyard—
anywhere I thought another demonstration might be possible.
Ivysearching, I labeled it—all one word, terribly ungrammatical,
almost thrillingly wrong from the viewpoint of a classicist like
myself. I Ivysearched with heady desperation. I was flouting the
rules of the English language the same way Ivy had flouted the
rules of the English.

I had shared none of this searching with Father. Not out of
distrust, or a fear he would misunderstand—more the opposite,
a fear he would understand all too well. Having Father assure
me he felt the same way about Evelyn Manning as I felt about
Ivy Earnshaw would mean I was not the first person since Eden
to feel this way. And maybe I wasn't; others had undoubtedly
experienced something similar to my own emotions, and might
naively assume we were going through the same thing. Only
this, I was certain, could not be true. The world *could not* be
filled with my feelings—no one would ever get anything done.
Besides, I had eyes, I could see, I could read, and I never saw,
never read about, people like me, people pulsing with, blinded
by, this particular buoyant suffering, this agonized joyful loneli-

ness. Oh, I knew about love—after all, I had three big sisters—but I also knew this wasn't it. I didn't love Ivy: that was ridiculous. I just . . . I just loved the *idea* of loving Ivy. I loved the idea of saving her, I loved the idea of seeing her again. But I didn't love Ivy herself, of course not. Of course not. Of course I didn't.

I took out my ticket and studied it. I had come over on the *Admiral Tully,* traveling with Father's youngest sister and her two children. The *Admiral Tully* was a stolid liner which had taken twelve boring days to chug from New York to Queenstown; I had read most of Robert Louis Stevenson by the time we'd landed, polishing off *Treasure Island* the day we docked.

Today's trip promised to be different. For one thing, it was a maiden voyage, which always meant both passengers and staff were a little giddier, a little looser, than usual. For another it was very much a *public* voyage—not for me, of course, but for the glittering London and New York millionaires who had proclaimed it to be *the* social event of the spring season. Third, and most important, I was traveling alone. No aunts to cramp my style; no eight-year-old cousins to bemoan the slow passage of time. I had total freedom: responsibility for my own pleasure, myself to blame for my own boredom.

The train hurtled south. My entire car was Atlantic-bound, and as our train lurched and settled, our miracle ship became the subject of all conversation. A number of people already had seen her, some when she was still an open hull in Belfast; others when she was launched; a few more just before her sea trials. They all claimed that not even the most respectful drawing, the most complimentary photograph, could begin to do her justice. They spoke of her as though she were a great but unphotogenic actress: you must see her in person, you must see her yourself. Her size, her lines, the sheer beauty of her construction—she was the bride of science, the sister of poetry, the firstborn child of the marriage of marine engineering and art. Her genius began with the brilliance of her watertight compartments and expanded upward to every corner. Whole rooms of spun glass. Stairwells of wood and silver. Tapestries. Pools.

I shut my eyes. I saw a pure white ship, translucent as ice. I could look into all the staterooms. They were filled with women in red dresses, drinking champagne and talking to shadowy men in evening clothes. One by one the lights in the staterooms went out, the men moved toward the women, the ship moved in the lift of the North Atlantic spring.

"How 'bout *you*, kid?" somebody asked me.

I opened my eyes, startled to be noticed, and saw a man in his early twenties. He wore glasses and had brown hair, a bit of a paunch, and the warmest and friendliest smile ever to pass my way in this lifetime. His voice held a folksy Midwestern drawl.

"You seen her yet?" he asked.

I thought of all the women I had been seeing lately, and blushed. "Seen who?" I asked.

"The ship," the man said. "Have you seen the ship?"

With all the boat talk surrounding me I felt guilty of a complex error, both social and maritime. "Not yet," I answered.

The man had his arm draped over a young woman who held a magazine in her lap. As I watched him, his hand brushed the back of her neck: a gesture she seemed, if the way she was arching her shoulders meant anything, to greatly enjoy. I wondered if Father had ever tried this with Evelyn Manning. Catching me gawk at this open caress, the woman flashed me a playful wink.

"She's amazing," the man was saying. "Lorna and I extended our honeymoon one whole week, just to go home on her. Plus we've been down to see her three times already, we're that excited.''

"We," mouthed the woman, pointing to the man, and aglow with the satisfaction of a successful gift-giver.

I simply nodded. Both of them radiated cheer, contentment, and sheer goodwill.

"Well, we figure it's worth it," the man continued. "Soon we'll be sitting at home with a houseful of kids, and who knows when we'll ever get the money together for this kind of joyride again.''

The woman smiled, first at her husband, then—almost as warmly—at me. "That houseful of kids," she said. "They're not quite as imminent as Jack makes them sound.''

My mind whirred: did everyone in the world, except my own family, speak about sex this openly? The man chuckled and patted my knee.

"Didn't mean to embarrass you, son," he said. "Besides, shoot, shipboard romance—I may wind up with a brand-new bride before this trip's over." He gave the woman a quick, bright kiss. "Where you from, kid?''

I told him.

"Traveling solo?''

"Yes, sir.''

"Boy, if I were your age, that'd be my idea of heaven!" the man—Jack—said. He stretched his legs. "But to tell you the truth, this is close enough. I'm an engineer—bridges, roads, dams—but I've always loved ships. Ever since they wrote this one up I've been following it.''

"And talking about it," Lorna said.

Jack kissed her again. He seemed utterly pleased by the fact that this woman dwelled in the universe. I watched him with envy. Just one person bringing so much happiness! I fingered the spine of my journal. Not even Miss M—— had given my hero what Lorna was giving to Jack.

A few minutes later he returned to me.

"Yeah, the most beautiful ship in the world," he announced. "Largest. Safest. Strongest. Fifty thousand horsepower, fifty-phone switchboard, wireless they can hear in Timbuktu. Eight hundred eighty feet long. That's three football fields. Minus a couple of downs," he added. Lorna rolled her eyes.

"I can't help it," said Jack. "Someday I'd like to design a bridge like that. Something people would point to and say, 'That's the best there is. The best, the biggest, the prettiest ever.'" His blue eyes twinkled. "Of course, that's about how I'd describe Lorna here."

The train howled, rounding a corner. A conductor popped his head into our compartment and announced our arrival in Southampton Station. A half hour later, we were at the dock, our tickets collected and luggage stowed—all the details of everyday travel discreetly dispensed with, so that nothing could distract from the floating vision before us.

She was so *long*. So sleek and so long, and so tall as she arched over the greasy water. Row upon row of empty portholes, then the sweep of her deck and that beautiful gold lettering. Layer upon layer of sparkling windows and mysterious protuberances, and topping it—dwarfing it—all, four gigantic funnels, each painted gold and tipped with black, and reaching like thick painted fingers up to the sky.

"My God in heaven," said a man next to me. "What a beauty. What a monster. Just look at that."

We looked and looked. Jack gaped as though he never had seen her before. Even Lorna looked impressed. There was an air on that dock of satisfied jointedness, as though her builders and her carpenters and her crew and her passengers had all created her together. She was a soaring, technological wonder.

I had been on board for less than ten minutes before I felt I'd been here for days. That strange, homelike feeling peculiar to great ships enveloped me; everything was so wisely, so logically placed that the newest arrangements seemed welcome, familiar friends. I ducked down to C Deck to find my stateroom: a maple door, numbered in brass, with a doorknob as shiny as ice. I opened the door and peered inside, abloom with unplanned delight.

For a room in a house the cabin was quite small. For a room on the average liner it was almost too large. But as a room for one person traveling alone for the first time it was perfect: plenty of space, plenty of air and light, but I could see into every corner. There was no place for shadows, for the mysteries of newness which transform chairs and tables into uninvited midnight visitors. This stateroom, designed for thousands of future anonymous guests, nevertheless seemed fashioned especially for me.

I closed the porthole, already comfortable in my sanctuary. The rosewood writing desk reminded me of my desk at home. The lamps, with their pale aureole of daytime electricity, looked like the lamps in Mother's bedroom, globular and sturdy. The bed, almost four feet wide and fluffy with pillows and a deep silk comforter, promised a safe place to sleep and a sweet place to read. I stuck my journal under the cover and went on deck.

It was just before noon. All about me, people were saying good-byes, exchanging last-minute instructions and presents and messages. Everyone except me seemed to have someone to part with: I felt cheated by this self-sufficiency, and I looked around for Lorna and Jack; surely one of them would have a bright comment for all of this fervent sentimentality. I could already hear Jack saying, "Didn't they know until now that this was a *ship?* That some folks were actually *leaving?*" But I couldn't find them in the crush of tearful farewells, so I slipped to the rail and looked out at the crowded dock. Everyone around me was waving, so I chose a kind-looking woman's face on the pier and waved too. She looked at me, puzzled, then continued calling to a middle-aged man behind me.

"Good-bye, good-bye!" the man responded. "I'll write! As soon as I get there! I'll send a wireless!"

"I'll write!" I repeated, waving. "A wireless! I promise!"

The waving and shouting continued.

After a while I noticed the ratio of guests to passengers, equal to begin with, was starting to shift. At first it was subtle, just a little fewer of Them, a little more of Us. . . . Then, suddenly, it was fixed. No more embraces, no more tears or farewells; the only people on deck were travelers, eyeing one another with nervous concern. For we all understood that from now on out we had only ourselves—for amusement, for desire, for moral fiber. Our voyage was ready to start.

A whistle shrilled. A wharfside clock clanged twelve times. Far below us, the massive engines started to rumble. Almost immediately their heavy thudding achieved a pattern: *push/stop, push/stop,* a soft, pounding rhythm which was perfectly in stride and utterly familiar; almost not felt, yet already something that was always there. Like one's own heartbeat, miraculous and dependable. Slowly we started to move. But the ship was so large, and seemed so solid—so much more a gigantic earthbound building than a vessel—that it felt as though the dock, not the ship, were moving. The waving crowds on the pier, it appeared, were the ones who were making the trip, while we stood on the deck of this lovely new liner, unbudging, forever. As we gained speed the illusion mounted; the pier continued to glide by us, faster and faster.

Suddenly there was a loud snapping sound—totally wrong

and alarming, like ice cracking in sunlight. Snakes of thick, braided rope flipped through the air. At the same second a smaller ship, the S.S. *New York,* appeared directly below us. We stood, the crowd on the ship and the crowd on the dock, breathless with horrified surprise. The churning of our great propellers had sucked the little liner from her mooring and was dragging her, pilotless, into unwilling suicide.

Whistles blew frantically as our gigantic bulk drew the helpless *New York,* as if magnetized, right into our side. Then, just as collision seemed unstoppable—so inevitable it was already accepted—we managed to halt. Smoother than an automobile, smoother than a train: our engines simply ceased their thudding, and we came to a perfectly timed dead stop, inches from the other liner. Artificial surf on all sides of us receded. Two tugs scurried to the little ship, nudging her back to safety. On the dock and aboard, we all cheered.

Next to me a man said, "One of these days maybe they'll learn how to steer these things."

I looked at the man who had spoken. He was extremely handsome, tall and slender, with a runner's body, long black hair, and sharp cheekbones. His eyes were the startling green of an indoor fern. He was wearing a full-length camel's-hair coat and holding a book with a misty, pastoral painting on the cover. As the space between our ship and the little liner widened, he narrowed his eyes.

"Safe this time," he said. "Oh, well. Better luck tomorrow."

It was a hard comment, on board a ship, to ignore. Several passengers looked at him—men, coldly; women, too, but with interest. He stared them all down; nobody spoke. He started to move away.

I have always found the role of playing straight man to the sardonic irresistible: cynicism, which I mostly lack, fascinates me. "I guess you think it'd have been more exciting if we'd crashed," I said.

His green eyes flickered. It was clear he had meant to be overheard; equally clear, not by a child.

"Exciting, I doubt it," he said. "Rewarding, possibly."

I giggled nervously. "Not for me!" I said.

"Well, then, you've chosen the right ship."

I giggled again, embarrassed. His reassurance, I felt, was an apology: nobody wants to frighten a child. Eager to please, I chose to entertain; pointing to one of the gigantic funnels, I said, "Look at the size of that thing! It said in the brochure you could drive two locomotives through it and still have room on both sides!"

He gazed up at the funnel, then out at the port, staring as if the piers and the tugboats and the waving crowds had already melted away, and we were days deep into the North Atlantic.

"A locomotive," he said dreamily. "Fascinating. I wonder if they'd like someone to test that claim."

I gawked at him; he smiled, a very slow crescent which made him look even more somber, his mouth smiling, his eyes spookily veiled. Strange: he was in his mid-twenties, only four or five years older than Ivy Earnshaw, or friendly and funny Lorna and Jack. But they were all moving forward; they even leaned forward when they talked. This man spoke as though he already had passed, burning, through life, and now wanted only water and rest.

I mumbled that maybe he could talk the captain into taking his offer: great liners, they say, are made to please. I hadn't meant to be taken seriously, or actually even heard; he did hear me, though, because he said, in a voice so monotonic it was impossible to say whether or not he was joking, "Well, perhaps I shall. Sea captains and I go a long way back."

Before I could ask him more, he raised his book in a slow

salute and walked off. I watched his tall figure vanish into the crowd, disapproval trailing after him like a hail of dull arrows. Nothing stuck.

I turned from the man to the sea. Just as he had receded, so had the shore: slowly, coolly—maybe a little disappointingly— something was being withdrawn. By the time he was gone, the pier had become a soft blur, set in a still softer, blurrier city. I looked around, unaccountably depressed by all that vagueness, and somehow expecting the ship to display some flaw which would confirm my depression. But no. She was far too beautiful, far too worldy and gay, for moodiness. Instead she sparkled at me, clean, friendly, beckoning, a paid companion good at the job, begging only to entertain. Specifically designed to replace nothing you cared about, just to move you happily from one world to another. Like a rocket, a comet; like a fresh new moon. I decided to go exploring.

For the next seventy hours I never saw the water. The ship was so large, and equipped with so many playthings, you could easily spend the entire voyage totally unaware of the existence of the Atlantic Ocean. I spent hours in the gymnasium, which was outfitted not only with dumbbells, punching bags, Indian clubs, and trapeze bars but also with full-size bicycles, each fitted into a frame so that the wheels never touched the ground: the perversity of such cycling—pedaling yet going nowhere—fascinated me. There was even a mechanical camel which actually bucked when you rode it through its timed electrical desert. The gym master, probably sensing I was too shy to refuse, invited me to supervise the women and children; I stood stiffly by the exercise bike while Mrs. John Jacob Astor giddily pedaled one sixth of a mile. "Are you here to make sure I don't have a collision?" she asked me.

Mesmerized by the rhythm of her pedaling, and amused to the point of speechless bedazzlement by the fact that the wife of the wealthiest man in America wore a motoring hat to go stationary-biking, I simply adjusted the resistance knob, praying she realized that I, like her, was a First Class passenger: she should not offer a tip.

I swam. Not only was this the first ship to have a pool; this was the first swimming pool I had ever seen. I loved it. I had swum before, but only in lakes and the ocean, where you had to pay attention to not drowning. Here there was absolutely nothing to distract you—no waves, no pebbles, no nipping crabs, no hectoring lifeguards. The attendant, exquisitely polite, spoke only French. "In case I get a cramp," a fellow swimmer asked me, "you got any idea how to say 'Help!' in frog?"

"Same way you say 'Help!' in English," another man answered, before I had a chance to show off my languages. "Cross yourself, yell three times, and pray you float."

I floated. I lay on my back on the skin of the pool's smooth surface, spineless and weightless. I dove. I plunged into the totally clear, fresh seawater and touched the mosaic floor with my fingertips; the tiles felt like a jigsaw puzzle welded together with industrial glue. Men swam separately from women; the hours were posted. I swam and dove and floated, accepted without initiation into this aqueous fraternity. I kept hoping to see Jack at the pool, or even the handsome man with the green eyes; minimal as my conversation with both had been, they were the closest friends I had on board. Neither ever appeared; I swam in silence.

Afterward I visited the wireless room. A young British man, thin, pale and intense, sat hunched over the equipment. He wore headphones and was so raptly concentrating that all expression was wiped from his face, leaving him looking as mechanical as his mechanism. Bright sparks leapt from his receiver, dancing like blue lightning through his fingers. Messages were tacked to the wall, incoming on one side, outgoing on the other. Seeing me reflected in his instrument, he waved me inside without breaking the spark's insistent spell.

The room was precisely designed to hold one man, one cot, one curtain, and one set of wireless equipment; with both of us there, it felt rather cramped. Pressed up against a wall and hypnotized by the metallic tapping, I started reading messages: "Good luck, Bob and Jeanette"; "We miss you, Mother and Daddy, love, Andrew and the boys"; "Don't forget the sheet music. Franklin." One message read: "Attention R. T. Scanlon: Sell Burlington Northern ASAP. Urgent. Over." It looked as if everyone—except, as usual, me—had been sent a wireless. "Good luck, Sumner and Ivy, we miss you," I wrote myself, signing off, "Ezra Pound and James Joyce."

In a separate section were messages to the captain. Most were congratulatory and heavily metaphorical: "A trembling maiden atop the ocean deep," "A crown for the newborn queen of the North Atlantic"—that sort of thing. One, signed by the Belfast Metalworkers' Union, read, "Maiden Voyage— 'Made in' Belfast." A few telegrams, from other ships far to our west, spoke of quiet seas, clear skies, and ice fields.

After a long time the traffic stopped. The operator, Mr. Phillips, turned around, ripping off his headset and grimacing as he rotated his stiff neck. "Now that you've read all these private messages," he said, "care to give it a try?"

I nearly hooted with excitement. "You mean transmit a wireless? A real one?"

"A real *short* one," said Mr. Phillips, and handed me the receiver. It was heavy and unwieldy, two thick metal bands and a pair of headphones which fitted loosely over my ears. The bands acted as clamps, anchoring the set to my head, and me into the dancing current of a universe of electrical signals, all of which seemed capable of sizzling me into deafness.

I listened and listened, thoroughly spellbound. I had no idea what anything I was hearing might mean: that it was *there* was meaning enough. For it was a starry and great revelation: alone, on a ship, in the middle of nowhere, I had worked out a way to end loneliness forever. Out there—out where?—in the air, in the ether, all around, all the time, men and women were speaking to one another, strangers becoming friends, intimacy not only without touching, but without *anything*—without seeing, hearing, ever meeting, or even wanting to. Just tapping and receiving a perfectly sane, economic, and universal code.

"Hear anything interesting?" asked Mr. Phillips.

"It's wonderful, but I don't understand any of it."

"Probably not worth understanding anyway. Here."

He handed me a notepad and pen. "Write it down," he said. "Dots and dashes and spaces. Then we'll translate." I hesitated. "Go on! Outside of the ice and weather messages, most of this stuff is gibberish *after* you decode it. Give it a try."

For five minutes I transcribed while Mr. Phillips rummaged through a pile of dusty papers, a dictionary, and an atlas before finally locating a crumpled instruction sheet. It was an English alphabet with Morse signals beside each letter. Mr. Phillips pointed to the dots and dashes, then to the alphabet sheet.

"Dash-dot-dot, that's a 'D.' Dot, that's an 'E,' " he decoded. "What do you want to bet the next two are 'A' and 'R'? D-E-A-R M-O-T-H—. Well, either he's courting a butterfly or he's writing his mother. Right, here's the 'E-R.'

" 'Dear Mother,' " he continued as I scribbled. " 'Gladys had twins and all are well.' Bless you, Gladys! and your two moths. 'Will meet the ship but without Uncle Bob.' What's a homecoming without Bob? If I were Ma, I'd go right back to England. 'Bertie has weasels'—believe that's 'measles,' old man —'but is fine now. Much love Andrea.' Over and out."

The message's banality deflated me; I put down the receiver. "Little less breathtaking than it looks, right?" said Mr. Phillips. "Well, that's technology for you. Personally I prefer the semaphore. Look, here's something interesting."

He pointed to the alphabet chart. The letters C, Q, and D were bright red.

"Come Quick—Danger," said Mr. Phillips. "International distress call. Anyone sends that, he's saying, 'Somebody give me a hand here, right this minute.'"

"There's a man at the pool," I said, "who was wondering how to say that in French."

"Don't get down to the pool much," Mr. Phillips sniffed. "But you can tell him this." He picked up the pen and drew three dots, three dashes, and three dots. "S-O-S," he said. "They just recently changed the signal. Figured C-Q-D only made sense in English, maybe. Tell your swimmer friend any Morse-man in the world can understand dot-dash-dot. May save his life."

At the end of my fourth day at sea it occurred to me that with the exception of eleven words from Mrs. Astor, I had not spoken to any passengers since leaving England. I had met several officers, who all seemed chilly, preoccupied, and terribly busy; they answered every question with brisk and staggering politeness but never volunteered anything. I also had met three crew members, all Cockneys, all friendly, and none much older than twenty-one. One of them told me he still could not figure out the quickest route from the engine room to the Boat Deck: "She's so bloody *high,* you know?" Another one took me to some of the ship's most advanced and impressive features: her amateur darkroom, eerily glittering with wet negatives, and the infirmary, complete with operating theater. A third, the youngest, got me all Saturday morning. He bustled me down, then up, then back down a labyrinth of iron stairwells, pointing out the coal holds, the boiler rooms, the baggage and mail holds. He carefully explained the ship's revolutionary system of watertight compartments; I didn't quite understand, but I imagined Jack (and probably Lorna) would have, and wished they were with me. At last he showed me the massive reciprocating engines, pumping and churning in perpetual motion, pounding lodestars of solid steel.

Then we reversed direction and climbed back up. Up, up, up almost twenty minutes of stairs and corridors and ladders, until, with a blast of light and fresh air and blinding color, we reached the Boat Deck.

It was my first sight of the open sea since I had boarded. What a contrast, what a revelation! Compared to the ship, the ocean seemed so simple, so—so untechnological. Waves in neat, surfless bundles; cool misty air the color and opacity of lemon soda; staid flat blue sky. Nothing changing, nothing challenging, nothing requiring any brains to figure out. Just a good idea that worked.

I stared, dazzled by the ocean's blandness.

"The Atlantic whore," said Buckley, my guide. "Remind me never to join the Navy."

"I was just thinking how peaceful it looks," I said. "Like paradise. Sort of dull."

Buckley spat into the peacefulness.

"Dull!" he said. "Storm season starts the day after Hallⁿ-een. Lasts till Easter. Icebergs till summer. Then your assorted gales and contrary gales and warm-weather cyclones. Then hurricanes. Paradise on ice, all right."

He pointed over the side of the ship. "Goddamn W.N.A. line's practically scraping the bottom of the ocean," he muttered.

"What's a W.N.A. line?" I asked—I couldn't bring myself to repeat "goddamn." "I can't see anything."

"Load line," said Buckley. "How low she sits in the water when properly loaded. You can't see it from here. But W.N.A. —Winter North Atlantic—is the lowest load line in all the seven seas. On account of the North Atlantic in winter is the deadliest ocean in all the world." He spat again.

"This ocean's a year-round horror," he said. "There's even a poem about it."

I'd always admired disaster poetry. "Really?" I said. "How's it go?"

Buckley hesitated. "I'm not sure I remember it all," he mumbled.

"I'd really like to hear it," I said.

He blushed. "I'm not a great one for public speaking," he said.

"There's only me here," I wheedled.

"I didn't write it, mind," he warned.

"That's O.K.," I said. "Whatever you remember."

"Right." Buckley paused a few moments, then threw back his shoulders, glared at the unloved ocean, and said:

"July, stand by. August, you must.
September, remember. October, all over.
Then back to Winter North Atlantic once again."

Flushed and relieved, he glanced at me. Remembering all of the critics at Father's party, I did my best not to look disappointed. "That's it?" I asked.

He nodded.

"Kind of short," I said. "But . . . really effective. Like a haiku," I babbled. "Very, um . . . Japanese."

"I like a bit of poetry," Buckley, now expansive, confided. "You know any?"

Now it was my turn to hesitate. In addition to "The Martyrdom of Charles Sumner,'' I easily knew at least five hundred poems by heart, but I feared Buckley might not understand them, nor have patience for their excessive length. I decided to go with my all-time favorite, the only poem to have touched me so deeply I had memorized it without trying—that is, I had read it so often that one day I had turned to reread it and found I didn't need the book.

"It's about bravery and sacrifice on the high seas. It's the best poem ever," I said, and began:

> "The boy stood on the burning deck,
>   Whence all but he had fled—''

Carried away as always by the story, my voice started trembling. Buckley nodded and excitedly interrupted:

> "The boy stood on the burning deck,
>   Eating peanuts by the peck,
>   His father called, he would not go,
>   Because he loved those peanuts so."

I gawked at him, flabbergasted, feeling myself wince as I realized what he had done. My beloved poem!—I would never be able to read it the same way again. Why hadn't I just kept my mouth shut? Now it was ruined forever. Too late, I realized Buckley had noticed my horrified reaction.

"Guess we know different versions," I finally said.

"I learned that poem at school," he said. "Word for word."

"Maybe I know the American version," I said.

We gazed, now both terribly uncomfortable, at the endless water. Waves rippled and shimmered like dunes in a blue Sahara. I tried to think of another subject.

"How come you're a sailor," I asked, "if you hate the ocean?"

"Figured it was either shovel coal at sea or shovel coal on land," he said. "Either way I'd be shoveling something."

He removed his cap and stared into its stained interior. The thin sunshine ignited his red hair and washed out his freckles. Hatless, and paled by the ocean and sunlight, he looked even younger than me.

"I'm pretty ignorant," he said. His voice was neither resentful nor regretful, just informative: I'm Buckley, I'm British, I'm ignorant. "I only went to school the four years. Barely had time to learn reading and sums. No Japanese. Not like you."

"Please—" I said, helplessly embarrassed.

"My da's a miner," he continued. "And his da, too. And my brothers. And they all hate it, and it's all but killed them. And half their friends it *has* killed. So when the union came to sign me up for apprenticing, I asked myself the big hard question. How would I rather die, drowning or suffocating?"

The ship shimmered and whinnied, cutting ferociously through the unoffending water like a jackknife through cotton: much too much force for so simple an enemy, much too hard a question for such a young man. A small wave tickled the bow; Buckley, observing it, nodded casually, as though reading a clock. Time had passed, back to work. "Sorry I ruined your poem," he said, and stuck out a thin hand.

"Sorry I was so obvious," I answered.

"Hope you enjoy your trip," he said, and frowned, maybe at the water, maybe at hearing his own formality. He touched the brass of the Boat Deck railing. Then he jammed on his cap and walked away, leaving me alone, surrounded by lifeboats and the lapping, sucking silence of the middle of the ocean.

I continued to watch the Atlantic. *Enjoy your trip,* I repeated.

I was not enjoying my trip at all. I was becoming, instead, proficient in the language of loneliness. For every five minutes with a Buckley, there were ragged chunks of endless speechless hours, long afternoons of emptiness, of silence, of nobody at all. I was discovering loneliness was a word and condition of infinite, painful subtlety. Being stuck in a study with Latin declensions while the rest of your friends go sledding was one kind of loneliness; being shut out of a suffrage planning session because you already can vote is another. Seeing people talking and laughing with one another and never, never with you is a third.

I had observed, on this trip, so many people, having such a good time. People strolling along promenades, playing squash, dancing—all talking, laughing, all making contact. But nobody contacting *me*. They saw a child and therefore saw nothing: I was my parents' responsibility, or problem, or possibly solution; at any rate, they wanted nothing to do with me. I wondered if Jack and Lorna would treat me like this when and if we finally met again. Jack had spoken of shipboard romances. Perhaps his friendliness on the train was a male variation.

I moved away from the railing. Another problem, less Byronic, was that I was very, very hungry. Unable to cope with the idea of sitting at a table with people who all knew one another and would only patronize or ignore me, I had simply munched fruit in my stateroom. It was beginning to become obvious I could not keep this up for eight days; in fact, suddenly it became clear I couldn't maintain it another moment. I rushed down a deck, combing my hair with my fingers, already rehearsing what I would eat.

The Verandah Café, glossy with oiled wood and weirdly tropical with its indoor palm trees, contained neither dining room nor restaurant. I peeked into the smoking room, hoping for some sort of dessert buffet. The room was spacious and silent, almost empty, the air heavy with hazy blue smoke from last evening's cigars. A few men sat slumped deep into leather cushions, reading four-day-old newspapers and sipping highballs; melting ice gently tinkled in half a dozen frosty glasses. No one seemed to be eating; no one, as usual, noticed me.

I entered a new smoking room. This one, for Second Class passengers only—and decidedly more austere than its First Class counterpart—was equally foodless. I kept on walking. A buzz of voices and an arrow discreetly painted on the wall pointed me toward the Café Parisian.

The "Caf" was a low-ceilinged room, bright with sunlight, and crowded with round wooden tables and wicker chairs— probably very chic, but definitely what Mother would label "lawn furniture." The walls were lined with trellises on which nothing yet grew. Most of the tables were occupied by laughing couples all interested more in each other than in the trays of cookies and chocolate pastries being offered by five passing wait-ers. I sat down at the table closest to the door. An eclair and a cup of milky coffee were set down before me. Another waiter offered three butter cookies. A third suggested a German-sounding something which turned out to be jam and whipped cream lathered onto four crispy pancakes. A fourth offered sil-verware, water, and ice.

I scooped up a small hill of whipped cream and pancake. I almost had it deposited into my mouth when I saw the only subject at that moment marginally more interesting than food.

In a far corner of the room, at a tiny table cluttered with coffee cups and half hidden by shadow, sat the green-eyed man from embarkation. But that was not what was interesting. Next to him—*very* next to him—was a blond woman who even from that distance was breathtakingly, shockingly, hunger-dispellingly beautiful. He was leaning close to her, one hand enclosing her gloved fingers, the other expertly caressing her neck. As I watched, he moved her even nearer—then nearer yet. It was like maneuvering a statue; he never moved himself, but somehow he inched her closer, lining her mouth up with his while continuing to bore into her face with those minty eyes.

Then he kissed her. Right in the open. The clatter of cups against saucers and forks against plates continued for everyone, stopped for me, maybe for her, obviously not for him: even while kissing her, he somehow managed to summon a waiter, who deftly removed their coffee cups. I gawked, impressed, amazed, envious: he was kissing this woman the way Father had kissed Evelyn Manning, but not in a bedroom in private in the dead of night, but out here in broad daylight, and in front of at least three dozen people. His arm slid lower, encircling her waist; still kissing, they rose, a single unit, and walked through the room. Some people looked up; I immediately looked down, studying my pastries, which now seemed cloyingly sweet and totally inappropriate for my new hunger. As soon as they had left I left too, scurrying toward my stateroom one deck down.

Somehow I got lost. C Deck, where my cabin was located, was much too logically laid out for someone like me, who never approached it the same way twice: my stateroom appeared to have vanished. For ten long minutes I wandered in wretched impatience down the lamplit hallway. A sign on the wall read PORT, but I'd forgotten whether ''port'' meant left or right—I knew there was a trick to remembering, but I'd forgotten that too. I walked down another companionway and emerged on D Deck. Scents from a dozen French provinces wafted through the air. I passed several large, locked rooms and prodded an open door. I took a few more steps and found myself in the single largest room I ever had seen in my life. It was the First and Second Class galley.

The first thing that struck me was the height of the ceiling. It positively soared, and the men standing beneath its vastness worked in white-robed silence, sober monks in this secular cathedral. One table nearly the size of a barge was completely devoted to lamb. Twelve dozen cutlets, each encased in a pink paper tutu, sat peppered and waiting for the oven. Four dozen rolled roasts stood guard, thermometers sticking out of thick rolls of gashed fat. Various other chops were scattered about, with small notes attached to each. On a similar table, over three hundred quartered chickens, their puckered skins studded with garlic, glistened in the clean white light. Twenty pots, ten gallons each, bubbled on five white stoves.

I wandered over to one of the pots. A young man no older than Buckley saluted me with a wooden spoon. One of the privileges of being a First Class passenger—and somehow people always seemed able to tell—was that you could go anywhere and be welcomed, or at least tolerated. The stirrer lifted the lid off one of the kettles. The odor of beef broth, spicy and winey, like salty maple syrup, filled the air. The broth was so concentrated that even its steam was brown; it spread to the ceiling in great caramel-colored poufs. The young man tossed in a handful of rock salt.

I kept walking. Machines I never had seen before whirred and hummed. Someone was feeding apples into an apple-press fitted with teeth and a humming electric motor; in went three hundred apples, out came ten quarts of fresh applesauce. A boy stirred in almonds and white raisins, an ounce at a time; the applesauce shaded from smooth pinkness to chunky gold. Next to the apples was a fruit and vegetable juicer. Clear pint jars shimmered with essence of celery, carrot, tomato, persimmon, and lemon.

I passed another table. At least five thousand shrimp were swimming in buckets of icy water, next to ten dozen lobsters, while two aproned men were swiftly arranging the execution yard. Water boiled ominously in ten wide pans. One of the men picked up a lobster. Seeming to sense what was coming, the lobster balked, legs and claws and antennae all waving in horrified excitement.

"In the pot, buddy-boy," said the man. "Prepare to meet your maker!" He lowered the lobster into the boiling water.

"Now don't be shellfish," the second man said to the dying lobster. Both cooks laughed, then, glancing at me, laughed even harder. I looked hastily, and a little desperately, toward the door.

But I couldn't find it: someone had opened a freezer, blocking all exits. I moved uneasily forward, hoping to avoid, if not more dead animals, at least the process of doing them in. The smell of salt and shellfish gradually faded away, replaced subtly, then outrageously, with yeast and sugar and eggs. Holiday memories washed over me. The bakery!

The greatest desserts of the Western world were being assembled on three vast counters. Eclairs bursting with custard and blazing with chocolate; puffy meringue angels with perfectly singed coconut wings. Puddings and mousses; ice cream sandwiches packed in dry ice. Cookies shaped like horses, lions, apples, roses, the ship herself. Cream puffs, with slivers of chocolate mixed with the cream; they slid down the slopes of the puffs like skiers caught in an avalanche. Trifles. Charlottes. Five hundred crêpes. Glazed fruit. Candied fruit. Poached fruit. Fruit ice. Tortes. Pies. You name it.

It was strange. In spite of my previous hunger, in spite of the heavenly, comforting scents and the obvious love and skill that had gone into all these treats, nothing looked good. Nothing looked real. Everything I looked at seemed somehow flat; even the thickest wedges of chocolate cake lacked dimension. And the attention that had gone into all this lacked dimension too, or at least perspective. It seemed to me this much effort, this attention to detail, just wasn't worth it. For literature or art, yes. For politics, definitely. For love, absolutely. But not for dinner.

A chef weaving sugar-nests noticed me, and said something loudly in German. Probably he simply was offering some of his just-spun candy, but I didn't speak German, and like most non-speakers found anything said in that language aggressive-sounding and forbidding. In German, even "Please pass the salt" comes out like a war cry; a man standing near a kettle of boiling sugar shouting only-God-knows-what seems like Attila. I scurried forward and out a swinging door leading to the elevators.

Back on the enclosed promenade, I stared glumly out the window. The most beautiful ship in the world, charming people, a smooth sea, and a swift, silent sailing. What more could anyone want?

A million things. I wanted a friend. I wanted home. I wanted to sit with people I knew, eating something familiar and talking about subjects I cared about. I wanted America. I wanted Boston. I wanted my mother.

Tears surprised me by flooding my eyes. I gazed, blinking, at the bobbing horizon. A woman walked by me, holding a newspaper.

Ten seconds later, I realized it was Ivy Earnshaw.

CHAPTER SIX

IN LESS THAN A SECOND, LESS THAN A LURCHING HEARTBEAT, everything changed. The cloak of loneliness that had fit me so well fell away; I felt happy, lucky, and incredibly excited. The true purpose of this ship finally became obvious: she was the backdrop for adventure and romance, for the most blazing, improbable, yet totally possible thrills.

I ran without thinking down the closest companionway, trying frantically to recollect what colors Ivy had been wearing—what I should be looking for. But she had come and gone too suddenly, and I was too giddy to exercise my memory. I emerged on the hallway of First Class cabins on B Deck and looked at the first doorknob. Could this really be her stateroom? Was my luck really holding up like this? I stood helplessly before the door, weighing the possibly unpleasant ramifications of disturbing a total stranger against the breathtaking payoff should I be right. But *l'audace, l'audace, toujours l'audace:* if Frederick the Great could do it, so could I. I lifted my hand to knock.

"Sir, may I help you?"

I dropped my hand and turned around; a steward holding a tray of steaming towels stood watching me.

"I'm seeking Miss Ivy Earnshaw," I said stiffly, trying to

sound both adult and foreign—I thought this would give me more panache. "I believe she is on this deck."

"I believe she is not," said the steward.

I found this a very difficult sentence to respond to; not really rude, it was certainly uninformative; and it made Ivy seem like a jewel which was going to be much harder to locate than I had first thought.

"Perhaps if you asked the purser," the steward said. He shifted the towels, getting a firmer grip; he obviously intended to stand guard in his corridor until I left. That was one of the understood amenities of ships like this: First Class or not, no loiterers allowed.

"The purser," I repeated. "Yes. *Merci bien.* Perhaps I shall." But I knew I wouldn't; for one thing, I wasn't exactly sure what a "purser" was. Also, I definitely did not want Ivy to know anyone was asking about her. Not that she seemed the type to panic, but I wanted to surprise her—to spring myself upon her unannounced, suffrage credentials undeniably impeccable, urbanely amused by the accident of our sailing together. I looked down the shadowy corridor of locked, painted doors, wondering what to do next.

Almost in answer, a bell chimed. Automatically I began counting. Six o'clock. Here was my solution. Dinner began at seven. Ivy undoubtedly would be dining in the First Class dining saloon. I would meet her there, and incidentally eat my first meal since boarding the ship.

I scooted past the watchful steward. God, how easy life is when you have a direction!

Now on a mission, I took only a second to zip down the companionway and arrive at my own cabin door. Some people walked by, nodded at me, and smiled. Suddenly I realized these same faces had been smiling at me for the past four days.

Blinded with loneliness, I had failed to understand I was part of a community; all that time I had felt so alone, there had been neighbors, people who noticed me, people who kept at least minimal track of my comings and goings. I grinned as I opened the door to my stateroom, and when I realized this was my first smile since coming on board, I grinned even wider.

I stopped grinning when I passed a mirror. Impossible as it seemed, I already had outgrown the slacks and long woolen jacket Father had bought me in London. Obviously I would have to change; but when I surveyed my wardrobe—all carefully unpacked, ironed and hung up by someone during one of my expeditions around the ship—everything looked wrong. Too warm, too heavy, too practical, too childish. What made the situation worse was that I had no idea how to correct it. I could not begin to imagine what sort of clothing was appropriate at this kind of dinner.

I sat down on the edge of the bed, feeling feverish and baffled. Was I to be defeated by the inadequacies of my wardrobe? At home, in this situation, I had only to ask Melville, our butler, for advice, and a half dozen suggestions would be immediately proffered. Melville knew how a man should dress for any occasion, from funerals to clambakes. But there was no Melville here.

There was, however, a private steward. His name was . . . Perry, Porter, something with a P. . . . I opened the door and peeked into the hall. A much friendlier-looking man than the B Deck steward stood at the far end of the corridor, talking to one of the passengers. I could hear atonal laughter, those strange jangling chuckles when two different classes are sharing a common joke. I waited several moments and then, for the first time in my life, summoned an unknown servant. The C Deck steward hurried down the hall.

"Ah, Mr. Jordan. We haven't seen you at dinner these past nights. How may I help you?"

Bowled over by my boldness in calling for him, I forgot even the letter his name started with. "I, uh, you . . . ," I floundered.

"Percy, sir."

"Of course. I was wondering, Mr. Percy—"

"Just Percy, sir."

"Of course," I said again. I was not going to let this bother me: Melville was Melville, Percy naturally was simply Percy. "I was just getting dressed, uh, Percy, and I wondered if you could give me a hand."

"It would be my pleasure," Percy said. "You'll be wearing your evening clothes, naturally?"

Oh.

"Naturally," I answered.

Percy strode to the closet and authoritatively began shoving aside coats and jackets. He seemed to know my wardrobe better than I did. Almost immediately he located my best tuxedo, blue-black and spotless, its creases steam-pressed into brutal sharpness.

"This is quite nice," he said, holding the jacket out for me while I slipped out of my sweater. "Now the pants, sir . . ."

A few minutes later I was dressed. Percy and I studied the mirror, I with horror, Percy with some concern. My socks showed almost an inch below my pants, and my blazingly white cuffs shot like a comet out of the dark sleeves of my jacket.

"I've grown a bit," I said apologetically.

"Not to worry," said Percy. He dropped to his knees and started to pull and adjust, a quarter inch here, an eighth inch there. "Two centimeters," he mumbled. "Two point five, perhaps two point six . . ." He stood up, took out a small notebook, and made some notations. "The most minor of problems,

Mr. Jordan," he said. "Nothing our tailor can't remedy with needle and thread. I'll have him drop in tomorrow morning."

"But what about tonight?" I asked plaintively.

Percy smiled. "I'm sure the others will forgive a young man the presumptuousness of growing. Let me finish you up."

For the next five minutes Percy hovered over me, pomading my hair, massaging my cheeks, rubbing some kind of lime-smelling lotion into my neck. From time to time he cooed complimentary half sentences which, while movingly polite, nevertheless sounded convictionless. Finally, wishing me a most pleasant evening, he escorted me to the elevator, where we waited silently. Just before the car arrived, he gave my collar a final wrenching tug.

"Smashing!" he said.

I rode down to D Deck in a gust of uneasy excitement. In a way, I wanted the ride to last forever—though of course, having thought that, we took almost no time at all, arriving in under a minute. The car stopped, the door opened carefully, deliberately melodramatic—like a slowly rising curtain, like a vaporetto approaching Venice. I stepped into the magical vortex of total luxury.

As with so much else on that beautiful ship, the First Class dining saloon was so exquisite, and in so many ways, you almost laughed with outlandish pleasure. The room glittered like a great nighttime city, its skyline a necklace of wood, mirrors, and paintings. The curves of the wineglasses matched the curves in the silverware; the whorls in the birchwood panels echoed the painted gold whorls of the plates. From inside the room, voices and laughter, modulated by concert-hall acoustics, enticed and invited. I forced myself to savor the moment, not to hurry, not to appear rushed. . . .

Then I saw her. She was sitting with five other people, at a table near a far wall. She was laughing; so was everyone at her table. Her left hand held a fork. It traveled to her mouth in a silvery haze, as I watched in a total dither of admiration and desire. God, on top of everything else, she was a southpaw!

I stood as though rooted at the dining-room door. I wanted to make an impression, but could not decide which would work best, a noticeable arrival or a quiet but dignified entrance and later an introduction. In almost every case I could imagine, the second choice was correct: it suited me both socially and psychologically, and furthermore it had the advantage of being far less easy to muff. Yet, somehow, in this circumstance, with this particular person . . . Ivy was beyond question theatrical. Surely she would admire drama in another.

I tried to envision how anyone else might do it. Mr. Pound would dance her a hornpipe on the nearest tabletop. Mr. Phillips would teach her to SOS. Buckley would recite another poem. I thought of the green-eyed man from Wednesday afternoon. Would he amuse Ivy by telling her he was sorry the ship wasn't sinking?

"Excusez-moi, monsieur, vous attendez quelqu'un?"

I started. The maître d' was standing puzzled but helpful before me, a seating chart in his hand.

"No," I admitted. "I'm not waiting for anyone. Just—just waiting."

"Ah," he murmured—that one syllable that says it all. He looked down at his list, then across the room, scanning, I was sure, for some table both unlucky and polite enough to accept me as a dinner partner. I twitched my right shoulder in Ivy's direction.

"Perhaps I could sit there," I mumbled, nearly choking with nervousness.

The maître d' observed Ivy's party. Where I saw pleasure and helpless fascination, he saw a table with no empty chairs. "I think I have more room a little further back," he said, in a voice which combined observation with suggestion and direction. He walked, and I meekly followed, to a largish table which was six yards and two intervening parties from Ivy. Two elderly couples and a woman my grandmother's age looked up with pleasant smiles as I was introduced.

"Mr. and Mrs. Gibson, Mr. and Mrs. Hannant, Miss Mayhew, this is, ah . . ."

"Sumner Jordan," I said, still looking at Ivy. She was engaged in what I was sure was a spellbinding conversation with a silver-haired man. Spellbinding from her side only, of course: whatever he was saying, I knew I could say it better.

"It's a pleasure to have you join us," Mr. Gibson said. "We could use a little young blood around here, right, Emily?"

"Oh, yes." Mrs. Gibson smiled. She patted the back of an empty chair. "Sit right down next to me, young man, and give me your opinion on everything. We were all just agreeing how none of us understood your generation one whit."

One whit? Everyone gently chuckled. I sat down, resignedly realizing the logic of the maître d's table selection: these people were as paralyzed by their many years as I by my few. Perfect match.

"Traveling *tout seul?*" Miss Mayhew asked. Her long garnet necklace glittered dully, like a lei of frozen roses.

"*Tout seul,* yes, ma'am. Completely alone."

"My, how courageous!" she exclaimed. "Don't you ever get lonely?"

I nodded bravely, the boy on the burning deck. "I read a lot," I mumbled.

"Oh, how pathetic!" said Mrs. Hannant.

"Pathetic, my Aunt Clara!" Mr. Hannant snorted. "If he's been so busy reading that he hasn't made it to dinner in three nights, she must be one hell of an interesting book, right, boy?"

I blushed as red as Miss Mayhew's darkest garnet. Across the room I could see Ivy tasting her soup. She did this with much less delicacy than any of my sisters, a characteristic I found strangely alluring. I looked back at Mr. Hannant. He was smiling at his wife the same way Jack had smiled at Lorna, the gleam of their love burnished and deepened by time. The entire room seemed to quake and sparkle with lovers and potential lovers, with good people, with kindness, with joy.

"Tell me, young man," said Mrs. Gibson, "do you turkey-trot?"

Thus commenced one of the most peculiar meals of my life. Throughout, I found myself marveling at the human condition—how it can change so radically, so quickly, and so very often. Had I been assigned to this table without having seen Ivy, I would have had a delightful evening. The Gibsons, the Hannants, and Miss Mayhew were extremely friendly, and they were utterly fascinated by my adventures in England, the demonstration, and Mr. Joyce especially. And they were all more than ready to tell me everything about themselves. I learned that Mr. Gibson ran the largest insurance company in Philadelphia; that Miss Mayhew had studied ballet in New York City in the 1870s and had once performed before Lillie Langtry and the Prince of Wales; that Mr. Hannant had worked himself out of a Manchester cotton mill to become the head of a lucrative cotton cooperative in northern Georgia. All interesting, all thought-provoking . . . yet, throughout, I could not stop looking at, and thinking about, Ivy Earnshaw. Perhaps that was why my own conversation—devoid, for once, of any self-consciousness—was so sparkling. Everyone at my table was laughing at my observations, agreeing with my analyses: yes, I thought Wilson would win the election; yes, I thought Sun Yat-sen could save China; yes, I thought Germany was itching for war. "What a clever young man!" Miss Mayhew trilled, and Mr. Gibson, rather shyly and gravely, offered me a job when I turned sixteen. I accepted everything, the praise, the approving laughter, even the job, while all the time nodding and smiling and staring at Ivy.

She was beautiful tonight. But beautiful in a very different way from the demonstration. She looked elegant, stately, almost regal—rather like Mother when presiding at a formal dinner. Her hair was piled in a complex chignon, braided with black ribbon; her dress was black, too, velvet with a square black silk panel, like a schoolgirl's pinafore—only what a school! The dress rested on her wide, jewelless shoulders like a spuming wave, its blackness turning her skin white as surf. The effect, considering its North Atlantic setting, was almost ludicrously poetic: the phrase "an ocean upon an ocean" popped into mind and lodged there, obviously meant for insertion into a poem. I sat back, still watching. Ocean, potion, lotion, motion. Devotion.

Ivy appeared to have a great many actual and potential friends and admirers on board. Men, women, American, foreign, they all came up to her table, chatted, chuckled, giggled, and whispered—leaned over to deliver private comments which probably were only greetings but looked to me like secret communiqués. At the start of every course—there were seven—I resolved to walk up to her table as soon as I finished eating, introduce myself, and enter her happy circle; but at the end of each course I was still sitting with the Gibsons, the Hannants, and Miss Mayhew. I knew there was no way I could sail effortlessly up to Ivy's table the way all her other fans could; there was *no way,* because I was only a child.

Just before dessert, and the fading of my last intention to make contact with Ivy this evening, a fantasy fitted itself into my head. It was, even for me, surprisingly detailed; and for the moment it lasted it was as satisfying as a dream. I excused myself from my table and strode with the grace of my sisters'

ballet instructor across the room. I passed vaguely familiar faces
—Mr. Guggenheim, Mr. and Mrs. Straus, Mr. Ismay, president
of the White Star Line. Mrs. Astor, remembering me from the
gymnasium, smiled prettily. Finally I reached Ivy's table and
identified myself. But although it was my name I gave her, it was
neither my face nor my body I offered. I had become, instead,
the green-eyed man. I was certain that if anyone could make an
impression on Ivy Earnshaw, he could, with his wide, haunting
eyes and that sardonic courtesy. Naturally, everyone at the table
would instantly dislike his distant politesse and baffling cynicism.
Everyone except Ivy, who, I believed, was in her own way distant and cynical too.

I opened my mouth to speak to Ivy. The illusion of actually
having approached her was so strong I was astonished when I
was interrupted mid-suavity by Miss Mayhew's nervous and embarrassed giggle. The Gibsons and Hannants were absorbed in
some argument—incredibly enough, they were discussing the
merits of my comments on Woodrow Wilson. Only Miss Mayhew noticed my eyes fixed across the room.

"She's very pretty," Miss Mayhew said.

Dessert arrived at that point: everything I had seen in the
kitchen, plus. With the fervency of psychoneurotic hunger I
consumed three plates of baked Alaska and a goblet of charlotte
russe, while my tablemates drank tea, nibbled cookies, beamed
as I ordered another glass of milk, and in general continued to
treat me with deference and kindly charm. When we finally
finished, Ivy was gone—but, to my surprise, this was not devas-
tating. In fact, discovering her absence was rather pleasurable, in
spite of how much it hurt: of course I regretted I'd failed to
make contact, but this way I could still roam the virgin territory
of anticipation, where the season is always springtime and you
never do anything wrong. Besides, I was sure I would see her
again; the ship was large, but not that large. Meanwhile, I had

these pleasant fellow diners to eat with and show off to. Not bad for one night's work.

The Gibsons and Miss Mayhew were on my deck, the Hannants above; I escorted everyone home, then returned to my stateroom, dug out my journal, and started to Ivywrite. Two hours passed and I still was writing, full of energy and charged by creative potency—and all those desserts—into that state of sleeplessness in which you know you'll never be tired again. I decided I needed a break. Carefully I slipped my journal under my pillow and went out on deck.

Arid Arctic night slapped like a knife. The air was astoundingly cold, and at the same time dry, the way I imagined cold on the Russian steppes, totally uncomfortable, with no history of sunlight or warmth. I rebounded at once into my cabin, my cheeks so cold they felt singed. I grabbed my fisherman's sweater, buried my face in the soft warm cable, then pulled it on, sticking my dinner jacket over it. My shoulders, suddenly padded by all this wool, looked enormous: Smashing! as Percy would say. I went back outside.

All was still, yet comfortingly so: the familiar stillness of home. Ten feet below me, something mechanical rumbled; eight feet above, a door slammed shut. Entwined through these specific noises was the faint constant pounding of the engines, still as perfectly balanced and rhythmed as on their first day.

I walked down corridors and up companionways and through the same large rooms, now deserted, which seemed so recently to have promised such undeliverable happiness. I felt a tremendous calmness, as though I were walking with an Ivy I already had known for twenty years. No surprises, no more of those spine-stabbing flashes, just the peace and comfort of easeful friendship. In a haze of contented future memories I walked into the First Class lounge.

It was in all respects a perfect room: large and airy, with

deep-cushioned chairs and rugs so plush you wanted to lie on the floor. I was hoping nobody would be here this late, and I was in luck (all of a sudden, wasn't I always?); this handsome retreat was mine alone. I wandered over to the bookshelf—glass and wood, with the wood even shinier than the glass—and pondered my choices. The selection was eclectic: a solid row of classics; novels; much military history; lots of Westerns. I opted for Coleridge; they had the Gustave Doré edition, the one Mother wouldn't allow in the house, with its gruesome detailed drawings and Life-in-Death squatting and beckoning on the shrinking deck. I sat down in a shadowy corner behind a pillar and began reading, cocooned in that gentle luxury of being alone without being lonely.

After a while, a clock chimed midnight. I read on, sucked in as always by the rhyme and the weird, familiar story. The Mariner murdered the albatross. One o'clock. His ship and his doomed companions passed the equator. Two o'clock. My own ship became quieter and quieter. Three o'clock. The night pulsed outside, blacker than black. The only sounds were the distant engines, as stalwart as windmills, and me, carefully turning pages within the peaceful silence.

Suddenly the door on the opposite side of the room crashed wide open. The glass in the bookcase shuddered, reflections rippling; a vase on the mantel fell to the floor. I felt my heart slam into action as I jumped to my feet. I knew it was, had to be, was, naturally, Ivy.

It wasn't. The man with green eyes tossed a book onto the nearest table, observed, puzzled, the vase he had caused to shatter, and walked to the single, half-empty shelf devoted to science and technology.

I watched as he studied the books. Like me, he wore evening clothes, though he was impeccably dressed and minus the Irish sweater. He looked much as I remembered, tall and slender, with a tall man's posture, lounging and casual even when standing straight. He picked up a book and slid his fingers through the pages, much too rapidly even for skimming. He picked up a second book, then a third. He appeared tense and a little impatient, and suddenly I remembered the lovely blond woman I had seen him with. Had I accidentally stumbled into an assignation site? A public lounge seemed a most perverse place for a tryst; on the other hand, this man somehow did not appear unacquainted with perversity. I realized that if he intended to meet someone here, then I would be very unwelcome, and the idea of having those dreamy eyes and that dazzling, arrogant smile focused upon me was not appealing. I decided to walk to the door, mumble something, and get out as quickly as possible.

Then I decided not to. I decided, instead, to remain in my corner, staying quiet and hidden, and see if I could discover with this man and his lover the heart of the mystery I had missed with my father and Evelyn Manning. I carefully placed my book on the floor and crawled backward onto the chair, facing the door. My knees dug into the velvet seat.

Five minutes later my legs were thoroughly cramped, no blondes had appeared, and the man had not moved from his third book. Taking great care, I shifted my weight a little off one knee. A spring in the chair squealed, and the constricted muscles in my right leg immediately froze. The man looked up, startled. Then he strode right toward me. Helpless, still frozen, I watched him approach.

He saw me. His eyes widened. It was so obvious I had been spying it seemed pointless to apologize; I could only wait for him to point out the total despicableness of my position. I rubbed my cramped leg and slid to my feet, braced for humiliation.

"Hello," I mumbled.

The green-eyed man said, "Oh, hi."

I blinked, disbelieving. This wasn't exactly the opening I was expecting. Not from him, under any circumstances; under these circumstances, not from anyone.

"Knees O.K.?" he asked.

I tested them both and nodded.

"I do that one myself," he said. "Plus sit-ups, running, biking. Whatever'll keep the muscles loose. The last thing you need is to have your knees lock."

I backed off a few steps to look at him. I didn't trust these pleasantries, not at all; there had to be chastisement lurking here somewhere. This, after all, was the man who had said . . . but it was hard to remember just what he had said, especially now, as he took off his dinner jacket, tossed it into a corner, and stretched out full-length on the carpet, stomach to the floor, and started doing push-ups. His black hair fell into his eyes. I started counting. One, two, three . . . eleven, twelve, thirteen . . .

"I figure that under the best of conditions you're asking for trouble, begging for it, anyway," he said. "In fact, that's the appeal of it all, right?" His voice seemed totally remote from his exercises; he didn't even pause to breathe. "Right," he answered himself. "So let's say you spend an hour or two a day preparing for something that maybe'll give you a couple of extra seconds when you really need them. If it turns out you never use them, then all you've done is lost some time. If it turns out you do, well, then, of course, you were right." He flipped over and began doing sit-ups. "Of course what probably really happens," he said, "is you end up needing eight more seconds, and the exercises give you six; so you're still missing two and you end up dying anyway, but you get six extra seconds to review your life, or admire the flames, or do whatever you can think of to do in six seconds, which in my case would be to regret I didn't do more for my mother or less for my father, but in your case might be something entirely different, such as true love, or false love, or—"

"What are you *talking* about?" I asked.

He stopped abruptly and looked at me, worried.

"I'm sorry," I said, "but I don't understand."

His eyes fixed on mine for several seconds. Then he said, very cautiously, "I'm talking about whatever you were talking about."

"I wasn't talking about anything!" I said.

"Certainly you were." He lowered himself to the floor, then sat back up. He looked very concerned—not for himself, but for me. "Does this happen to you often?" he asked politely.

I was thoroughly baffled. "Does what happen?"

"Forgetting." He stood up quickly, one sleek, continuous movement, and I at once backed away, as I did automatically for all standing adults. He reached for his jacket and put it on, an instant reminder of how such a garment should fit.

"Forgetting's a sign, you'd better be careful," he said. He patted his pockets. "I forget just what it's a sign of. Just kidding. But if Freud—you know, Freud?—if Freud were in this room, he'd say you forgot whatever it was because it had overtones—sexual overtones—although maybe undertones would be a better word—that made you uncomfortable or excited or embarrassed. Which pretty much leaves the field wide open, because just about everything on earth is either uncomfortable or exciting or embarrassing and usually all three."

"Oh, yes," I said fervently. I was so swept away by astonished agreement with that last statement I forgot—forgot!—I had not initiated a single word of this rambling presentation.

"You have to be ready," the man continued. "I just always feel you have to be ready for anything. And the less you know what that 'anything' is, the more ready you have to be. I personally have no idea what anything is, so I'm much more ready than

anyone I know. Except when I fly. It's impossible to be ready
then, because there're so many things going on—going wrong
—at the same time. And you're supposed to be concentrating
on all of them, when all the time there's this outrageous tug on
you just to look. Look down, look up, look around—my God,
that's a roof, that's a tree, that's the sun, that's you. And there's
a feeling that you're becoming engulfed, entangled, all that air,
all that energy, it's like making love except all the time you just
want to keep looking, looking, looking, looking. My name's
Pierce Andrews. You got a cigarette?''

I shook my head, utterly flattered and bedazzled. *Me* being
asked for tobacco? *Me* having someone compare something to
lovemaking, expecting me to comprehend? *Me* having this conversation, which itself sounded like flying—soaring from subject
to object, fancy to image—nobody asking how was I doing in
school, how was my poetry coming along, my classmates, my
grades. This man obviously didn't give a damn about grades—
mine and, I was sure, sometime past, his. Oh, I thought, this is
how *adults* talk, and what they talk about. I didn't understand
most of it, but that didn't matter—what made this moment so
marvelous was that this Pierce person *assumed* I understood.

''I don't smoke,'' I said.

''God, that's all I do,'' Pierce said. He patted his pockets
again; I giggled.

''You just did that!'' I said.

''I know that,'' said Pierce. ''I never forget the important
things. I was just hoping for a miracle, that's all. Look, what's
your name?''

I told him.

''Look, Sumner, I've got to go to my cabin for a couple of
minutes. Dig up some smokes. You planning to be up awhile
longer or shall we call it an evening?''

I was no more willing to let Pierce out of sight than Ivy out of my daydreams. "Can I go with you?" I asked.

"To my cabin? What for?"

Because I know once you leave you won't come back, I thought. You'll decide this conversation was fine but enough's enough and now you'd like some real company. "Just to see it," I finally said. "See somebody else's place."

"It isn't that interesting."

"That won't bother me."

Pierce's eyes flickered with the barest darkening of impatience—not really annoyed, just unfriendly enough to remind me of my first impression of him.

"I'll just be a second," he said. "Really."

"Please," I said, a sudden surprising desperation making my voice squeak.

"No," Pierce said.

I stared at him; I wasn't used to people being rude with such total lack of apology.

"Look, Sumner, I'll be back in five minutes. I'm just going to get some cigarettes. I'm not planning to jump off the side of the ship."

That was something I hadn't considered. Now I did: not whether he intended to do it, but why he had mentioned it. Pierce smiled, then added, quite gently, "And I'm not planning to duck out on you. So just give me five minutes, O.K.?"

"O.K." I sighed, unnerved at being so obvious, unhappy at having so little choice. Pierce took a step, then noticed my book, carefully tucked under its chair. His surprisingly kind smile of fifteen seconds ago burst into a grin.

"You're reading pornographic novels?" he said, swooping down to the floor with a swimmer's fluidity. "In public?" He observed the title and stood back up. "The guy kill the bird yet?'' he asked, and walked out of the library, slamming the door. I listened to his footsteps in the predawn ultrasilence: it was like listening to a dancer walk across an empty stage—light, precise, unconsciously theatrical.

I sat in my chair, thinking over what just had happened. Never had I heard someone zip through so many moods and modes of expression in so little time. His monologues; his talk about air and sex and energy; his cruel, surprising rejection and his mind-reading reassurance. That crack about the albatross. That crack about pornography! And push-ups in the middle of the night—in the middle of the ocean! You've got to be kidding!

It occurred to me, as I sat in the deflated stillness created by Pierce's absence, that he must be Drunk. That's how I thought it—capital D. If he was, he would be the first drunk person I ever had met. In fact, he would be my first drinker. Nobody at home drank—we didn't even eat fruitcake. But I knew all about drinking from Melville, who was against it, as he was against most things. Melville contended that drinking made men untrustworthy, undignified, false. Once they had had a few ''belts''—great expression!—they inevitably turned sentimental and friendly on you; and Melville, who was neither, loathed this artificial conviviality,which, he lectured, always disappeared by morning. Now that I thought about it, Pierce's behavior seemed to tally up pretty well with Melville's description of a gentleman drinker. The only thing was, one wouldn't expect a drinker to perform calisthenics. They'd make him dizzy. And the other thing was . . . well, Pierce had sounded as though he meant it when he said he'd return. Of course, Melville would answer: drunks *always* meant it.

I waited in the library nevertheless. Five minutes passed, then ten. I knew if I left and Pierce returned, it would make no difference to him and all the difference in the world to me; therefore I had no choice but to remain. Just five minutes,

Pierce had promised. I tried to tell myself that no one can accomplish anything in five minutes; Pierce merely had meant he would be back soon. I picked up my book and slogged through a few stanzas. God, Coleridge could drag! Finally I heard the door opening, and Pierce's already-familiar footsteps; I slammed the book shut and looked up joyfully.

The cold air had narrowed his eyes and pinkened his cheeks; he somehow looked both infernal and angelic. "Jesus, it's quiet out there," he said. "Sorry I took so long, but I've never heard —not heard—anything like that." He cocked his head as if still listening. "I like silence," he said. "When I listen to music I try to hear the silence between the notes."

The silence between the notes. I tapped my book. Was this a possibly brilliant way to appreciate music or the confiding babble of a drunkard? Pierce took out a cigarette case, long and slender, and tapped it on the edge of a table. An engraved bird soared across the case's narrow silver surface.

"That's very pretty," I said.

"What, the case? Yes, it is. People always seem to be giving me things with birds on 'em. Guess it's hard to distinguish between a flier and an ornithologist."

"I know," I said. "I write poems, and people are always giving me something dumb, a thesaurus, or a rhyming dictionary, or the collected works of somebody really awful, Thomas Gray or someone—"

Suddenly I stopped, terribly confused. Yes, people did give me those presents; I had duplicate sets of all the great poets, and rhyming dictionaries for Italian, English, and French. But until this moment that had never struck me as silly or odd; in fact, it always had seemed very sweet: Sumner wants to become a poet, give him the tools of poetry. I glanced at Pierce. What was it about him that had inspired my first trip into cynicism?

Pierce flipped open the cigarette case. I noticed a message, engraved inside and surrounded by curlicues, and raised my eyebrows. He passed me the case. " 'To my beloved Pierce,' " I read aloud. " 'With love. Remember me forever.' " I returned the case.

"Actually I don't remember her at all," he said. "I think she had red hair and we met in Algiers, but it might have been brown hair in Athens or maybe Brindisi." He studied the engraving. " 'Remember me forever.' Lady, I wish I could. 'Remember forever—' . . . You know, I think this might be from my mother. My God, what a mix-up! Well, she did have red hair."

"Your mother?" I repeated, mystified.

"Dead," Pierce said. "Terminal boredom, contracted upon her marriage contract. Endemic among women, I understand. She just couldn't take another day of the Admiral's—that's my father—another day of the Admiral's lectures on Roman seapower, or Confederate seapower, or German seapower. I can see her point; five minutes with my father and I'm ready to drown myself, just to make a comment on American seapower. Plus she had the added pleasure of receiving his well-thought-out opinions about her only child. His too, incidentally."

The idea of being motherless was so sad to me, and the idea of being flip about it so astonishing, I could say nothing. Pierce gently tapped his cigarette case, the silver bird between his long fingers fluttering like a lost albatross.

"She just ran out of things she cared about," he said quietly. "She just stopped being curious about outcomes. Everything seemed continuous—her life, my life, the Admiral's life. She tried to explain, but I couldn't understand. I told her she had to unfurl herself, throw herself against the rocks, anything as long as it made her feel. Life is meant to be lived!—all that stuff. She just listened, nodded, and reached for the laudanum."

Pierce closed his eyes. I tried to remember whether any other adult had ever spoken to me like this before. It was a shocking world Pierce was revealing: the familiar pain and self-doubts of childhood lasting and jabbing the rest of your life. If this was adulthood, then his mother was right; if this was maturity, then what—besides sex—was the point of growing up?

"She was wrong," I said loudly. Pierce opened his eyes. "Your mother. She was wrong. There're lots of things worth caring about. And you're wrong too. They're not just things you have to crash into before you can enjoy them. They're just normal, everyday things."

Like what, anyone would have asked, but Pierce didn't; deference, or maybe indifference, to my outburst kept him silent. Granted this rare and total freedom of speech, I of course became speechless; the only normal pleasure I could think of was the pleasure of this discussion. But telling him that, I was sure, would annoy him, and I cast about for an example of a simple joy that I knew he would like.

The problem was, I didn't know what in the world Pierce Andrews liked. He seemed to like women but no one woman in particular. He seemed to like talking but spoke about listening to silence. He seemed to . . . I looked at his tapping fingers.

"For instance," I said, "smoking. Smoking is a pleasurable, normal activity."

Pierce looked as though someone had just cued him. "Oh, excuse me," he said, mechanically polite, "would you care for a cigarette?"

He pushed the case toward me: neat rows of sweet-smelling, machine-rolled cigarettes, trailing threads of pale tobacco.

"Sobranies," Pierce said. "Hand-rolled by Serbian anarchists, when they're not out blowing up each other's houses or prodding the tender underbelly of the Habsburg Empire. A wonderful country, Serbia: very beautiful, but nothing works. The opposite of Germany. I bought a towel in Serbia once and it didn't dry for three years. Please, help yourself.''

My hand hovered over the cigarettes. Pierce might as well be offering drugs, women, stolen diamonds; nothing could be more illicit for me than these trim, forbidden packets.

''It's hilly country there, though,'' Pierce continued. ''Nasty place for a war. But not my problem; I don't intend to spend the next war on land. Or at sea, either. No offense, Dad.''

He took out a cigarette and tapped it sharply on the edge of the table.

''Of course the Admiral wouldn't want to share an ocean with me anyway,'' he continued. ''And neither, apparently, would the U.S. Navy. They said as much when they asked me to leave the Academy—that's Annapolis, Sumner, not a *real* academy. They told me I had the instincts to be a good sailor, but unfortunately they were in the business of training officers, not sailors, so would I please get the hell out of there.''

I jumped at his ''hell''—my destination for smoking? We were moving away rapidly from the list of innocent pleasures I was supposed to be enumerating. ''You were a naval officer?'' I asked.

''Washed up,'' Pierce said. ''Bailed out. Little nautical pun there. 'Sunk without trace' would be more accurate. Missing presumed lost interest. God, though, the Navy! 'You're Admiral Andrews's son and heir, sir, are you not?' 'No, sir, I'm Admiral Andrews's single night of sexual abandon regretted ever after, *sir!*' 'Grandson of the hero of New Orleans, sniff, snort, grunt, yes, no, what?' 'Yes, sir, the grandson of the Union hero who supported the Confederacy but couldn't take the idea of working under Jefferson Davis, *sir!*' ''

Pierce shrugged, lighting his cigarette. A smell of cherries and wet sand rose from his hand. My own hand continued to dangle over the cigarette case. Wanting to withdraw, afraid to accept . . . everyone knew what smoking could lead to. Look, it had led to the grandson of a Civil War hero's being tossed out of the Naval Academy. But, I told myself, you're not a member of anything you can be bounced out of—and besides, who was going to know, other than the person offering, and himself indulging in, this sin?

I lowered my hand a few more inches. Cigarettes, I imagined, were probably like candies, etiquette decreeing that once you touched one, you were expected to consume it. If my fingertips should accidentally brush against a Sobranie . . .

"It's less wonderful than it looks," Pierce said.

My hand dropped, empty, to my lap.

"And less difficult," he said. "Like sex. Just take one."

"One what?" I squeaked.

"One cigarette." He picked up the case and pulled aside a narrow silver bar protecting the contents. Thus loosened and offered, the cigarettes moved beyond enticement, to possession. I grabbed at one.

"Not like that," Pierce said. "Delicately. Thumb and forefinger. Like picking up a needle."

I plucked at the cigarettes; with Pierce watching, my fingers felt sweaty and heavy, as though fitted with thimbles: totally incapable of finesse. Touching the Sobranies loosened a few more tobacco threads, and I could picture them disintegrating, a brown moist clot inside that lovely silver case.

"Try it again," Pierce said. "Pretend you're picking up a strand of a woman's hair."

The image astonished me; why would I be picking up a strand of Ivy's hair? I extracted a cigarette with tender care.

Pierce nodded, crushing the cigarette he was holding with one expert twist, like a gardener beheading a less-than-perfect rose, and took a box of Swan Vesta matches out of his pocket.

"There are three ways to light a cigarette," he said. "One, man to man. Two, gentleman to lady." He struck a match. "Three, lover to lover." He held out the flame. "Or maybe you're not that interested?" he asked.

I wasn't interested, I was *fascinated*. It must have shown: without bothering to wait for my enthusiastic affirmation, Pierce said, "Put the cigarette in your mouth. Good. Rest it just inside your lips. Perfect. Don't get it wet or you'll numb your gums. Okay, pull your breath in. Not quite so hard. There!"

And with that "There!" I was launched into the beguiling, engrossing, invigorating, heady, addicting world of smoking. With Pierce guiding me, there was none of the usual first-cigarette-turn-green business; smoke flowed smoothly down my throat, rolling back through my mouth and nostrils with no harshness at all.

"That's how a man lights another man's cigarette," Pierce said. "Did you see what I did?"

I couldn't remember. Pierce removed my cigarette, put it out, and slipped another one between my lips. He lit up a match and leaned toward me, cupping the match between his fingers and keeping his eyes fixed on the flame, as if in those few seconds he intended to understand the very physics of fire. The fresh cigarette sprang to life.

"The emphasis with a man is on the match," Pierce said. "With a woman, on the cigarette." He gave me a new Sobranie, lit a new Vesta, and bore the tiny wooden light to the edge of my cigarette, fitting the flame against the tobacco with the care of an engraver etching in platinum. His eyes watched my Sobranie with intense concentration: a young priest dispensing communion wafers. "You notice the difference?" he asked.

Nicotine, company, the sheer lateness of hour, and oddness of occupation were making me light-headed. "Show me the third way!" I begged.

Pierce smiled: an unusually bright student in this semester's Etiquette of Smoking seminar. "Ah, the third way," he repeated. "A combination of Methods One and Two. The first procedure, you'll remember, is very comradely. The most important thing is to perform a socially useful, physically measurable service: lighting a match. You could just as easily be offering an apple or pouring a glass of water. The second process is more formal. You're offering a solution to a problem: this lady's cigarette is unlit, you're here to help her. The third way merges camaraderie with formality, which is what the great love affairs are all about."

"That's true," I said wisely.

Pierce took out two more cigarettes, gave me one, and nodded for me to put it in my mouth.

"Now just use your imagination," he directed. "And your memories."

I nodded; I didn't have memories—at least not the sort I knew Pierce possessed—but I did have Ivy. Pierce slipped a cigarette between his lips, lit another match, quickly ignited his cigarette, then leaned over. The end of his smoldering cigarette seemed to have its own life and will, searching out my own Sobranie with a blind insistence. It was like watching a pin seeking a magnet, a baby seeking a breast. It was like—oh God. It was like watching my father's hands seeking Miss Manning, eyeless, mindless, moving, groping.

The two cigarettes touched: mine flickered and caught. I coughed, flustered and embarrassed. Pierce leaned back. He lazily drew in a deep breath of tobacco.

"See why people smoke?" he asked.

I puffed silently on my cigarette. It was just as I had sus-

pected, with Lorna and Jack, my father and Evelyn Manning—
even with Mr. and Mrs. Hannant. The entire world, every aspect, every encounter, every exchange, however casual, was
soaked with sex.

Pierce stood up and began pacing the room. How was it, I
wondered, for someone like him? He knew how he looked, how
he acted; he knew every woman on deck had watched him the
day we sailed. What was it like to open a door and enter a room
full of strangers, knowing everyone noticed? I rose and followed
him.

"Do you like me?" I demanded.

He was reaching for a book on the top shelf. "So far," he
replied.

"Then would you tell me something?"

His hand paused. "Depends. Tell you what?"

I pushed nicotine down my throat, and words back up.
"Would you tell me how to meet a woman?"

He continued reaching. His back was turned toward me,
and I prayed he wasn't laughing. If he was, then this entire, and
entirely pleasant, evening would be ruined; and instead of a
memory to hoard and embellish, all I would be left with was a
memory of smoking cigarettes with an admiral's drunken son.
Don't be laughing at me, Pierce, I begged wordlessly. I didn't
laugh at your calisthenics, or your mother.

When Pierce turned around, looking sober and interested,
passing the test, I wanted to hug him. But fellow smokers didn't
behave that way, so I said, "Would you? Would you tell me?"

"Academic reasons, or do you have someone in mind?"

"She's on board," I said.

"That's very romantic," Pierce said. "And convenient too.
What's her name?"

"Ivy," I whispered. It was the first time I had spoken her
name aloud, and the syllables sounded wonderful, comfortable

—what was it Pierce had said? Camaraderie and formality. "Ivy," I repeated.

"Ivy," Pierce said. We walked out of the shelf area toward the front door. He propped himself against a wall. "What's she like?"

"She's very beautiful," I said immediately. "And she's very . . . I think she's probably very intelligent. And she's very feisty. And she's very beautiful—"

"I get it," said Pierce. "Very very. And when did this *bel amour* kick in?"

I looked at the carpet. "It hasn't," I mumbled. "I just don't know what to say to her. How to approach. Serious or funny. Friendly or very proper. Casual or—"

"I recommend enthused detachment," Pierce said. "You want her to know you're intrigued, because that means she's intriguing. But you don't want her to know you're excited, because that implies your enchantment is because of her gender, not her. Play up the fact you think she's intelligent, but present it as a given, not a reassurance; most women already know they're intelligent, and they resent it when men act surprised."

Pierce took a cigarette out of his case. "Women are much more uncertain about their bodies than their brains," he continued, "so it never hurts to reassure them there. You can make a direct statement, although sometimes that sounds a little crass; so you might mention how something she's wearing complements some attribute of hers. Eyes are always good, and they match anything—"

"Pierce!" I interrupted. "What exactly do I *say*?"

Pierce peeled his back from the wall, stood up straight for several seconds, then abandoned the effort. I don't think he had ever considered my question in his entire life; he looked serious and confused, like a man trying to explain how he, personally, breathed.

"You don't say anything," he finally said. "You just . . . you just talk. You ask a question, she gives an answer. She does the same; you do the same. You talk about . . . uh, what she likes to do, what you like to do, where she lives, where you live, who she knows, who you know . . ."

I looked at him, disappointed. I live in Boston and I go to school. How long could it take to say that? Pierce's instructions, when you came right down to it, were not very illuminating: be polite, exchange small talk, appeal to the mind. I might as well be asking my mother.

Pierce seemed embarrassed; I think he knew his advice was a dud. "You might try finding a common interest," he said. "You two share any causes or hobbies, anything like that?"

"She's a feminist," I said.

Pierce said, "Oh."

"Is that a problem?"

"I'm not the one interested in her."

He lit his Sobranie. Apparently there was a fourth way: lighting your own. "Would it be a problem for you?" I asked.

"Nobody interested in his or her own emancipation ever causes me any problems," said Pierce. "It's people trying to emancipate me I have trouble with."

I looked out the porthole. The air was becoming chalky with intimations of dawn. This was the first time in my life I had stayed up like this, and I shivered with the sudden chilling fever of sleeplessness. Pierce opened the door, then turned around.

"There's a party tomorrow evening after dinner," he said. "Why don't you invite your young feminist to dance?"

CHAPTER SEVEN

I SLEPT UNTIL FOUR THE NEXT AFTERNOON.

Pierce had said there were three different ways of lighting a cigarette. I was discovering there were different varieties of sleeping, too. There was the usual school-homework-dinner-with-family sleep, awarded for virtue: you dropped off within twenty minutes, were awakened by noise in the hall, usually beat out the alarm clock, and never dreamed. There was Saturday sleep, where you went to bed two hours later than usual and then awoke puzzled the next morning, your eyes unfamiliarly flooded with late-morning sunshine. There was fever sleep—light, fitful, unrefreshing, hallucinatory. And finally there was compensation sleep, repayment sleep, the sleep you wrote out a check for and sent to your brain to square your account for the night before.

I owed myself all the sleep I could get, because dawn already was pinking my stateroom when I finally crawled into bed, drained by Pierce's confessions, observations, and advice. My eyes felt dry and swollen; my throat throbbed and itched, cross-hatched with irritating blisters. Nicotine leached from my gums, flavoring the minty tooth powder with a disgusting, punishing essence of tobacco, like unsugared licorice. Nevertheless I could hardly wait to see Pierce again, and to smoke more cigarettes;

and all these prodding discomforts seemed to me a natural and just aftermath to yesterday evening, and a price which any pub-crawling young gentleman should be willing to pay.

I awoke when the thought of what I was going to do this evening fell like an axed tree into my dreams. Ivy! Dance with! I shot out of bed. Where were my clothes? My shoes? My coat? Where the hell was Perry—I mean, Percy? Where the hell had the expression "where the hell" come from?

I bathed frantically, trying unsuccessfully to calm down. Soap refused to lather. Lotions refused to soothe. My hair seemed unable to dry, instead standing straight up in a stiff, wet gob, in spite of three towels and an attempt to dry it by cupping my hands and blowing up. When Percy showed up—"just to check things over, Mr. Jordan"—I was trying to blot my hair with a sponge wrapped in one of my mother's handkerchiefs. Silently he whipped out a square of porous flannel and toweled me dry.

"The alterations to your evening wear have all been taken care of," he announced. "Shall we give it a try?"

We tried. We succeeded. My trousers now fell perfectly, stopping at the precise center of my gleaming shoes. My cuffs, starched brittle, were near-totally hidden by the graceful folds of my lengthened sleeves. My post-Percy hair looked soft, even a little wavy. Not exactly another Pierce, but . . . As I looked at my reflection from as many angles as I could contort myself into, I was, for the first time since childhood, at least halfway satisfied with what I saw.

That night I needed no Percy to walk me to the elevator, no maître d' to show me my table. I sailed into the dining room, took in all that beauty and chatter with one cool glance, located Ivy, and found my own table. Pierce, to my disappointment, wasn't there to admire my sharp tailoring, but the Hannants and Gibsons and Miss Mayhew were; they waved at me across the room, gratifyingly awed by my transformation. "You look ten years older!" Miss Mayhew cried, catapulting herself with that one comment to the top of my Favorite Adults list. Our main waiter hurried over. I ordered lightly; I was not here to eat. I was here to observe Ivy Earnshaw the stranger for the last time. The next time we met, in this very room, we would have spoken.

Dinner went by quickly. Mr. Gibson and Mrs. Hannant discussed socialism, the theater, unions, and automobiles, while Mrs. Gibson and Mr. Hannant debated pure-food legislation (Mr. Hannant: "Caveat emptor"; Mrs. Gibson: "Have you ever actually *eaten* a hot dog, Clarence?"). Miss Mayhew and I gazed at Ivy, and it occurred to me that perhaps, in her decade, Miss Mayhew had been another Ivy: independent, well-traveled, well-spoken, single. Was she now what Ivy would become? Ivy reached for her wine. She could do worse, I decided, than to metamorphose into this gracious and kindly woman. Only I hoped I'd get forty years with her first.

After dinner my tablemates retired and I headed toward the dance floor. Then it occurred to me that Pierce had not mentioned where it was. This was no problem: the new Sumner had no trouble asking stewards, pursers, or anyone else for directions; in fact I talked to so many people that over an hour had passed by the time I finally rounded a corner and heard the clamor of "Alexander's Ragtime Band" drumming in the hallways. I walked into the Grand Saloon, with its great chandelier and its paneled walls and the blurred pastels of its Aubusson carpets. Excitement and trepidation elbowed for position with every step.

Somehow I had expected Pierce to be there; he seemed the type to skip a meal but not a party. But no, he wasn't; and beyond noticing that, I had no room in my mind for anything at all. For twenty feet, light-years, half a generation, five seconds away, Ivy stood: alone, in a green dress, holding a glass of punch. Waiting. For me. The sight of her cramped my stomach like hot strychnine.

I started to walk toward her. One step, one smaller step. Two . . . this was easy! Three . . . four . . .

Then the great net fell.

Shyness. Shyness so tightly knit I could not make a single move. Shyness so total it incapacitated. I was less than five feet away from her but we might as well have been in two different universes. Ivy . . . Ivy . . .

I stood staring helplessly. A man and a woman walked up to her. The man handed her a piece of cake. I could see every particle of that cake, the crumbs from each bite, the grains of each crumb, the granular texture of sugary, almondy frosting. Icing fell against Ivy's fork like collapsing snow. The woman said something; Ivy smiled, a rising sun. Yes, I could see everything: seeing caused no difficulties. My difficulty lay with getting my legs to obey my brain.

Ivy finally stepped away, into a crowd of people. Naturally, as soon as she moved, I was released, legs fine, muscles energized, neurons firing and receiving right on schedule. Only there was nowhere, nowhere, nowhere to go. I could not possibly plunge into that circle of Ivyadmirers; my behavior two minutes ago had demonstrated conclusively my inability to approach under even optimal conditions. I walked to a table and sat down glumly. Imagine bothering to ask Pierce what to talk to a woman about! What the hell—yes, what the *hell* had made me think I ever would get the chance?

A waltz started. I tapped the edge of the table and continued to look at Ivy. Now that I knew my limits, I could not even fantasize; and without the possibility of success, that outside shot at achievement which daydreaming confers, watching her was agony. The only thing more painful would have been to know she was near me, and not to watch.

"So, Sumner, how'd it go?"

My eyes moved off Ivy. Pierce was standing beside me, smiling the friendly smile one wears when thoroughly expecting good news.

"It didn't go at all," I answered sullenly.

"Sorry to hear that," said Pierce. "I'm surprised." He squatted down next to my chair, balancing himself like a catcher awaiting a pitch. I looked at him resentfully. It was tough blaming Pierce for my own shyness, but if I really stretched things, I could—*just*—blame him for my failure.

"You may be sorry," I told him, "but you really shouldn't be that surprised. You must have known everything you told me was totally useless." An ugly whine which I couldn't control buzzed through my voice. "You told me all I had to do was ask her," I said. "Just ask her, you said, and everything would be fine."

"I never said that," Pierce protested—a fair enough contention, which I chose to ignore. "I just suggested you give it a try."

"You made it all sound so easy," I continued. "Well, maybe it's easy for you. But it isn't for me. I'm shy, O.K.? You need it spelled out? I can't just sail up to someone I've never met and pretend I know what's going on. I look stupid when I do that. I look *silly*. And besides," I added nastily, "I think anyone else who does that looks stupid and silly too."

"Hold on a second," said Pierce, his voice quite pleasant, but somehow sounding capable of turning very caustic very quickly. "Were you actually turned down by the lady in question? Or did you never get around to asking?"

I didn't answer: answer enough.

Pierce arose, patted my hand, and sat down on a chair next to me; we lit Sobranies and puffed in silence. Across the room Ivy sparkled and beckoned, dancing with various idiots.

"Asking anyone for anything, even just a dance, puts you so on the line," Pierce said. "Sometimes I think that's why people rape and rob and murder. It's not nature, like the Darwinists say; and it isn't environment, like the settlement workers claim. It's just so much less risky to take than to ask."

"I didn't ask, I didn't take," I whispered. "I just froze."

"Why?"

Why. Not because of the obvious—that Ivy, seeing only an importunate child, would turn me down. And not because of the *less* obvious—that Ivy in real life would shatter my Ivy-fantasy. No, what had immobilized me was shyness in its purest sense: a fear of fear. My fear that fear would paralyze me had paralyzed me; I had been accompanied at every step across that room by a detailed vision of myself approaching Ivy and being unable to speak. So embarrassing, humiliating, unendingly awful had this image of failure been that I had failed beforehand, superseding my own imagination.

I took out my watch. Almost ten-thirty. The dancing, I knew, would end at eleven, or even earlier: I had very little time. On the other hand, you don't need much time if you're not doing anything. I glanced at Pierce. He was studying his cigarette with surprise; I really don't think he recalled lighting it. He tapped ashes into a swan-shaped ashtray of pearly marble.

"The first woman I ever asked to dance," he said, "pulled my hair, slapped my face, and tried to kick me in the stomach. Of course, I did have most of my arm down the front of her dress at the time. On the other hand, I was only five years old, and she *was* my aunt. It taught me to be very circumspect about whom one invites to go dancing."

He looked across the room. A group of girls about my own

age stood in a corner, hair carefully braided with ribbons and flowers, white velvet dresses nearly identical. Their eyes watched the dancing with almost as much longing as mine. "So," said Pierce, "which of these young Circes is Ivy?"

I realized then that there had been a massive failure of communication. Wordlessly I pointed in the opposite direction, where Ivy stood, surrounded by friends, tapping her feet to a bouncy waltz, shining like silk in the mild shadows. Pierce breathed an astonished gasp.

"Christ, Sumner, isn't she a little ol—" His tongue was pushing against his teeth; most of the word "old" was already out of his mouth. But Pierce was nothing if not cool under fire. ". . . old-fashioned for a forward-looking guy like yourself?" he finished: sheer babble, but totally appreciated.

"No, she's just right," I said. "And she's very modern. I told you. She's a feminist."

Pierce lit another cigarette, visibly gratified by that gesture's familiar lack of surprises. "She's certainly beautiful," he said. "No one would question your taste." He gazed at Ivy with bewildered appreciation, like an art instructor before a bumbling student's startling masterpiece. Then he looked at me.

"Don't you think you'd better get going?" he asked.

"Going?"

"Going across the room. Getting this show on the road. Moving. Doing. Asking."

"I can't," I said. "I already tried. I just can't."

Pierce stood up smoothly. "Well, I can," he said.

I jumped up. "No! You can't do that!"

"The hell I can't," Pierce said.

"But she—you—" I was so upset, so thoroughly thrown off-balance by this betrayal, I could only sputter. "I saw her first! She's mine!"

"Doubt if a feminist would appreciate that comment," said

Pierce, crushing out his cigarette. "We're not talking about a cow or a piece of machinery someone can say he owns. We're talking about a human being."

"Don't you turn pious on me!" I cried.

"Don't *you* turn unadorable. Hell, just last night you were extolling the simple pleasures of life. What's more pleasurable than watching a beautiful woman dance? And if she's not dancing with you—well, you've been settling for that all evening, it seems to me. I'll simply be one more dancer who isn't you."

I was so angry I couldn't think. All I wanted was to get out of there, away from them, all of them—Pierce, Ivy, even Miss Mayhew, if she was there. No wonder adults were so nasty to children; they knew how much children—at least the smart ones—despised them. I took two steps toward the front exit, then wheeled around. No! I was not going to be made a fool of! Hell, no! I had more in common with Ivy than Pierce Andrews would in a lifetime!

L'audace! I stomped across the floor. Dancers parted for me like the waves before the Israelites. If anyone tried to restrain me, I'd . . . I'd . . . But nobody tried. I soldiered onward.

It was only when I was within Ivydistance I realized how far into the room my rage had propelled me. By then it was too late: I was close enough for pure excitement to push aside any urge to retreat. I was conscious of two men on one side of her, two women on the other, Ivy set in the middle like a perfect emerald.

Please, God, please, Ivy, please, I instructed everybody. Please don't let me botch it.

"Excuse me, Miss Earnshaw," I said to her.

"Yes?"

"Would you care to dance?"

One of the men by her side gave a surprised snort; one of

the women chuckled. Ivy might be smiling, too: I was afraid to look. Instead I stared at her shoulders, at the slight pink indentation which the heavy fabric of her dress had carved into her flesh. Time passed, whole seasons changed while I stood motionless, poised to dive into a pool which might or might not be empty.

When she finally spoke it was so familiar: the voice from the demonstration, only lower now, less angry—still thrilling.

"It would give me," she said, "the greatest pleasure."

I was wound so tightly I couldn't understand a word she spoke. "What?" I said.

She looked at my stricken face and stuck out her hand. "Let's go," she said.

I walked her to the dance floor—a distance of ten whole feet—in a state of total, perfect perception. Everyone we passed, every scent, every shading of light, each harmonic, appeared to me in microscopic, fascinating detail. What care had gone into designing and furnishing this room! Into writing this waltz! I was stunned by how much more beautiful than necessary life was.

We began dancing—the "Milano" waltz. Ivy danced exactly the way I had imagined, though until that moment I hadn't realized I had imagined it. She felt both fragile and athletic, and she rocked a little as she danced, a characteristic I remembered my dancing teacher describing as "common." My only thought, as I felt Ivy's shoulder slide against mine, was, This should become more common. I kept my eyes on the edge of her hair, where it swept above her upper ear, leaving the lower half level with my mouth. I was in heaven, only it was so quiet.

Talk to her, say something.

What can I say?

Say anything! What would Pierce say?

Who cares? I'm me! I mean, I'm I! I mean . . .

Back and forth my private advisers yacked. Finally one made a usable suggestion: Tell her you saw her in London!

"I saw you in London!" I said.

Mouth at her ear, I spoke too loudly; Ivy's head jerked.

"At the demonstration," I explained.

"Which one?" she asked. "I was in . . . God, at least eight. Maybe more. *Would*'ve been more, anyway, only I got arrested."

Arrested? The ever-sweet, ever-helpful, may-I-be-of-assistance English bobbies arresting my Ivy?

"And they were real bastards, too," Ivy said.

My legs trembled, shocked at the word, and her using it, and all the time wondering what, exactly, a man had to do to Ivy for Ivy to call him a bastard.

"They finally sprang me because I'm American," she said. "The judge—excuse me, the 'magistrate'—told me to go home, little lady, and wreck family life in the United States. Leave English social chaos to the English." I felt the strong shrug of her velvety shoulders. "As if I'd let some minor-league Sheriff of Nottingham advise me on how to conduct my politics!" she said. "I was leaving anyway."

We moved farther into the crowd. "I saw you outside Parliament," I said.

The curve of her cheekbone lifted as she smiled. "Ah, yes. The strip-show riot." Her smile widened. "A personal favorite," she added.

"It was terrible!" I said. "I thought they were going to . . ." I couldn't finish; I couldn't say what I'd thought they were going to do, or how horrified—interested—I had been. "I was scared for you," I said. "Really worried."

"That's very sweet," she said. "Wish I'd known you were there. I was a tad scared myself."

It was as though Joan of Arc had said she was a tad scared of the flames. "It didn't show," I assured her. "You looked very valiant. Very stalwart. That guy didn't stand a chance."

"Well, I gave him several. But those kind of people . . . actually it's a gift they show up on their own. Because otherwise we'd have to go out and hire them. Bullies like him make rallies like ours come alive."

We continued dancing. Talking with Ivy was, really, surprisingly easy; I didn't even need to resort to Pierce's suggestions. If things became quiet for more than five seconds, she smoothly took over, submitting some neutral, riskless topic: the music, the weather, the food, our respective cabins (I found out she *was* on B Deck, just as I'd guessed, and I glowed, congratulating myself on being both smart and intuitive), our various notions of London. Ivy's London turned out to be far more interesting than mine; after all, no English police matron had tried to force-feed me, nor had I sat on the floor of a holding cell singing "La Marseillaise" with Fannie Pankhurst. But she listened carefully and politely to my softer recollections, and she always came up with the right questions.

"So what's he like, this writer?" she asked. "This Mr. Joyce?"

"I liked him," I said. "I liked him a lot. I think—I think maybe he changed my life."

I was instantly panicked: such a comment seemed lumpish —a terribly heavy burden to ask a first dance to support. But Ivy managed the balance.

"Changed in what way?" she said.

"He told me if you really want something, you have to make sacrifices." Her eyes rolled, impatient; I hurried on. "I know, I know—that's what everyone says. But he gave examples. And they were all so sad and so terrible, and he was experiencing each of them. He said you had to endure the most painful loneliness. Turn your back on everything you love. No friends. No ties. No community. That's the only way you'll be free for your own work.''

Ivy was silent.

"Do you believe that?'' I asked.

"No,'' she said briskly. "No, I certainly don't.''

"Oh!'' I was embarrassed—maybe a little hurt. "Oh, well . . . maybe I didn't say it right. Or left something out. Maybe I—''

"The first part's right,'' Ivy said. "You have to make sacrifices for what you want, of course you do. But being lonely, turning your back on everything you love . . . Well, maybe that's true for art. But I'm not an artist, I'm a political woman, and I don't want to reject my community, I want to *change* it. *That's* worth sacrificing for. But being isolated, not being involved . . . I mean, what's the point?''

We danced on. Actually, I thought, there *was* a point, in isolation, I mean—even the most political people, even people like Charles Sumner, who lived for change, and practically died for it, too, were isolated: their very desire to change their world isolated them from that world. On the other hand, the mere thought of my Ivy isolated or sad or alone or rejected was almost unbearable in the strength of its misery. For I didn't want her ever to sacrifice. I wanted to do it for her.

Some of this must have shown in my face—either that, or she was unaccustomed to bug-eyed worship, for after observing my close-range adoration for several seconds, she softly patted my shoulder. It was in all ways obviously meant to be a friendly, sisterly, sexless tap; my reaction of course was totally sexual, my whole body responding with grueling delight. She tapped again.

"Hey,'' she said, "stop looking at me that way. I'm trying to tell you something.''

I'm trying to tell you something, too, I thought.

Ivy said, "Listen to me. This is serious."

"I'm listening," I said.

She sighed. "No, you're not. You're just staring. But listen —I'm trying to warn you. It's the last thing you want from me, I know. But if you act like this with every woman you meet, you're going to end up suffering more than you can possibly imagine."

"I'm not suffering," I said. "And I wouldn't care if I were."

Ivy's face stiffened, then softened; for a second she looked like Mother, about to begin a lecture. But the waltz, at that instant, slipped into its lively "American" version, and in the couple of moments it took us both to adjust our feet and our rhythms, her warning, though not forgotten, died. Relieved and emboldened, I gave her my name—she nodded—and my mother's name. She knew all about Mother, of course, and she started laughing.

"Rebecca Jordan's son!" she exclaimed. "You're kidding! I've read her speeches! I collect her essays! You're the son of Rebecca Jordan? God, that's amazing!"

"Please," I said, modestly. "Just call me Sumner."

"Sumner," she repeated. My soul shimmered and fluttered, fragile as ice.

The waltz moved into its final movement. Behind me I could hear the click of other feet, the murmur of other conversations. A clock on the wall read twenty till eleven. Just twenty more minutes, it all would be over; hang on, Cinderella style, to every second . . . Then I heard hurried steps, a familiar voice, and a rustle of silk, all aiming my way. I looked around. Pierce, a black-haired woman wound tight in his arms, was scything his way through the weaving dancers, every woman, Ivy included, observing.

"Every time I see that man," she said, "he's with a different woman."

Pierce and his partner, he calmly, she a little breathlessly, arrived at our side. "Sumner, old lad," he said, and smiled at Ivy, as I glared.

"Miss Earnshaw," he added.

Ivy nodded. Pierce had pronounced her name perfectly politely, perfectly respectfully; yet somehow he seemed to be addressing her from within the cocoon of a most intimate, shocking embrace. Ivy noticed, smiled; I winced. What was she wanting, what was she thinking?

"Might I have the honor of a dance?" asked Pierce, in that same nonsuggestive, all-suggesting voice.

Ivy looked around. "Well . . ." she started, "perhaps—"

"Say 'No!' " Pierce hissed at me.

"What?"

Pierce gave my ankle a vicious kick.

"No!" I barked.

"Ah, well, some other time then," Pierce said. He smiled at both of us, tucked his partner back into place, and bounded away.

"Friend of yours?" Ivy asked.

Only then did realization of what Pierce had been up to earlier hit me. Of course he hadn't really intended to seek out Ivy for himself! Of course he had said all that only to get me moving! Of course, that was not to say that if I *hadn't* gotten moving, he wouldn't have . . .

"Yes," I said, "he's a very good friend."

Someone else broke in then, someone less interesting than Pierce; Ivy and I switched partners. I danced with two young women from the opposite corner; I danced with one of Ivy's girlfriends; I danced with an elderly lady who wore pink pearls and murmured in French. The lights began dimming and the band began playing more softly and slowly; one by one, couples walked off the dance floor, adjusting wraps and jackets, bidding happy good nights. Pierce and his dancing companion wandered out of one door; my Frenchwoman and her monocled husband left through another. Soon there were only a dozen couples waltzing in the sudden quiet. I was once again partnered with Ivy.

Dark outside blackness filtered through the windows; the lights turned lower, electric blue. Ivy's face was alabaster, expressionless, washed with enormous shadows. I closed my eyes and felt her against my arms. The air between our faces surged warmly, in springlike puffs; her fragrance smelled like incense, like attar, like words in a poem. I felt the room behind my eyelids grow even dimmer, heard the music become even lower, even slower. It was a moment of astonishing loveliness, luck, and silence, lulled peaceful and satisfied, dancing in the dark with Miss Ivy Earnshaw.

CHAPTER EIGHT

I WAS LYING IN BED, STILL DANCING.

Ivy was everywhere. In my hair, my skin, my clothes; on my lips, behind my eyes. She curled around me, purred beneath me; I hovered above her, kissing scented memories. She flowed through my empty cabin like music in darkness: nothing to see, but impossible to ignore. Ivy waltzed through my brain.

I moved my right hand; a flash of white cuff darted mothlike in the black air. I took a deep breath, sniffing Ivy's perfume, Pierce's Sobranies, the starch of my shirt. All three odors melded together, an olfactory rainbow, me and my two favorite people in all the world.

I had thought dancing with Ivy would be the most wonderful thing in my life, but I was wrong. Remembering was even better. Remembering refined, highlighted, the very special seconds: Ivy taking my hand, Ivy touching my shoulder, Pierce flying across the room, checking my progress, whirling away. Ivy smiling. Ivy talking. The tremble in my bones. Her utter calmness. Her kindness.

At that point I tried to remember an example of Ivy's kindness, but I couldn't. That, perhaps, was the greatest kindness of all. She had treated me totally as an equal, as an adult. As a fellow suffragist.

Hadn't she? Sudden doubt sat me up. I reached for our conversations, pulled them apart. Could anything be interpreted as condescending? Time marking? Time killing?

I looked again at our movie, studying every scene. Sumner enters from left. Walks across room, sees Ivy, hesitates. Confesses to Pierce. "I cannot do it!" reads the title. Pierce gesticulates violently. Sumner springs across room, asks Ivy to dance, Ivy accepts. They waltz. They talk. Angle on Ivy, smiling. Angle on Sumner, face ridiculously radiant.

The reel was almost finished when I discovered what I was looking for. Focus on Ivy, staring at Pierce for that half second before she realizes simple courtesy requires she refuse him. Pierce smiles, bows, capers away; camera on Ivy; fade out; end.

I blinked, resigned. I must not, *must not,* become jealous of Pierce—that would lead nowhere, solve nothing, change nobody. Besides, jealousy of someone I liked so much was pointless, self-crucifying; trading enthusiasm for masochism was a most bitter bargain. I studied the film once again. I had to admit, it still delivered. Slowly, very slowly, like water flirting with boiling, my happiness began once again to bubble and surge.

Then something happened.

Or, rather, *nothing* happened. Nothing *was.* I looked around, puzzled. I felt an absence, a falling-away of the familiar. I switched on the lamp and looked around me. Nothing looked different, nothing seemed missing. . . .

Then I realized. The muffled pound of iron surf which had been murmuring for five nights straight had vanished.

The engines were dead.

I swung my legs out of bed, then wondered why; certainly nothing was wrong, and the deep silence outside my door told me no one else on the deck was worried or stirring. I retreated back under the blankets, ready for more memories. But none arrived. Part of what had always made my bed so welcoming, so appealing, was that faint sigh of power and steam which was now missing; without the growling engines, I felt uneasy, as if there were no longer a dependable barrier between myself and the sea. I rose again, stuck on my oldest and warmest coat, and walked upstairs and outside, onto the Boat Deck.

Night stretched blackly, still and without horizon; the dark air sparkled, moonless, starry and clear as ice. It would have been beautiful, only it was so cold. My lungs ached simply from the effort of breathing; my throat throbbed, rubbed raw by the stinging chill. A few other explorers walked by me, murmuring theories for our silent engines; nobody shared them with me.

Then, to my utter delight, on the other side of the deck, I saw Lorna and Jack.

They were standing arm in arm, both gazing nightward and somehow managing not to look cold. Jack was whispering, Lorna shaking her head. A man passed them, mumbled something. Jack disappeared down the stairs.

"Lorna!" I said.

She turned around, her smile cool, then warming in recognition. How pleasant, I thought, those suspended moments when your definition passes from stranger to friend. "What's going on?" I asked her. "All the engines stopped."

"I don't know. We were just lying in bed"—my head jerked; lying in bed?—"and we felt a bump. Jack thinks we hit something." She gestured vaguely into the darkness. "Something out there," she said.

"Where?" I peered into the black night, but there was nothing to see, absolutely nothing to hit. The ship was motionless, sitting in that nothingness with perfect posture, meaning-

lessly immobile. Coleridge slithered uninvited forward. *As idle as
a painted ship / Upon a painted ocean . . .*

I shivered, coldness blunting good manners. "I was sort of
hoping I'd run into you two sooner," I said.

Even in the cold darkness, I could see Lorna blush. "I guess
we've been busy," she said. "We haven't been on deck that
much."

Always one to let others' embarrassment embarrass me, I
blushed too. "Well, we *are* married," Lorna said.

"Ah," I said, neutral as Switzerland.

"How about you?" Lorna asked. "Has it been a good voyage?"

She was the first person to ask. "Oh, yes!" I exclaimed. "I
met . . . It's been wonderful. Better than the best thing that's
ever happened to me."

She smiled. "Can't ask for much better than that," she said.

I smiled back, and we continued to look out at the blank
Atlantic silence. I suspected we were both remembering ec-
stasies so recent the joy still smarted. Jack walked up behind us.

"This is the damnedest thing I ever heard of," he said.
"Look what we hit."

He reached into a pocket and took out a thick white stick of
glass. He held it upward, to catch the deck light; a prism of
greens and violets skidded off the crystal. Then I noticed: there
were droplets on the glass, melting down Jack's hand, puddling
the deck.

It wasn't glass. It was ice.

"There's about three tons of this stuff down below on the
starboard well deck," Jack said. "That's what that bump was.
We grazed a growler."

"What's a growler?" I asked.

"Iceberg," said Jack.

Iceberg. Suddenly I remembered Buckley, with his list of the North Atlantic's guaranteed sorrows. Where had icebergs ranked? Were they better than storms or worse?

"Does it matter?" I asked.

Jack didn't answer. We stared together into the night. Just the pale outline of our own gigantic reflection, and those tiny, distant stars. Jack tossed the shard of melting ice over the side. It disappeared; then, an infinitely long time later, so much later I'd forgotten he'd thrown it, it splashed into the sea. A long, long way down.

"Don't *think* it matters," he finally said. "The deckhands say we'll be under way in just a few minutes. And everything *vibrates* right." He tapped the deck sharply with his foot, then rapped the railing. "Bad construction has a certain feel to it," he explained. "A kind of tenderness. Like a bad lung. You learn to sniff it out, even when it's hidden. Especially when it's hidden." He tapped again. "Like the Vanier Bridge," he said. "It looked solid but it tapped hollow. And it never looked better than the day it collapsed."

"That's certainly reassuring," Lorna said.

"Fear not!" Jack stomped and listened. "Granted, this isn't terribly scientific," he said, "but she sounds safe to me."

We started for the stairs leading below. I felt a sharp stab of envy for Jack—not only for Lorna but for his vocation. If only I too were an engineer, tutored to build and to comfort! Being a boy poet was so boring. I beamed at them both.

"It's so nice to see you again," I said.

"Sumner's been having a hot old time," Lorna told Jack.

"Yeah?" Jack looked pleased for me, but not totally pleased: something else had caught his attention. He took a few steps and frowned.

"You have a marble?" he asked me.

I was immediately insulted: only children carry marbles. On

the other hand, yes, I did happen to have one; the pockets of all my coats were always full of marbles, combs, pennies, old chewing-gum wrappers. I handed it over. Jack carefully poured it down the length of the deck. It rolled perfectly, straight and true.

"Thought I felt a list," Jack said, returning it. "Guess not. Nice purie, by the way. Look, Sumner, it's getting a little chilly. We're going below. I'm sure everything's under control, but just in case it isn't, let's meet here in an hour. All right? We'll be up anyway."

"O.K.," I said (for what else could I say?). They disappeared down the stairs; I watched them descend. They somehow looked a little awkward, a little stiff—a little off balance for people who obviously spent so much time walking arm in arm. Then I descended myself.

When I did I felt the same oddness I had observed watching Lorna and Jack.

Probably it was the sort of thing only someone who had explored the ship staircase by staircase, as I had, would notice. But one of the liner's more marvelous minor architectural features was her mathematically calibrated companionways, designed to minimize muscle strain as you lifted and lowered your legs. Now those stairs, usually so comfortable, were infinitesimally off. Somewhere deep within the ship's hidden center of gravity a fulcrum had shifted, realigned. We were perfectly balanced, yes. Yet the stairs tilted.

I looked down the hallway for Jack; this observation, I decided, required a technical explanation. But he was gone, and I didn't want to interrupt his honeymoon for engineering reassurances. Instead I experimented with descending and mounting more stairs on other decks. I passed occasional passengers—some, like Jack, bearing chunks of ice; I passed a few officers, a steward, a maid. Nobody appeared at all concerned or worried;

that we should have struck an iceberg, and were now sitting motionless in the middle of the ocean, seemed perfectly fine with everyone. And everything felt—*vibrated,* Jack would say—perfectly fine too. Except that you had to shift your left knee half an inch to comfortably descend the stairs.

I walked down a few more companionways and found myself outside the squash court. From within I could hear thumping—back and forth, up and down, side to side—the unmistakable ricochet of a closely played match. I listened and grinned: on the only ship in history which made hitting an iceberg boring, people ignored the collision but played squash! I pushed open the door to watch.

The court was deserted. But the thumping continued.

I stood bewildered. A squash court with nobody on it is much like an empty church, or a school with no children—being unused renders it useless, and uselessness renders it pointless. But *was* it unused? This insistent, repeated rhythm—where was it coming from? Were there adjoining rooms I had somehow missed? Or was the ship also toting, unbeknownst to me, a tennis court?

I stepped farther in. The pace of the thumping was disciplined and unbroken. It was as if a championship tournament were being played—played without players, without equipment or audience; yet nevertheless played with great skill and vigor. The walls echoed with precisely that same dull thud a ball makes against wood; the floor soaked up the sound, then the thumping started again, against the far wall. The ghostly volleys were growing in strength and volume, becoming louder, much louder, and more rapid. The spaces between the thumps shortened; now the roar was nearly constant.

Then, suddenly, the entire far wall caved in.

The wooden panels exploded, green seawater rushing across the court in a foamy tidal wave over eight feet high. The noise was louder than any machinery—louder than any ocean was this caged ocean. I imagined myself lifted, splattered senseless against the floor, tossed toward the ceiling. I was a city of one, in the path of a maddened dam. My poor mother. Poor Ivy. Poor Sumner. *Move!*

I jumped out the door, idiotically locking it behind me, and raced down the hall, terrified my heart would never stop pounding this loudly, almost as loud as that water, a pain like drowning in air. I ran up deck after deck after deck. Thank God for my earlier loneliness!—I knew just where to go. Collision! My God! Rescue in the middle of the North Atlantic! Oh, Jesus! What terrible, deadening, saddening pain. What fear.

I burst into the wireless office. All was clean, dry, busy, efficient. Mr. Phillips sat hunched as usual over his machinery, one-handedly accepting messages from utterly calm officers. With his other hand he was rapping out the letters of his magical syntax. For one breathless second I listened. It was the new signal: SOS, SOS, SOS.

I tugged the arm of a nearby officer.

"Excuse me, sir," I said, still panting, "but are you aware just how bad off we really are?"

"You shouldn't be here," he said.

I was sure he'd misheard me. "No, no," I said, "I mean, do you realize we're sinking?"

"You shouldn't be here," he repeated.

"Believe me," I said, emboldened by fear, "I wish I were anywhere else."

We both gaped at my rudeness. "Does anyone know the squash court's completely flooded?" I demanded. "Does anyone care?"

"I care," another officer said. "I've scheduled a match for tomorrow morning."

"Better bring a sponge," somebody said.

I couldn't believe it. SOS, SOS, Mr. Phillips calmly contin-ued to tap out. SOS.

"Give them lat and longitude," a third officer instructed. Mr. Phillips signaled and listened.

"They say four hours at the earliest," he reported. "That's *Carpathia. Frankfurt* says longer."

"Tell them four hours isn't good enough."

"Not good enough, old man," Mr. Phillips mumbled as he signaled. "We're taking on water on F and G." Without turn-ing around, he added, "Squash court flooded."

I shivered, attention paid to me. Electricity squawked.

"Fellow wants to know," said Mr. Phillips, "if a flooded squash court is what formally constitutes an emergency on this ship. Guess that depends on whether you wouldn't mind playing water polo instead. What's my reply?"

"Situation critical," an older officer replied.

"Situation critical," Mr. Phillips transmitted. "As will be," he added to himself, "the Board of Trade and the stockholders. Sideswiping a berg, indeed. Goddammit!" he shouted at the cackling apparatus. "Don't ask *me* why we didn't heed the bloody ice warnings!"

The officers looked at one another.

"Anyone care to answer that?" Mr. Phillips asked.

Nobody did. The room became very silent, filled with the humming queries of distant ships. Mr. Phillips decoded the in-coming messages in a flat voice. *Titanic,* what is your location? *Titanic,* have you begun firing rockets? *Titanic,* how much time do you have? . . . time do you have?

The older officer grimaced. "Tell them," he said, very slowly, his voice weary, "we have time to lower lifeboats in orderly fashion. We have little more time than that."

Mr. Phillips threw the transmittal switch.

His action seemed to energize everyone; the situation clearly defined at last to the outside world, there were specific duties one could attend to, places to go, life-saving missions to perform, in logical, predetermined maritime fashion. Briskly the officers began backing out of the tiny room, heading purposefully toward the Boat Deck. The older officer looked at me and smiled, a terribly strained smile, more a reflexing muscle than anything else—an instinctive attempt, in the middle of all this, to reassure a passenger.

"Young man," he said, "don't waste any time. Go at once to the lifeboats on the Boat Deck. We'll load women and children first."

"But I'm not a child—"

"Your family will be fine," he said. "Everyone will be saved. Just go on deck. You'll be assigned a lifeboat. Don't worry. Don't worry."

He passed his hand tiredly over his face. "We were so wrong," he whispered. "We were right she was beautiful, and we were right she was strong. But she was never unsinkable. We drove her too hard, and we killed her. She is dying. She already is dead."

He dragged himself up the tilting stairs. By now they were listing at an angle of more than ten degrees. I trailed him as far as C Deck.

Then I suddenly stopped. A vision appeared, vivid, precise —as clear as a saint's, or a madman's. And I knew, at that frozen moment of this amazing, improbable, impossible situation, exactly what to do.

I would *not* go on deck as instructed. That was out of the question. I would, instead, go to my stateroom. There I would pack up my journal, put on my sweater, and wait.

For what? It was simple. For time to pass. For adventure to beckon. For the women and helpless children to be lowered away in anticipation of the moment when I could come forth, to be saved along with the rest of my sex. For adulthood, with its attendant responsibilities, sacrifices, and instinctive heroism. For manhood, Charles Sumnerhood, to arrive at last.

I walked to my cabin. People were milling about in the passageway, confused and exhilarated, repeating outlandish rumors: we had run aground off Newfoundland; we had been hit by torpedoes; we were already in New York Harbor. Percy was everywhere, dispensing life preservers and calm advice: not to worry, just go on deck; not to worry, just go topside. Some people had taken the time to don furs and woolens; others were still in nightclothes, plucking at their life belts, pulling the strings. In the general hubbub, nobody noticed me; I darted into my stateroom, carefully locking the door against anyone mistakenly altruistic enough to attempt to save me before my time.

After the companionway, the stateroom was wonderfully silent: no voices, no high-pitched demands for explanations, no questions, no instructions. It was all extraordinarily peaceful and restful. The perfect environment, I told myself, the perfect setting, for a rite of passage.

I recalled other rites of passage I had read about. Young men deposited on isolated Peruvian mountaintops, dazed with hunger, drugged into hallucination; children of the veldt, shivering in the Sahara sunshine, bodies feathered, painted eyelids too parched to blink. I sighed. My passage to manhood seemed almost too tame: the promise of triumph without the challenge of pain. No formalized suffering, no blood—also no witnesses. A decision made in a stairwell, to remain in a locked cabin and save oneself later rather than now. No fear. No snickering, lurking danger. No death.

I slipped on my sweater. This must be what manhood was like when you grew up in Massachusetts instead of Africa. A little uneasiness, maybe a little tension, a weird foreboding—but no real flash. I thought about Charles Sumner, reeling in blood and righteousness through the United States Senate. *There* was an American who had undergone a genuine rite of passage; *there* was the challenge, *there* was the pain. True, Senator Sumner had been a bit older than the average initiate; in his mid-forties, I recalled, at the time of Bloody Kansas, and still a virgin (something else we had in common). Nevertheless there was no denying that his rite of passage, bloody and brutal as it undeniably was, had a certain beguiling purity to it. At least Senator Sumner had *felt* something. I wanted to feel something too.

I leafed through my carefully written journal, rereading the mythical Sumner's affair with Miss M———, now substituting Miss E——— and enjoying it quite a bit more. I looked at the section when our hero defends the cause from the outraged howlings of antifeminist thugs. Meanwhile I thought about what might be going on on deck. We had hit the iceberg so gracefully that most people had probably slept right through. Jack and Lorna had felt it, of course, but they had been, well . . . I wondered whether Pierce knew about it: he seemed to have spent his life colliding with icebergs nobody else could see. I wondered what Ivy knew.

Ivy. The officer had told me they would be loading women and children first—a chivalry so offensive it had stuck me down here for half an hour, and that was because of age, not sex. What would be Ivy's reaction to this gracious and courtly offer to be lumped with the helpless and weak, and hustled to safety?

Her reaction? Are you kidding? Ivy would never, never get into a lifeboat first. She wouldn't budge off that deck until at least two thousand people had been classified as less capable than she in the art and science of self-preservation.

I stood up suddenly, as two thoughts collided and pulled me toward the door. The first was that this deflating—when you came right down to it, this disappointing—rite of passage might have its good side after all. I had failed Ivy at the demonstration;

I could make up for it here. I would locate Ivy (perhaps she was still in her cabin? in her bed? in her nightgown? I could only hope), carry her bags, escort her to a lifeboat, and then, using all the powers of persuasive rhetoric which had earned me a lock on the "Boston Schoolboys Remember Paul Revere!" competition for three years straight, convince her to get on board.

Yes. I could save her. Even though there probably was nobody on this ship less in need of a savior, I could save her. And having done so I could truly be said to have become an adult and a man. And as an adult man I would then save myself.

The second thought—which hurried me down the hall and up to her stateroom on B Deck—was less a thought than a blurred flash of memory and arithmetic. There were twenty-two hundred people on board the *Titanic*. I did not recall, when I stood swapping verses with Buckley, seeing lifeboats for anywhere near that number.

B Deck, when I arrived, was nearly empty. Far, far down at the other end of the hall I could see somebody knocking on doors. It was the steward who had so nonplussed me yesterday as I'd stood before Ivy's imagined stateroom. Now he saw me and nodded—that same eerie recognition of First Class passengers the whole crew possessed.

"Just checking against looters," he explained. "Can't be too careful."

"Looters?" I repeated.

He nodded. "There's a lot of immigrants down below. Somebody up here goes off leaving his door unlocked, the place'll look like the second sacking of Rome."

I fiddled with the sleeves of my sweater.

"But we're sinking," I said. "Who cares how it looks?"

He checked another lock.

"Oh, no, laddie," he said, "no, no, no, no, no. Sinking's no excuse for bad behavior. People should leave this ship in the same state they boarded. No little help-yourself gifties just because we had the misfortune of a collision.''

I started knocking on doors. ''You can stop knocking,'' the steward said. ''Miss Earnshaw left her room almost an hour ago. In the company of a tall, green-eyed man who was behaving extremely badly.''

A tall, green-eyed . . . Pierce? ''Badly how?'' I asked.

''As though he was frightened,'' the steward said disdainfully. ''As though he didn't think the situation was under control.''

''Which way did they go?''

''C Deck.''

C Deck was me. So Pierce and Ivy were looking for me. Quite a shadow, this, on my dawning manhood! I peered down the companionway, hoping to catch them and cheer them up with the joyful gleam of my new identity—hoping to reassure them that the three main adults had joined forces at last.

But Ivy and Pierce were not in the companionway. I saw only lights—the boxy electric guides fitted into each stairway, seven decks deep. Floor after floor after floor of trim yellow squares. Except . . . except . . .

Except from E Deck downward, the boxes were green.

I blinked. The green lights shimmered and wavered in the clean, empty air. Then I realized it all was illusion: the air was neither clean nor empty—there was no air. The lights were green because they were submerged under tons of North Atlantic seawater.

I stared at the lights. They were beautiful, so bright in the water, and somehow so calm, so reassuring, still managing their electric glitter in spite of the pressure of all that ocean. It seemed to me that nothing really bad could happen in a world where a ship could sink with her lights on; and I could picture all of us, passengers and crew, floating peacefully in our lifeboats, waiting to be saved, our wait illumined by a sparkling *Titanic* burning beneath the sea. I went up the stairs to the Boat Deck. I hoped I could find Jack and Lorna, Ivy and Pierce, and we could watch the ship go down together.

The Boat Deck, nearly deserted the last time I had been there, was now packed, and more and more people were streaming up the stairs every minute. All was quite calm, as friends and families exchanged shrugs and inconvenienced smiles; the only loud noise I heard was the bark of a dog, balking as it was handed into a lifeboat. I saw Miss Mayhew, standing in line to enter one of the tiny wooden vessels. Only four or five people stood behind her, and there were dozens of empty seats in the waiting lifeboat. She saw me and waved.

"I know I'm being silly, but my steward insisted," she said, gesturing to her place in line. "Everyone else is telling me to just stay on board until help comes, but, my dear, I just don't know . . ."

I peeped over the side. "It looks like a long way down," I said.

"It does," she agreed.

"Come along, please, madam," said an officer.

"Sumner, come with me," Miss Mayhew said. "Keep me company. We can be panicky fools together."

"I can't," I said. "They're only loading women and children."

"That's okay, sonny," the officer said. "You qualify."

I tensed. In a world where Miss Mayhew was "madam," certainly I should be "sir," not "sonny."

"Thank you," I said to the officer, "but I believe I'll wait with the rest of the men. And, Miss Mayhew, let's be sure we're table partners at our next breakfast." She smiled wanly, entered the lifeboat, sat down, and closed her eyes. Her boat swung out over the side.

I continued walking the deck, still miffed at the officer's age classification. By now the ship seemed to have righted herself; the list was gone, the floor felt level. I passed a cluster of men, all in black evening dress, smoking cigars and exchanging little jokes. I recognized William Stead, the famous British editor whose tastes ran to "strange religions"—Mother's term for anything non-Congregationalist—and Archie Butt, President Taft's personal aide and adviser. I saw John Jacob Astor, a man who could stand on the deck of a sinking ship and still look richer than anyone else, and I exchanged greetings with his wife.

"They tell me the gymnasium's underwater!" she said. "Guess I'll have to substitute swimming for stationary-biking!"

I passed lifeboat after lifeboat. Some were slowly filling up; others left nearly empty, ten or twelve people sitting comfortably in a vessel easily fitted for fifty or sixty. Eventually I noticed that not everyone leaving was either woman or child: a number of men were filing forward too. On the port side of the ship ("port" meant "left," I finally remembered), these men were all turned away; on the right, though, the officers in charge—having looked around, called several times for more females and youths, and found none willing to leave the shelter of our huge knownness for the blue-black unknown looming below—were letting men board, generally accompanied by muttered speculations about hysteria-prone landlubbers.

I plodded scornfully on. Those men were cowards: the obviously correct thing to do was just what I was doing. Stay on board, help where needed, see my woman to safety. My woman? See my Ivy to safety.

Eventually I came to where Jack and Lorna had agreed to meet me that long hour ago. Neither was there; I looked around, and to my surprise saw Lorna sitting in a lifeboat suspended from a davit between the Boat and A decks. She cheerfully waved.

"Jack insisted!" she shouted. "He promised it'd be an adventure!"

Something twinged in my stomach, a hard, swift surge, as if someone had just sliced something sharp against my flesh. Every impression I had of Lorna and Jack raced through my memory. They seemed designed to share everything—their lives, their love, their adventures. Why would Jack want Lorna to enjoy this adventure alone?

"Sumner!"

I wheeled around at that familiar voice. Ivy was stalking across the deck toward me. Clumps of people stood in her way, but somehow they seemed flat and painted and two-dimensional, while only Ivy seemed rounded and real. Ivy, and Pierce.

They both looked grim. In fact, with their dark hair and quick strides and serious expressions, they looked rather alike. And they did not, to my relief, look at all interested in each other. Instead, they seemed very interested in me—too much so, suspiciously so. I smiled uneasily.

"Where the hell have you been the last hour?" Pierce greeted me.

I gasped, smile disappearing. Pierce's eyes were wide and dilated, his mouth twisted, biting off words like a Gatling gun spitting out bullets. "What's the matter with you anyway?" he demanded.

"Pierce—" Ivy interjected, while I weighed her pronunciation of his name for potential affection, "Pierce, don't bother—"

"I was in my cabin," I said defensively.

"Like hell you were."

"I was too!"

"Goddammit!" snapped Pierce. "Don't lie to me! I went right to your cabin the minute we hit, and you weren't there. So

I ask that bizarre whispery little steward that spies on everyone on your deck, and he tells me he may have seen you go upstairs, so I go to Miss Earnshaw's floor and waste twenty minutes getting the third degree from *her* steward before he'll even tell me which door is hers—''

"Pierce, it doesn't matter—" Ivy interrupted. But Pierce seemed unable to stop talking.

"—and of course she hasn't seen you since the dance, and doesn't have the faintest idea where some idiot little kid might disappear to when his ship hits a goddamn iceberg, so for the past hour we've been traipsing through this floating coffin—"

Stinging hurt feelings prodded like nettles. Idiot little kid? Oh, Pierce.

"You didn't have to try to find me," I told him. "Nobody ever asked for your help."

"Thanks very much," Pierce said. "Pity you hadn't made that obvious earlier."

"Pierce, shut up!" Ivy said. "Sumner, you too. You boys can finish this fascinating debate later. We've got to get into a lifeboat. All of us. Right this second. Now."

This was all going totally wrong; I was supposed to be saving *her*. "No, no," I said. "You're the one who should get in the boat. I came up here looking for you."

I heard Pierce mutter "Jesus!" under his breath. It was hard ignoring his expression—a cross between a sneer and an edgy, worried frown—but I found, if I looked only into Ivy's restful eyes, I could do it.

"I just want to make sure you're all right," I told her. "That's all I want to know. Then I'll wait with the rest of the men."

"Look, this isn't some chivalry contest," said Pierce, "this is—"

But Ivy at that moment had her inspiration. "But, Sumner," she said, "I can't do it. I can't get into that boat without you."

"You can't?" I asked.

She smiled, beautifully, totally, calmly. "What would it do to your mother," she said, "if you didn't come back alive?"

I stiffened.

"I have every intention of coming back alive," I said. "You needn't worry about my mother. I'm simply trying to be a gentleman."

Ivy's smile hardened; in her eyes flickered that same anger I had seen at the demonstration: impatient, derisive, destructive.

"I don't have any more time for this," she said. "Get in that lifeboat before I have to drag you in."

I backed off from them both. Tears flooded my eyes. What precise pain those you love can inflict. Pierce's insults, Ivy's commands—nobody else on the face of this planet could have shot with such accuracy. I swallowed. I hoped for only one thing; I hoped, when I answered, my voice would not quaver.

"To hell with you both," I said. "I'm staying. I shall leave this ship with the rest of the men. I'm not going to be a child anymore."

Pierce reached out and grabbed me, his fingers wrenching my shoulders.

"You're going to be a corpse if you don't get moving!" he whispered furiously. "There aren't enough lifeboats!"

My mind turned dark and cold and dead; I remembered the Boat Deck arithmetic; and at that moment the first rocket went off.

Rockets at sea. Nothing is more sickening, more purely terrorizing. High up in the air they stream, blue-white, gleaming, iridescent. Their shriek is muted, even as they explode: the cry of a victim into a pillow, the despairing scream everyone knows no one can hear. Then they disintegrate, hot sparks falling, flaying your upturned face, your lips, your chilled, bloodless skin. Your skin, which is soon to feel so much more pain than mere fire.

There followed a silence. A silence even Dante had failed to include in his circles. The silence of contrast. Breathing, or drowning.

Now there was an urgency, a sudden more businesslike hustle, to the loading of boats. The officers' faces betrayed no fear, only seriousness; they looked like students hurrying to finish a test before the end of the hour. Ivy took my hand and led me firmly to Lorna's lifeboat. I watched my feet moving across the deck, watched myself unprotestingly get into line. Ivy was holding my hand the way one holds a valuable package: not with love, but with great concern for the contents. Thoughts of alternative lines of action presented themselves, but none clearly enough to follow. What would Charles Sumner have done? Senator Sumner, born for martyrdom—would he go to his death willingly, like a true hero? Or would he tote up the incredible stupidity of hitting an iceberg and insufficient lifeboats and find the equation too foolish to die for? What would he do? What should I do?

What should I do?

I tugged on Ivy's hand. Her grasp was firm, but not so tenacious I could not break away. Only—break away and do what?

Drowning in its every horrifying facet presented itself. I remembered reading somewhere that drowning was one of the quickest ways to die. But how could anyone say for sure? And what if, like me, you could swim? I pictured myself starting to go under, mouth, eyes, nose, lungs all full of blueness, so cold, no air, no revival, then saving myself in spite of myself, saving myself only to rise to the surface and start dying all over again.

Did you die, in the end, of suffocation or hysteria? What would it be like to open your mouth . . . to open your mouth and have it be full of water and nothing else? To try to kick yourself upward to a lighter surface you could see but not reach? To breathe in wetness, no air, just that explosion in your ears, behind your eyes? Would it hurt? Could you think? Could you make it go faster? Could you make it hurt more, only let it end, let it end, let it end quicker?

I couldn't. Couldn't. I couldn't face it, not willingly. Couldn't face that cold, that pain, that bright blue eruption of my own airless blood. Must prevent it, if I could. Please God, let me control it. Don't let me die. Not this way. Not to-night.

We shuffled forward a few more feet. Hands reaching out, offering safety. I was a child; I passed the test; I was a legitimate recipient of salvation. I shouldn't have to feel guilty. And I was so, so terrified. Drowning, I now understood, would take forever: I would never be dead, always be dying. Please, please. Please let it happen to somebody else.

Ivy released my hand to take the outstretched hand of a loading officer. Pierce was somewhere behind me, where he couldn't reach me; I was, for this second, and perhaps only this second, free of them both. This was my chance. I could reject my safe passage, turn around, and die like a man, painfully, horribly, heroically. Or I could live. Live like what? I couldn't imagine. But . . . live.

The officer settled Ivy into the boat and reached for me. I wanted it all—heroism, yes, but also the chance to survive to enjoy it. Was that so greedy? I looked at Ivy and the drop to the water, sixty feet down. Maybe it was meant to happen some other time. I let the officer take my hand.

He settled me in next to Ivy. Incredibly enough, she seemed glad to see me, even proud, as if I had passed with distinction the test I already was damning myself for failing. I looked quickly around the lifeboat. We had room for perhaps seven more people, while high on the deck above me I could see seven times seven, dozens, crowding the officers and gesturing. The officers let one person board, then another, another.

But Pierce was not one of them. He was not even in line.

A crane grunted and our lifeboat shuddered. No, wait! I thought, and as if in response we fell several feet, then rose to a shouted command. For several long moments we hung parallel to the Boat Deck while blurred bodies rushed before my eyes. Then I saw him.

He saw me, too. He smiled at me. His smile from last night —amused, relaxed, enigmatic. He waved, our arguments forgotten. He lit a cigarette. A man walked by him, said something; Pierce shrugged, answered back. Another man joined them. Someone produced a bottle; the three of them drank. It occurred to me that this was the first time I had seen Pierce in the company of men. Tonight, finally, irrevocably, he was not an outsider among his own sex. He had rejoined his brothers. He would leave me forever. He had already left.

I suddenly wanted the ship out, dead, gone, sunk to the bottom. I wanted it over, wanted him dead; he had died already, died in his own mind, and in mine, and I could not abide watching him live this illusion. I should have known from the beginning that he would die; known from the second we met, with his strange smile, his comments that spoke of death, cupped it hidden within every conversation. My throat ached, still sore from his cigarettes; my ankle still throbbed where he had kicked me, cued me into becoming Ivy's champion. He lifted his hand, brushed back his hair: graceful, martyred, already sanctified by his future chosen destruction.

I wondered if he had wanted to make love to Ivy. I wished now that they had; it was all I could think of to offer that he might value. His hand touching her warm body, remembering it when he reached out and touched nothing but seawater . . . Would it comfort him, that memory? Or would it only make dying more bitter?

I started crying, lonely, so lonely and so ashamed. Feminine voices rustled toward me, whispering, soothing.

"Sumner, Sumner, it's all right," Ivy murmured. "It's all right, my baby. It'll all be all right." Lorna reached out and patted my hand.

Then an officer peered into our boat and started yelling, shattering my sobs. "Who's the seaman on this vessel?" he demanded.

Lorna adjusted her shawl. "I wish Jack had gotten on with us," she whispered. "He knows how to handle a boat. He's probably driving somebody batty right this minute, telling them what to do."

"We can't let you people go without an experienced sailor!" the officer bellowed to us over Lorna's confidings. "It's too dangerous!"

People in the boat exchanged glances; a few feet shuffled, bodies starting to rise. Fear rolled over me, a great smothering, stifling, smoldering blanket. Reboarding that ship, given what I knew, seemed like marching to my own living burial. I felt myself starting to shake.

Ivy jumped up. "Nobody move!" she shouted. "We're better off on our own than back on that ship!"

The passengers halted; the officer shook his head. "Lady, you're giving these people some bad advice—"

"And look what *you've* given us!" Ivy cried.

The officer's face clouded. He stood staring at Ivy, telling her, warning her, begging her not to shout what he knew she knew, and spark off a panic. I slowly stood up and walked to the front of the boat. Ivy tried to grab me but I shook off her hand

and climbed with very careful steps back up the rope-and-chain ladder which led to the Boat Deck.

"Excuse me, sir," I said to the officer. "But I know who could take charge of our boat." And I pointed to Pierce.

The officer turned around. "Sir!" he called to Pierce. "Could you come here for a moment?"

Pierce looked puzzled.

"This boy says you can handle a vessel," the officer said. "Is that correct?"

"Would that it were," Pierce answered politely. "But unfortunately, no. Absolutely not."

"He's lying," I said.

Pierce said, "This child is hysterical."

"I am not hysterical!" I screamed. "He's a seaman! He went to Annapolis! His father's an admiral! He told me so!"

"Must have the wrong man," said Pierce. "I'm a flier. And my father's just some poor anonymous loser."

"God, Pierce, why are you doing this?" I moaned.

The officer looked back and forth at the two of us, uncertain whom to believe: Pierce, well-mannered, reserved, remote; me, twitching with sobs. He made up his mind, reached into his pocket, and pulled out his service revolver. He pointed the revolver at Pierce's temple.

"Sir," the officer said sternly, "if you cannot steer this boat, then you are a brave and good man to admit it. But if you can, you owe it to these people to assist them."

"Or you'll shoot me instead of drown me?" said Pierce.

"Or else you'll create your own victims," the officer said, very quietly. "And the point of your dying a gentleman will be lost."

Pierce studied the edge of his cigarette, watching its glow as flame gnawed slowly at the tobacco and crisp paper. Wordlessly I begged him, prayed, telegraphed him to make the right decision, all the time realizing I had no idea what the right decision really was. Above me the officer's arm, still trained at Pierce's head, began trembling. Pierce was gazing at the Sobranie as if it were his own flesh burning. Then, abruptly, he tossed the cigarette over the side of the ship.

"Oh, hell," he said, "what's the point of dying if there's no point?" He watched the Sobranie tumble, sparkling, into the darkness, then slipped into the lifeboat. He entered so expertly his weight did not produce even a tremor. The officer lowered his arm, flexed his elbow, then lifted his hand to signal to lower away.

It was like descending along a rainbow whose only color was blue. Every foot we fell we entered a different world, a world colder and darker and deeper blue than the world up above. For us, nothing happened quickly: other boats stumbled, jerking as they fell, or tumbling almost freeform before righting themselves with a screech of chain; we glided quietly, slipping along as smoothly as a wooden bead down a velvet necklace. The ship stayed always the same distance from us as we passed row after row of flickering lights, deck after deck of silence. It grew darker and colder and bluer.

We passed a passenger deck. Maybe even my own, deserted now, the portholes blank, the bedding in every stateroom still earnestly arranged for sleep. It all looked so cheerful, so happily, uselessly cozy: blankets turned invitingly back onto carefully fluffed pillows; fresh sheets and lacy cotton pillowcases, their white dyed weirdly purple by the blue air. I saw a single bed with a lamp still on, the floor a tumble of quilts and sweaters; I remembered lying in such a bed, blistered with joy, so happy it hurt to breathe. It seemed impossible, it fit into nothing real, my being there then, and here now. Slowly the glass of the portholes darkened, filled with our own reflection. So sad, so accusing, such a terribly wrong thing for a ship to see.

"Ah, sir?" I turned around. A middle-aged man in a thick plaid coat was talking to Pierce. "Shouldn't we be hurrying?" he asked.

Pierce said, "No."

We touched down softly, the hungry water parting eagerly. We were huddled up tight to the huge black cliff of the ship, three other lifeboats beside us, four more a few dozen yards away.

"Okay, folks," Pierce announced, "fun's over. Now we're going to get the hell out of here."

A man in a tuxedo, with foresight having tucked a blanket over his legs, jerked his head in instant disagreement.

"Get out?" he snorted. "That's completely ridiculous. You nautical geniuses get us into these jams, then you don't even know—"

"Nautical geniuses?" said Pierce. He stood up carefully; the boat quivered. "You want to run this vessel?" he asked. "Yes or no. Decide right now. You want to be responsible for the lives of all these people? Fine, great. Because I don't. Just give me a second to switch boats, will you?"

Ivy turned savagely to the tuxedoed man. "You'd better have gone to Annapolis too," she hissed.

"Of course I didn't go to Annapolis," the man snapped back. "But you don't have to be a maritime expert to know we'd be fools to just let ourselves drift."

"Well, tonight's little mishap suggests maritime expertise may not always go hand in hand with maritime survival," Pierce said. "I repeat my suggestion we get this boat moving, fast. We can debate why later."

"But if we're too far away, we'll never get picked up!"

"No one will see us," another man joined in. "No one will even realize we're gone."

A woman near Lorna groaned. Behind my back, I was twisting my hand over the side of the boat, edging and creeping until, finally, I could just trail the tip of a fingernail into the swell of the sea. The water was so cold it pinched. I lifted my throbbing finger. The idea of drifting, unseen and unmissed, through this unendurable coldness was almost as bad as—as bad as—worse than—drowning itself.

I looked at Pierce, suddenly wondering if he had any idea what he was doing. He had stepped forward until his face was just inches from the man in the tuxedo.

"The last thing in this world you should want," he said quietly, "is for me to keep us here."

"And would you mind telling me why?" the man rasped.

Pierce dropped his voice further. It was only a whisper: a whisper we all could hear.

"Do you really want the people in this boat to never forget?" he asked. "To never recover? To spend the rest of their lives wishing they'd died too? Do you really want them to watch their loved ones scream for help, beg for it, and know the only help they can possibly offer is to make room for another body by dying themselves?"

The tuxedoed man swallowed; his eyes turned inward, noncombative. Near me, one of the white-robed young ladies whom three hours ago Pierce had called a "young Circe" began crying.

"Do what you think is right," the man mumbled to Pierce. "Just keep us alive."

Pierce backed away a few steps and clapped his hands.

"O.K., everybody!" he called. "We all need to face the rear of the boat. Now pick up the nearest oar. Good. Perfect. Now we're all going to try to pull in unison."

Ivy stood up, her expression critical. Pierce gave her his best airman's smile.

"What's your opinion, Miss Earnshaw?"

"Make sure the men and the strongest women are seated farthest inside. It'll give better leverage."

Pierce nodded approvingly. "Excellent suggestion."

"Just elementary physics."

"Ah. I must've missed that lecture at the Academy."

A few halfhearted chuckles: Ivy looked at Pierce, suddenly suspicious. "All right," he continued, "we're going to assume Isaac Newton and Miss Earnshaw both know what they're talking about." He offered his arm to an elderly woman and gently shuttled her to an outside berth. Ivy observed, then extended her own arm to another older woman. For the next ten minutes the two of them skillfully braided male and female, young and old, weak and strong. The boat became absolutely steady, stable as an ark.

Lorna leaned over and whispered, "Your friends are wonderful! That fellow reminds me so much of Jack!"

I nodded politely. Where *was* Jack?, I suddenly wondered, and immediately turned to look anywhere except into Lorna's eyes. I gazed at Pierce. He was earnestly trying to communicate with two women from steerage, his gentle murmur nearly drowned by their sobs. His face twitched with frustration.

"We're losing time," he reported to Ivy. "I want a good arm here but I can't get this woman to—"

Ivy turned around at once. "Get over there," she commanded me. "He needs you."

I stood up so quickly the lifeboat shuddered. Ivy gave me a warning look and a pointed shove.

"Get going," she ordered.

Making my way to the other end of the boat was like crawling in late to Symphony. "Excuse me, excuse me," I kept mumbling, feeling myself stepping on shoes, satchels, bare feet. It took almost five minutes for me to reach Pierce. When I did, he put his hands on my shoulder and fitted me onto a bench next to the third oar back.

"Once the rowing starts, don't be a hero," he said. "Don't try to go harder than anyone else or you'll break the rhythm. Just stay in time. Like a Sunday paddle on Jamaica Pond, right?"

"Yes, sir," I said.

"Never call me that."

"Yes, Pierce."

"Better. By the way, what languages do you speak?"

"English, French, Latin, a little Italian—"

"Great. Try 'em all. See if you can calm these folks down."

Pierce started toward the helm, then turned around.

"By the way," he said, "that was pretty quick thinking back there. About my being a sailor, I mean. You saved my life. Something I've never been able to figure out how to do myself."

I ducked my head. I could no longer tell if I had saved Pierce to save Pierce or to save myself.

"You're welcome," I whispered.

" 'Course, this is going to be a serious setback for the Admiral," Pierce added. "I can already sense him preparing my eulogy. But maybe I can manage to die for him some other day."

Before I could answer—with what? comfort? assurance?— he had stepped away. I turned to my charges.

One woman was still crying—crying in fear, in shock, and in what must have been terrible, untranslatable confusion. And some of it may have been plain embarrassment too: even the First Class ladies who wore only nightgowns and monogrammed robes looked far better dressed than she—and, incredibly, conscious of it.

"Ah, *parlez-vous français?*" I began.

No response.

"*Italiano?*" I asked. The woman sobbed harder.

Pierce cleared his throat. "All right, everyone! Let's pull on my command. Ready?"

We grabbed our oars.

"Pull!" Pierce shouted.

Nothing seemed to happen. The oar was much heavier than I had expected, and the suck of the ocean much more urgent. There seemed to be no connection between my efforts and the minimal movement of the boat. I took the hands of the crying woman and laid them on the oar. I placed her friend's hands on top.

"*Aidez-moi,*" I said. "Help me."

Whatever they understood—me, Pierce, the night, the situation—the next time Pierce shouted, they pulled too. Down the length of the little boat we all pushed and tugged, and slowly we slipped away, inch by grudging inch, from the shadow and magnet of the crippled ship. It was exhausting work, shockingly difficult, like running through sand; within seconds we were all, in spite of the painful and biting cold, slick with sweat. I could feel a twitch in my arm that moved, with every completed stroke, from my wrist to my shoulder; the twitch burned as it jumped, jumped as it burned, and I imagined every muscle in my arm torn loose, floating about in my blood, messy and befouled, floating just as we floated, a pulpy blob in the slimy sea.

After twenty minutes or so, Pierce said, "That's fine, that's enough. Everyone stop."

We stopped. Then, as though synchronized, as though it were something rehearsed, we all as one person turned around.

We were perhaps a quarter mile from the ship. She was listing, but not too badly; her bow dipped into the water as if testing its temperature, the way a bird dips its beak into a birdbath before taking the plunge, and she somehow still managed to look as if she could, if she wished, right herself, make herself once again whole and healthy and perfectly balanced. "Maybe we should have stayed on board," said the man with the blanket. "She looks O.K. from here. In fact, she looks safer than we do."

We kept looking. The awful thing was, he was right; she *did* look safe, with her great outstretched length and her lights still so merrily blazing. What's more, she *sounded* safe; the decks were crowded, but there was no obvious panic or even fear, just a lot of voices as passengers skittered about: there seemed an air more of excitement than anything else. It reminded me of the day we set sail, all of us wanting to be on deck so that those we were leaving behind could see us and be jealous of all the good times which were waiting for us and not them. The band was playing ragtime.

"It's true," I heard Lorna whisper. "She *does* look all right. Maybe we should have—"

"Should have what?" Ivy snapped. "Stayed on board? Are you crazy? She's sinking!"

"Maybe she's not. Maybe it's just a serious . . . I don't know what you call it, Jack would know . . . a hole, a serious rip—but it's not bad enough to destroy her."

"That's right," said the man with the blanket. "She's indestructible. Everyone knows that."

Pierce said to him, "Sir, do you have a name?"

"Tillson," the man said. "Hugh Tillson."

"Well, you, Mr. Tillson," said Pierce, "are a goddamn fool."

A giggle—less of amusement than of sheer surprise— spurted from my mouth. Hugh Tillson was president of the third-largest bank in the country, with a fortune which rivaled that of J. P. Morgan or John Jacob Astor himself; only someone like Pierce would not know who he was. Or perhaps Pierce did know, and simply didn't care.

Mr. Tillson said, "Watch your mouth. There are women and children on board."

"Yes, there are," Pierce said, "and I intend keeping them on board. So stop saying the ship's O.K., and please don't encourage anyone else. She's been gutted; everything inside her is ruined; everything that could save her is either hopelessly maimed or already underwater. What she looks like doesn't matter. She can't be saved, she can't be helped."

"That's your opinion," said Mr. Tillson.

Pierce pointed at the expanse of ocean between us and the ship. "There's the door," he said. Mr. Tillson glowered.

One of the steerage women murmured to me in a language I recognized as Italian. The only two words I could translate were "food" and "water."

"Non lo so'," I answered her. She repeated her question a little louder.

"What's she saying?" asked Pierce.

"She's asking about food and water," I said.

"Jeez, what a time to be hungry," said Mr. Tillson.

"I think maybe she's asking about supplies," I said.

"Supplies?" Ivy repeated. "That's a good question. Do we have any?"

Pierce prodded under the nearest bench. "Nothing here," he said. A few people started to whisper.

"No water?" said Mr. Tillson.

Pierce said: "I want everyone to check the space right beneath you. Just give it a kick. Don't check your neighbor's space, only your own. We don't want to start rocking."

I kicked and felt nothing. The Italian woman, after asking the question which had started all this, sat motionless, so I leaned forward, extending my leg to feel if there was anything

—a lantern, a canteen, crackers, a rope—underneath her. I noticed her feet were bare, and swollen with cold. I tried easing my own feet around hers, and lost my balance, falling against her shoulder. She recoiled, and the woman next to her tumbled into the lap of the woman next to *her;* within seconds our whole row was slipping, careening rapidly to the right. The woman at the very end screamed, clutched the side of the boat, and shoved back; we all lurched left. The entire lifeboat started to pitch.

"Sumner!" Pierce barked. "What the hell are you doing? Sit down and hold on to the oar!"

Hold on to the oar? What was he *talking* about? But I did, and the next time the force of the wave of panicky bodies toppled into me, I managed to hang on tight to the oar and not push back. Slowly the momentum petered out and the lifeboat steadied itself. Pierce said, "It might be a good idea if everyone moved around as little as possible."

"I'm sorry," I mumbled, miserable: Lord, how many more mistakes do You want me to make in one night? "It was an accident."

I wanted desperately for Pierce to say he forgave me, but he was already thinking of something else. "You know," he said, turning to Ivy, "there's not much to eat besides crackers, there isn't much water, nothing to use as a sail . . ."

"See?" said Mr. Tillson. "This boat's not safe."

"Oh, as if *that* one is?" said Ivy, arm outstretched to the ship, which, in spite of her definite downward tilt, continued to look so dependable—so determined, so able, to stop this disaster and save herself.

And then, suddenly, she stopped looking able to stop or save anything. With no warning, no hint it would happen, and happen *now,* her bow, which had been so daintily easing itself into the water, abruptly pitched downward, like an uncertain diver deciding to make the plunge. The entire ship shuddered—she actually rocked back and forth—as she attempted to straighten herself, and she was still buoyant enough to be somewhat successful. But only somewhat; and when a part of her bow reappeared, dripping, it was much less than what had gone down, almost as if she were absorbing the murderous water. Then her stern, which had been only slightly out of the water, rose significantly, and her bow immediately dropped back under, farther this time. And farther meant deeper. She was sinking by the bow, and fast enough so you could see it.

There was no longer any illusion that she could survive.

Now I began wondering if *we* could. I glanced at Pierce. He was watching the ship with such pity that his eyes had filled and a muscle in his cheek was beginning to jump. It hurt to look at him, so I looked at Ivy instead. She had turned away from the ship and was gazing at the ice. She gestured toward one of the floes.

"Maybe that's the one that did it," she said.

It looked too little. But there were larger ones in the distance, true icebergs, and in this extraordinarily clear air I could see how enormous they were, towering up against the horizon like something from the third day of Creation. I expected them to be white, but only their cores were; the rest was nearly translucent, like a shocking reminder that they too were made of water, that they too belonged here, and we were the ones who didn't. Under the steady light of the stars I could see the sides of the bergs mucked so thickly with algae the ice appeared painted a deep ferny green. The bergs trembled slightly in the almost motionless water, so huge that each time they moved, a different section of the horizon was blotted out. I remembered once reading that all visible icebergs were only one tenth above water, and I realized that what I was looking at was the barest fraction of what really was there, submersed, implacable, solid as diamond.

A whole hidden world of jagged peaks and salients, of protruding headlands and rugged, motionless cliffs; a whole hidden world of patient mountains and ancient precipices. A whole hidden world of traps, of unconquerable, undeniable danger.

What in God's name had we been doing here in the first place?

Behind me there was a dreadful crash and the woman next to me grabbed my hand. My eyes swiveled back to the ship.

She was deep, deep down in the bow, and her stern was raised into the air at almost a perfect forty-five-degree angle to the water. Everything on her was moving and falling, glass shattering into metal, wood shattering into glass. A piano caromed down the deck, flattening everything in its path; on another deck, every window exploded. Deck chairs, mattresses, luggage, bookshelves, benches that I remembered as nailed to the floor, chandeliers I remembered as hammered into the ceiling, all were tumbling downward, and sometimes outward, falling into some of the lifeboats that had remained too near; I could hear screams as a furnace plunged into one of the collapsible dinghies. I could hear screaming everywhere.

Already people were in the water, held up by their life jackets, kicking and shouting. More people were still on board, running vainly upward against the ever-steepening angle, and slipping as they ran, sometimes sliding downward, with sickening acceleration, for four or five hundred feet, until they disappeared into the water. I could see a man standing where Pierce had stood. He had both arms wrapped around what had been the door to the deck beneath him. That deck was now underwater. The door ripped itself free, and the man was flung overboard.

The forward funnel began shaking. It was like watching a steel mill caught in an earthquake; first trembling side to side, then up and down, until finally it fell into the water. A maelstrom arose, of soot and cinders and choppy waves; the swimmers caught in its path died at once, scalded and crushed. There were hundreds and hundreds of bodies in the water now, and yet hundreds more kept pouring out of the ship; it was almost as if she were not only dying but giving birth. The stern continued its slow climb upward. The lights began blinking, and then went out. Now she was only a cylinder, a great black husk, outlined against the sky.

And still she kept rising. She rose until she stood at a perfect right angle to the water. She remained pointed like that for more than a minute, impossibly balanced and poised: it was like watching a stake being driven into the heart of the ocean. Everything inside her was exploding. But the crying voices were even louder.

Then the explosions stopped and her stern drooped—a little at first, then faster and faster. By now she was already nothing but death and memory; there was no reason for her not to hurry. She slid under the water, and the sound of her suction was like a sigh.

She was gone.

Most of us sighed too. We were beyond emotion by then, and probably all of us knew—*I* certainly did—that limitless hours of sighing awaited us all.

But only limited minutes awaited those survivors still in the water. What before had been screaming was now a continuous howl, as the shock of the water's cold was replaced by the shock of how painful that cold was. Everyone in the lifeboats was looking at everyone in the other lifeboats. Pierce said, "We've got to go back."

I gasped—we all did. Go back into *that*? How could we even *get* back?—the water was so packed with bodies there hardly seemed room for us. But of course that was the reason we had to do it.

"Right away," Pierce said. "Everybody pick up your oar. Come on, make it snappy. No one can stand that kind of cold very long." He looked at me and the woman next to me, whose translator I had become. "Sumner, you start. Get her to start too."

Instantly I began rowing; so did she; so did Ivy, so did Lorna; so did about half of us. But only half; the rest were watching Mr. Tillson, who was waving his hands and shouting, "No, no, no, no, no!" And, of course, with only fifty percent of us rowing, rowing was twice as difficult; our progress, if you could call it that, was sluggish, not only much slower than when we all were doing it, but also more awkward, because those of us who were rowing kept hitting the arms of those who were not. "We all need to do this together or it's never going to work," said Ivy.

Mr. Tillson exploded. "This is totally wrong!" he shouted to Pierce. "It's the exact opposite of what you said earlier!"

"I don't even remember what I said earlier," Pierce said.

"You said we should get out of the way! That we shouldn't stay near enough to have to look—to have to remember!"

Pierce said simply, "I was wrong. I didn't know it would be this bad."

"But that's even more of a reason!"

Pierce frowned. It was clear that he wanted to go back, clear that he wanted to try to save some of the flailing and endlessly screaming victims—though the screaming *wasn't* endless, already there was less: people had already died. But it was equally clear that he hadn't forgotten what he had said, that seeing this horror up close would be a lifelong brand on all of our memories.

"I just think," he said, his voice hesitant, "we might feel better if we tried to help."

"You mean *you* would," said Mr. Tillson. "Why don't we

put it to a vote? Who wants to stay here where we're safe, and who wants to go back and risk being swamped by those poor dying people?''

It was all clear now. At least Mr. Tillson had had the grace to pity them before condemning them. As for Pierce, he looked suddenly drained; he wasn't the sort of person accustomed to taking charge, and the weight of all this responsibility was exhausting him. "Everyone do what your conscience tells you to," he said, and he methodically started to row. Mr. Tillson sat with his hands folded. I noticed him watching my pumping arms.

"You realize," he said to me, "that they'll all be dead by the time we get there."

Not if you'd stop just sitting on your big fat blanketed butt and give us some help, I thought. But one of the most dispiriting parts of this whole dreadful night was discovering my complete inability to alter my personality, even in the face of utter disaster; and part of my personality was not to be rude. "Maybe not," I said.

"And it's not like we're only half full, like some of the other boats," Mr. Tillson said. "If we find someone, where are we even going to put them? Those other boats should be going back. Not us."

But the other boats, for the most part, were not going back —not even the ones which were nearly empty. Instead they were either rowing in our direction, so that we passed them going the other way, or else they were simply bobbing about, three or four hundred yards from where the life-jacketed swimmers were crying for help. I looked at the faces of some of the people in the other lifeboats, expecting to see fear or guilt (or both). But the faces showed no expression at all, not even sorrow; they looked like the faces of people in hospital waiting rooms, waiting to find out not how the patient was doing but whether the patient was dead yet.

The first body we passed was that of a man about my father's age. He was on his back, his head and shoulders held aloft by his life jacket, and his mouth was stretched wide open, as if he had died calling for help. Three more bodies floated by. Their mouths were open too, and their faces were blue.

"They aren't drowning," somebody whispered. "They're dying of cold."

I wondered which was worse. A few more people picked up their oars. Two more lifeboats floated quietly by.

And then it was as if we had entered a city—a water city—of plague. There were bodies everywhere, some dead, some still alive, some roaring for help, some begging for it. Some not even bothering. Along with the bodies was everything which had not gone down with the ship: tureens, shoes, silver-backed hairbrushes; crates loaded with lemons and melons and berries reserved for tomorrow's breakfast; Morse equipment; embroidered napkins; children's toys. Five men and a woman were clutching a barber's chair; their hands were purple. A swell no higher than ten inches washed over their heads. All six of them disappeared. The screaming and crying and calling went on and on.

Pierce passed his hand over his eyes. "Oh, God," he said, "how do we choose?"

Not even Mr. Tillson answered.

The vast majority of the dead and dying were men—some fully dressed, some still in pajamas. But there were women and children too, most of them, from the look of their clothes, from Third Class. There were also many crew members, all of whom had obviously stuck by the ship till her final convulsion; many of them were holding passengers in their arms, and sometimes passengers were holding them. In all cases, such assistance had failed: holding someone proved too exhausting, and everyone died.

We spotted three men bobbing in unison. One of them feebly waved. Pierce directed us toward them. They had seized a washtub and flipped it over—it was a brilliant improvisation. Pierce nosed the lifeboat up to the tub. The first man let go with one hand and reached up with the other. We hauled him in with great difficulty; his water-soaked clothes made him feel as heavy as if he were shackled, and he was so stiff from the cold he could not even bend his legs, which banged into the side of the boat as we dragged him up. The other two men watched. Finally one of them said, in heavily accented English, "Us too?"

Pierce nodded. But it was already too late. A bed frame skidded into the tub and it foundered; both men let go and went under.

Meanwhile, from the other side, two more men, cautiously kicking, approached. We heaved them both up and laid them between the benches. Their shivering was so violent it rocked the boat.

Those three were the only people we managed to save.

During the next half hour, the calls for help became less and less frequent; people were still alive, but just barely, and there were no longer any appeals for assistance, only moaning and hopeless sobs. We were able to pull five more people—all men —into our lifeboat, but they all died within seconds. It began to feel pointless, what we were doing, and we realized that we were interlopers in this ocean of death—that only the dead, not us, had the right to be here. We stayed anyway, because leaving seemed just as disrespectful as remaining. When all was quiet, we paddled away.

Behind us, in the finally tranquil silence, we left fifteen hundred souls who had perished with honor to sleep in peace.

CHAPTER NINE

UR RESCUE SHIP, S.S. *CARPATHIA*, APPEARED JUST BEFORE SUN-rise, slicing over the curved horizon in a blaze of rock-ets and flashing lights. Watching her coming to us was like watching the coming of God.

It took her four hours to locate us all: so much drifting in circles, so many bodies. Her officers and crew emptied each lifeboat with tender attention. The air was chilly, the water was choppy and full of ice. She started to hunt for the dead.

She finished searching just before nine. Somebody shouted an order, somebody offered a prayer; signals flew; engines started to hum. She turned, plunging into the western skyline. The sun rose higher. We were going home.

We who were left.

The *Carpathia* offered a kindly and thoughtful salvation. Her crew was ready the instant we stepped on board; they greeted us all with shawls and blankets and sweaters and gloves, then guided us each by the elbow to her dining rooms, where vats of simmering coffee and soup and cocoa awaited, with brandy and Scotch for the men, sherry for women (neither for me). As we sipped we were given coats and pillows, linen and towels, scarves. A steward with a notepad quietly moved from group to group.

"Your name, sir?" he asked me. I gave it. He carefully wrote it down and insisted I check his spelling. "For the survivors' list, sir," he explained.

Of course.

The first list, stamped PRELIMINARY in five different places, was posted by noon. It was separated into CREW and PASSENGERS, then subdivided by class, sex, and rank. It was blurrily printed, unalphabetical, and contained two third pages. It screamed of inaccuracy. Or so we hoped.

Mr. Sumner F. Jordan. Alive.

Miss Ivy A. Earnshaw. Alive.

Mr. Pierce G. Andrews. Alive.

Mrs. Lorna M. Farraday. Alive.

Mr. Harrison Gibson. Alive. Mrs. Emily Gibson. Alive.

Miss Alicia Mayhew. Alive.

Mrs. Clarence Hannant. Alive.

Mr. Jack Phillips, wireless operator. Missing believed dead.

Mr. Clarence Hannant. Missing believed dead.

Percy, my steward and fashion adviser. Dead.

Buckley, fellow poetry lover, and my guide to the lifeboats. Dead too.

The gym master. Dead. The maître d'. Dead. The lobster cooks. Dead. The pool attendant. Dead. The man who was wondering how to say "Help!" in French. Dead. The band that had played the waltz Ivy and I had been dancing to. All dead, drowned, gone.

Mr. Benjamin Guggenheim. Dead.

Colonel John Jacob Astor. Dead.

Mr. Isidor Straus. Dead. Mrs. Straus. Dead.

Mr. Jack Farraday. Still missing.

The day wore on. The ship became more and more silent.

The scale of our losses embarrassed and shamed our untragic saviors; they didn't know what to say—whether to curse or to comfort, to pray or to weep. The result was, they did the precisely right thing: they left us alone.

And we left each other alone as well.

Nobody planned it. It was just that as time went by, the solace of safety, of personal survival, slowly faded, replaced by the realization, over and over and over again, of who was missing. We ran out of energy, all of us. Out of energy, out of gratitude, out of all sense of blessing or luck. Grief clamped our hearts. And, for some of us, guilt.

I could not believe how I had acted. I simply could not believe it. How had I been such a coward? Not even a coward, oh, no, nothing so dignified, nothing so literarily pedigreed, just such a . . . just such a *chicken*. My whole life, longing to be a hero, longing to be the new Senator Sumner, to behave like a man, like a knight, like—like—the way Pierce had behaved— hell, the way *fifteen hundred* dead heroes had managed to behave. Yet what had I done? Taken the first excuse, the most obvious, transparent, falsely forgiving excuse imaginable. I am a child. Somebody save me.

Ivy. What must she think of me now? If, that is, she was thinking of me at all. I remembered her eyeing Pierce as he tried to balance the lifeboat; she had looked like somebody watching a motion picture. Such mesmerizing drama—if life were a play and Pierce were awarded the supreme gift of writing his own script, he could not have concocted a more perfect climax: a man ready to face death, yet forced for the sake of others to live. And it was clear, more than clear, that Ivy had noticed this excellent casting. They had worked so well together on the lifeboat, each so respectful of the other's wonderfulness. Two perfect, gifted, heroic saviors, both stuck, somehow, with me.

Now I began to wish everyone were a coward and a failure.

I pictured Ivy at her demonstration, whimpering and crying, I manfully having to stride to her rescue. Or Pierce, sneaking onto a lifeboat ahead of a crippled old woman, then saying that that young man up there, that Sumner Jordan, is a sailor, and the officer forcing me at gunpoint to get on board. Or Charles Sumner, begging Preston Brooks to stop it, stop it, stop beating him, and he would defend slavery in his very next speech.

O Cowardice!—so much more than Misery loving of company.

Tea was served just before four. I wandered into the main saloon. I saw no one I knew, not one familiar face: it was almost as though we had sunk again, this time finishing off all the survivors. Where was Ivy? Where was Pierce? Were they together? Where were the Gibsons? Was that Miss Mayhew, there with those ladies, though of course not looking up, not noticing me, not *wanting* to notice, not *wanting* to greet me. . . . And who could blame her?

Where was Lorna? And where was Jack?

I bleakly accepted tea and a shortbread, and sat down by myself in a corner. I noticed that nobody, not even those in the deepest mourning, seemed to be here alone. I dipped my cookie. I tried to remember how Mr. Joyce had told me he liked to sit by himself at parties—how he purposely searched for a peaceful shadow to hide himself in. But the memory of this confidence failed to comfort me, for I was no wallflower at a party—I was a murderer at a wake.

Then Lorna walked into the room, and I wished to remain by myself forever.

One look at her face was all it took. It was both pale and flushed, as if she were running a chill and a fever simultaneously, and her mouth was moving but made no sound. A pulse worked in her neck. The eyes beneath her puffy eyelids were wet and staring.

I stood up at once and hurried to join her.

"A new list," she said.

"Jack?"

She nodded.

I took her hand. I thought of Jack rolling my marble. He must have known all along.

"Oh, Lorna. I'm so sorry. I've been praying he'd somehow —I don't know what to say, I just wish—"

"I don't know what to do," she said.

"You don't have to do anything," I said. "Sit down. Let me get you something. They'll do it all for you. They're already doing it for—"

"For the other widows," she said.

"I just meant you don't have to decide anything right now. You don't have to think anything or arrange anything."

She sat down and stared at the floor.

"Your friend," she said. "The man who was running the boat. Last night I was so grateful. Now I just hate him. I hate everyone. Myself of course. You. Miss Earnshaw. Jack most of all. I wish he had died of cancer. At least we'd have had a minute to say good-bye."

"He was a nice guy," I said—all I could think of, and how many nice guys it applied to. "He wouldn't want you to hate everyone."

"You don't know *what* he'd want," she snapped. "And he's only been dead twelve hours. Stop trying to redefine him."

I looked down too. "I'm sorry," I said. I looked back up.

"And stop saying you're sorry," she added.

"Then there's nothing to say," I murmured. She shrugged. And the minutes of the afternoon of the first day slowly passed.

•   •   •

Much later I found my quarters. Designed to sleep four, it now served eight—its tenderhearted original occupants plus me and a trio of wide-eyed survivors, none older than five. Nobody spoke to anyone all night long, and when I awoke, they had all gone to breakfast. My face creaked, brittle with drying tears.

I went outside. The air on deck was warm and gentle, almost tropically sunny—a lovely morning, furnished by mocking nature at her most ironic. A cold, somber, storm-studded day would have been far more appropriate; instead, we had to conduct our grief amidst the feathery haze of spring shadows and cordial tradewinds.

And there was much grief: circles of women in every corner, holding each other's hands, patting each other's shoulders; dazed half families—husbandless mothers and fatherless children—staring into the sea. As for our crew, they had almost all perished, and those few who had survived appeared deeply embarrassed, in spite of our knowledge of their remarkable heroism, their stoic calm: the survivors' grapevine had flourished rapidly. One deckchair contained a woman whose face appeared cast in a mask of permanent woe. Next to her sat a stoker. In the world of Before the Iceberg they would never have sat so close. Now both of them lifted their heads to the honeyed sunshine and closed their eyes.

I walked to the railing. The ship knifed through the water, creating wedges of blue and spumy white. Awhile later, maybe an hour, or maybe at the end of the day, somebody touched my hand. Pierce.

"We're making good time," he said. "Little ship like this, I wouldn't have thought she could go so fast."

I couldn't bear looking at him. Whatever expression he wore—pity, loathing, deliberate nonchalance—could only offend, could only embarrass, remind, rebuke. I nodded, eyes fixed on the waves.

"You already can feel the air getting warmer," he continued. "We should be home soon. Couple of days at the most."

I stared at the water. Minutes crawled by. Pierce cleared his throat. I heard, behind him, the rustle of wood and wind.

"Are you not talking to me," he finally asked, "or just not talking, period?"

I turned to him then. "I'm talking to you," I said. "I'm talking to everyone. What is it you want to talk about? How I feel? I feel terrible. What I think? I think my behavior—I think my behavior was just what I should have expected. I think you did everything right. You did everything right, I did everything wrong. I wish I were dead. Anything else you want to know?"

Pierce blinked. "Well, no," he said, when a couple of seconds had gone by. "No, that seems to pretty well cover it."

"Then leave me alone."

He didn't move. After a while he said, "I guess I don't see what you did that's so terrible. I can understand your being sad; I'm sad too—Christ, how could anyone *not* be sad, seeing all this? Sad, angry, distressed, depressed: kind of nips at your faith in the meaning of life, doesn't it? That is, if you had any to begin with. But all this self-hatred, I don't know, it's all so . . ."

Tears thickened my vision. Wasn't he ever going to leave? "It's all so what?" I demanded. "This self-hatred, it's all so what?"

He sighed. "To tell you the truth," he said, "I just don't see the point."

"It's all I have left," I said. "All this self-hatred is all I have left."

"That and your life," said Pierce.

But I no longer wanted my life. I wanted his.

CHAPTER TEN

I HAD KNOWN SADNESS BEFORE THE *TITANIC*. I'D LOST ONE CLASS-mate to double pneumonia, another to diabetes; one of my cousins was hit by a streetcar and died in the hospital two hours later. I still missed them, still mourned for them —still half expected to see them again, strolling whole and happy across the Common, the victims of nothing but misinformation. So I knew how it felt to be sad. What I didn't know— and didn't know I didn't know—was how it felt to grieve.

Everything set me off. Not set me off weeping, which I might have preferred—weeping is physiological, after all, it does have limits; no matter how heartsick, you can't cry forever— but set off my mind: my memories, and my remorse. And these were limitless.

No one could say anything, do anything, that was right. When they expressed joy that I had survived, I heard it as disapproval for not having died. When they expressed pity for those who died, I heard it as condemnation for having survived. When they asked me to tell what had happened that night they seemed unforgivably ghoulish, and yet when they finally stopped asking, their stony indifference appalled me. At school, for a couple of weeks, I became a hero—a nightmarish irony, utterly unresolvable, all attempts to explain being chalked up to modesty and promptly ignored. And at home . . . at home I became, over the course of the summer, more and more moody, and more and more somber, and more and more ashamed.

And more and more in love. For if I had loved Ivy in London—and I had, I had; I realized that now—and on board the *Titanic*—and I did, I did; I realized that too—I loved her even more now, on dry unromantic American soil. She lived, it turned out, in Manhattan—somehow, in the course of our dance, I'd neglected to ask this most obvious question—and when the *Carpathia* had entered New York with her seven hundred lauded and stunned survivors, she'd introduced herself to my mother, who of course had come down to meet me and praise me for managing not to drown. Since then she and Mother had been in weekly correspondence regarding female suffrage—especially, lately, its newest and trickiest challenge: namely, how and to what extent did the sinking of the *Titanic* and the tragic loss of life resulting therefrom affect the women's suffrage movement? More specifically, what was the impact on female suffrage of "Women and children first"?

People heard right away about "Women and children first," just as they heard right away about not enough lifeboats, and iceberg warnings, and the first SOS, and dogs being saved while Third Class passengers perished: the first interviews appeared in the papers the afternoon of the morning we docked. But it didn't occur to anyone, in the immediate wake of the tragedy, that "Women and children first" could be seen as more than one type of bravery among a dozen others: the captain's going down with his ship; Mr. Phillips's last-second Morsing; the arm-in-arm Strauses; Pierce. Over the course of the summer, though, people had time to think. And to accuse. And to condemn.

It was to combat this condemnation that Mother was holding tonight's dinner–cum–strategy session. Although held in response to a large problem, it was a smallish affair: my mother, who believed in democracy but not in too much of it, sought advice and opinion from fairly limited circles. In attendance was Ivy, in her dual role of survivor and American feminist; George, Marcella's fiancé; Marcella herself, of course; my other two sisters, Cornelia and Julia; and Mrs. Enid Northfield, my mother's closest confidante among the leading New England suffragists. I'd been invited too, although mainly because I lived there and the meeting included dinner: the fact that I too had survived had not concerned anyone—had not even occurred to anyone that it *should* concern anyone. Which actually made its own horrible sense. For the problem being confronted had nothing to do with the saving of children.

In seven days a memorial service was to take place on Boston Common to honor the *Titanic* dead. At that time a statue was to be unveiled, after which the mayor would speak, and a choir would sing, and the clergy of several religions would attempt to explain what a tragedy of this magnitude had to do with the infinite mercy of God. Similar statues, accompanied by similar services and similar speeches, had been erected in other cities throughout the summer; Cornelia, visiting cousins in Rhode Island, had gone to a couple, one in Providence, one at Woonsocket. She'd found them quite moving—respectful of the dead, she had said, and as comforting as possible to the living. "Women and children first," she reported to Mother, was of course mentioned, but always without elaboration; it was a gallant and praiseworthy act by those who performed it, period, and the speakers at these memorials—unlike certain editors, and certain senators, and the authors of certain recent and savagely critical columns and letters and pamphlets—described the recipients of this gallantry, if they described us at all, as nearly as blessed by receiving such ultimate goodness of heart as those who had perished were blessed by the chance to have died with such power and grace. Nobody—until last Friday—had expected this dedication to be any different.

Then the poem began appearing.

George saw it first; it was circulated in his boardinghouse, and later he saw it being passed around Harvard Yard. Then Mother saw it, tacked to a tree outside her milliner's. Then I saw it, stapled to a bulletin board in the public library and bordered in black and red.

"Votes for women!" was the cry,
  Looking upward to the sky,
  Crashing glass, and flashing eye,
"Votes for women!" was the cry.

"Boats for women!" was the cry,
  When the brave were come to die.
  When the end was drawing nigh,
"Boats for women!" was the cry.

Below the poem, in addition to the date, time, and place of the dedication ceremony, was an open invitation to "all citizens sharing our Verse's Viewpoint" to show up at the unveiling of the statue. The paper was signed New England Women for National Household Stability. Neither Mother, Ivy, Mrs. Northfield, nor anyone else they knew had ever heard of them.

Now Mother coughed. It was a cough everyone recognized —polite, very low, slightly raspy, not really a cough at all but a signal that dinner was done and she wanted attention; Louis XIV, I'd read, coughed like that too. All conversation ended at once. I sneaked a quick look at Ivy—my one-hundred-thousandth of that night.

"What I fail to comprehend," my mother began, "is where

this group was in April, when it actually happened? Why are they starting now?''

Cornelia responded first. ''Oh, April was far too early,'' she said. ''It takes time to transform an actual disaster into a morality play. Especially a disaster accompanied by newspaper photographs. You've got to wait until it becomes a little less real. Then you can really sentimentalize it.''

''Well, they couldn't get much more sentimental than this,'' George agreed. '' 'When the end was drawing nigh'—I mean, really . . .'' He rolled his eyes.

But the end did draw nigh, I thought. You weren't there.

''George, dear,'' said Mrs. Northfield, ''no one's disputing the quality of the poem. It's what it says—who sacrificed what for whom, who died, who didn't—''

''They're saying,'' interrupted Marcella, ''that we're hypocrites. That we're willing to let men die for us but not vote for us.''

''Does that mean if I'd been willing to go down with the ship, they'd have slipped me a ballot?'' Ivy snapped.

Marcella blushed. ''I'm not accusing you of anything, Ivy,'' she said quietly. ''You saved my brother's life. I'd be proud to have done what you did.''

''Yes, but he *is* your brother. Saving him would be natural. It's leaving him there that might have looked odd.''

I felt stricken, argued over like this. Mother shook her head.

''I don't believe our best argument is who survived and who didn't,'' she said. ''It's obvious to any thinking person that not enough people survived. It should be equally obvious that the tragedy would have been just as great had more men survived and more women died.''

''Women did die,'' George said. ''They just happened to be steerage women, so nobody cared. Men survived, too, for that matter.''

Was everyone looking at me? Was anyone? I lowered my eyes. But there is a certain flow, a certain alignment of air and energy, when people are watching you, and I didn't feel it. I looked back up. No one was watching. No one except myself, it was clear, had made the connection between men's surviving and my surviving.

"That's a very interesting observation, George," Mother said. "And, I think—if rinsed of some of its class connotations —a useful one too."

George looked flustered, both flattered (praise from my mother was rare indeed) and annoyed (being a socialist, he did not consider class connotation something one "rinsed" away). "I think it's a major mistake," he said, "dropping class out of this. The people who died on that ship died in direct proportion to how much money they had."

"But that's not what this poem is about," Marcella protested. "This is a feminist issue, not a socialist issue."

"Perhaps it's both," he said.

"Perhaps that's not up to you," Ivy said coldly.

George blinked. Cornelia and Julia snickered. Marcella sighed.

I eyed Ivy again. Her face nicely sheened with late-summer perspiration, she looked somber, reserved, somewhat uncertain —very different from how she had looked our last night on the ship, when she had looked certain of everything. I thought back, as I always did, to our dance. We had sunk the same night; in fact we had hit the iceberg within an hour of our gavotte. What sort of evil, disgusting, selfishly desperate beast would still be unable, after all this time, to decide if the dance wasn't worth the disaster?

"We need a strategy," Mother said. "This poem, whether we like it or not, is simple and to the point. Our response has to be even simpler. We can't discuss class and we can't discuss money and we can't even discuss what the poem discusses—who lived and who died. We have to focus on the calamity itself: its enormity, its gravity, its tragedy, its sheer waste. I believe this is the only way we can avoid getting bogged down in the specifics of men dying versus women dying, or poor women versus rich women—"

"Argue this how, Rebecca?" asked Mrs. Northfield. "And where? Are you suggesting the New England Women for whatever they're for would even provide us a forum?"

"It's not up to them," Mother said calmly. "My thought is to call on the memorial's organizers tomorrow morning and simply inform them we wish to speak at the ceremony. They can't say no: it's a public event. Perhaps it's something we should have been planning to do all along."

She nodded to herself. "Yes," she said. "Our position is clear. We agree the sinking was a disaster—an utter catastrophe. But we add that all those who would take this disaster and make it a stage for the denigration of female suffrage are guilty of the most appalling lack of respect for the dead. That they are reducing catastrophe to politics, and genuine heroism to mundane decision-making. In other words, we accuse the accusers."

"Accuse them of what?" I asked—much to my shock (and everyone else's). "What have they said that's so wrong?"

Mother looked startled. But just as she couldn't be refused a forum at the unveiling, she couldn't refuse me a forum at her table—at least not for a couple of sentences.

"I just said what's so wrong," she replied. "Wanting universal suffrage does not necessarily mean you want to die in a shipwreck."

"Yes, but people who *do* want universal suffrage let people die in a shipwreck for them!"

"But what does one have to do with the other?" said Marcella. "The link between men dying and women voting is tenuous, to say the least—"

"So change the word 'voting'!" I cried. "There's a link between men dying and women living, because a whole lot of women didn't die, and neither did lots of children, and the reason they didn't is because men died instead! Died *for* them! Nobly! Bravely! Facing death, and knowing exactly what kind of death they were facing, death by drowning, death by freezing, death while hundreds of people are drowning and freezing all around you, no one's possibly going to help you—"

"Sumner, relax," George said. "No one's denying how awful this was. And no one's denying anyone's bravery either. We're just saying there's a lack of connectivity, that inferences are being made based on inconclusive or inconsequential data . . ."

Connectivity? Inferences? Inconsequential data? Was this dolt really going to be my brother-in-law?

"We *are* denying their bravery!" I exclaimed. "Their bravery's inconvenient, so we're denying it, or calling it something else, or better yet, hiding it, saying it's a tragedy, so it's everybody's tragedy—so no one's a hero, no one's a coward, we're all just tragic. But that's not how it was. Some people *were* heroes, some people *were* cowards. And some went beyond heroism! Some people lived who wanted to die! Who intended to! Pierce intended to—"

"Sumner, you're making a fool of yourself," Ivy said sharply.

I sprang from my chair as if cannonaded. I could hear Mother's voice as I ran up the stairs.

"He's a child," she said. "Nobody's saying they shouldn't have saved children."

I slammed shut my bedroom door.

• • •

My bedroom was blessedly silent. I locked the door, leaned on it, checked the lock. I was panting and almost crying. I rechecked the lock. Then I went to the closet and took out two tea towels and a handkerchief.

I laid the towels out flat on my bed. They were blue linen, with hefty, embroidery-laden borders—probably part of my mother's trousseau. The handkerchief was my own; it bore my initials, three stern brown letters against a plain tan background. I remembered the process of choosing them—the samples, the swatch books, Melville's endless suggested designs. What I wanted, I had explained to the salesman, was simple—something manly yet elegant, strong and austere. I rolled up the towels, carried them both to the door, and knelt down. There was a quarter-inch gap between the bottom of my door and the floor; I fitted the first towel into this space and laid the next towel on top, tucking the edges into the door frame until they created a perfect seal. Then I wrapped the kerchief around the doorknob and stuffed the edges into the keyhole. I stood back up, walked to the open window, and knotted the curtains away from the glass. I gazed out the window for several unhappy minutes.

Then I walked to my bank of dustless and tidy bookshelves, reached behind *Tennyson: A Collection* and drew out a packet of Sobranies.

I had resumed smoking—secretly, naturally—sometime during my third week home. At first it was mostly a form of solace, of trying to blot out the pain of our sinking by focusing back to the hours and days before—the pleasure of meeting Pierce, the sizzle of meeting Ivy. By now, however, I needed to do it constantly: I took two drags the instant I got out of bed, like a dose of Madeira, or morphine; I then planned the rest of the day around those precious and private moments when, uninterruptedly, I might sneak a few more. Before school had shut down for the summer, I'd gone to the trouble of casing out settings for future indulgence: the janitor's stairwell looked good, and so did the teachers' bathroom, provided one crouched on the toilet farthest away from the door. I also had learned, from the smell, which public library patrons smoked (also which librarians); following my nose, I then figured out where. I even had sneaked a few puffs in the graveyard outside the church, while reading the headstones of those who had died the way people were *meant* to die—that is, any way but in a shipwreck.

Mostly, though, I did my smoking at home, standing beside the window and craning my head to the left so I could look at the river and watch the ships. A few times I smoked in bed, staring out at the night and counting the stars. One time I stood in front of the mirror, practicing looking like Pierce: man to man, man to woman, lover to lover . . .

Despair is both a disease and a wound. It infects everything, and what it can't kill with memory it poisons with self-accusation and feverish midnight wails: "If only . . . what if . . . I should have . . ." Sometimes it stabs, sometimes it merely gnaws; sometimes it even retreats, a gift of remission lasting hours, maybe whole days. But it always returns, and for me its return was like the *Titanic* hitting her iceberg: I never could see it coming. When would these poems and speeches and statues and eulogies ever stop? When would anyone talk about, write about, think about, something else? When would I?

I laid the cigarette on the windowsill, walked to the closet, and pulled out a wooden box. Life, when you got right down to it, was, for the most part, not all that the word "life" promised; in fact it was pretty terrible, actually. It was so hazardous,

and so haphazard, and, and . . . it was just so meaningless.
Good happens whatever you do, bad happens whatever you do,
it all just flows; there's no intervention, not by man, not by
God, not by love, not by history. This was all very different
from what I'd been raised to believe: I had been taught that
people and actions matter, and virtue counts, and intervention
works; and that intervention by active and virtuous people can
and will change the world. This no longer seemed true. Good
men had died on that ship; their death was now being used to
attack a good cause; that good cause was counterattacking by
attacking those good dead men. No one had warned me the
setup was this damn cynical.

I opened the box. It had once contained white-ribbon fudge,
and it still smelled of sugar and nuts and vanilla and butter—a
kitcheny odor, familiar and soothing. I sniffed, although less to
enjoy the smell than to keep from weeping. For it seemed to me
at that moment that only the well-known contents of my
wooden box could offer me what I needed—the comfort of the
predictable, of the known, of the unsurprising. I dug, hungrily
and tearfully, into my scented treasures.

Most of the box was filled with newspaper clippings. A few,
hastily torn from the *Boston Globe,* were about me: poetry contests I had won; my prize-winning essay on the true meaning of
Christmas; a spelling bee conducted entirely in Latin. But these
were not, just now, what I needed; I wanted to escape myself,
not see myself praised. I kept on digging. I found several articles
on the architecture of Fenway Park, as well as the stubs from a
game I had gone to in early May. I'd had a terrible time at the
game, I remembered: I had felt guilty for being there, doing
something so flighty only two weeks after the sinking, plus
which I'd hated everyone else for *not* feeling guilty. But most of
all, I had felt sorry beyond belief for the stupid and innocent

Sumner who had been so happy to receive the tickets—long, long ago, as a Christmas present. I had envied him, too, and wished I could have his stupidity, and his innocence, back.

My Sobranie was ashes. I rose, brushed the dust into the street, tossed the butt into the bushes next door, and lit up another. Below the Fenway articles were my London journal and some Civil War medals of Grandfather's; also a note from Father, inviting me back to England "as soon as your mother permits." Under that was a letter from Pierce.

Pierce's letter had followed six lengthy missives from me, all sent—since I'd never gotten his home address—to the Naval Academy. His letter read as though he'd neglected to mail the first page; he had just begun writing, distant yet intimate, rambling and plaintive. Exactly as I remembered him.

I especially like the idea of your sending my mail in care of the Academy, since the Navy and the Post Office Department have a great deal in common, both managing to perform essential tasks in the most cumbersome manner possible. You certainly can continue writing there if you wish; however, my civilian address is on the envelope [Pierce lived in Georgetown]. Write to me c/o the Admiral; I believe he's the only one on the block. *He* certainly believes it.

Why is it I still live with the Admiral? you ask. I ask it too. They say the best tortures are often the simplest, and this I suppose is the best way to torture both him and myself. There is something about the look on my father's face when I drag myself home at seven a.m. that I find more precious than freedom. Or maybe coffee just naturally seems to taste better when somebody's watching your lips for the first blisters of syphilis.

We did have a bit of a man-to-man over my still being alive. I attempted explaining it was all your fault and I tried to die, Dad, honest I did. But he kept responding with allusions to the Spartans and the Carthaginians and the Charge of the Light Brigade, whom I can never keep straight one from the other. Gee, Pop, I said, would it square things if I filled up my pockets with rocks and took a nice dip in the Potomac? He replied with a quotation on the pleasures of conscience satisfied and duty well-tended. I never can tell whether he's quoting the Bible or Robert E. Lee.

In response to your question about novels: I think I read one once. Can't say I have a ready-made list of my twenty favorites, like you, though. As for what book I would take if I knew I'd be stuck on a desert island—well, I guess I'd take along a book about that particular island. Better yet, an atlas on what are some of the nearby islands and how do you get there. Truth is, I never much saw the point of fiction. Life seems unreal enough as it is. My mother read fiction, though, and look where it got her, mistaking the Admiral for Count Vronsky. Very serious error. I read aeronautics journals instead.

The flying continues! Most of it, of course, is not flying, it's mechanics—tightening one thing, loosening something else, smoothing, shearing, polishing, replacing. Five hours of fooling around on the ground for five minutes of fooling around in the air. Talk about a coy mistress!

I'm working on a new wing design which I hope lessens drag on the tail when you're going against the wind. Only moderate success so far—I'm getting very steep descents and taking too long to straighten out. This rather seems to be a metaphor for my life. Don't think anyone would go for the patent, do you?

A friend of mine, another flier, recently died. In flight, in the air. His name was Rex Stone. You may have heard of him. He set a record at the Albany Air Show this summer—he beat me to do it. Then we did a doubles routine together. That was June. Now it's August and he's dead.

I miss him a lot, Sumner. Sumner, I saw him die. He was trying a loop and he couldn't come out. He collided with a water tower and his head hit something. We couldn't tell what; it looked as though he had hit *everything*. If we hadn't known it was Rex, we wouldn't even have recognized him—his nose was smashed, something had poked out half his right eye, a lever was jammed in his throat. And that goddamn water tower didn't even collapse.

Will I be hearing from you again?

Your friend, Pierce

Your friend, Pierce. I put down the letter and walked to the window. The evening was hot, and as humid as Brazil, with ribbons of summertime lightning unspooling above the trees. Mother's meeting must just have ended; I could hear, from below, the singsong echo of voices saying good-bye—first Ivy, then Mrs. Northfield, then George with his murmured and private farewells to Marcella. I lowered the window and stuck the cigarettes under my pillow. Then I gathered the letter and clippings and boxed them back up.

My friend, Pierce. I removed the towels. What is the difference—or is there one?—between friendship and love? Love and desire? Desire and envy? I dreamed about Ivy every single night, my longing for her was as total as it was sharp; at the same time my envy of Pierce was so massive I dreamed of him too. Yet my longing for Ivy, my envy of Pierce—they were both nothing, nothing, compared to my new involvement with, interest in, this new guy—this dead friend, Rex. Had the situation been somewhat different, I wondered, how would Pierce think of me? Your friend, Pierce. My friend, Sumner. Was the price of a throttle jammed through my windpipe worth Pierce's writing to someone that he missed me? What if the person he wrote to about me was Ivy?

I unlocked the door and slipped into bed. I wanted to fall asleep fast, but I knew that would never happen; I was far too laden with despair ever to sleep again. I could hear Mother's shoes on the stairs. Her footsteps were firm and heavy: her stricture and exhortation mode. I remembered my earlier out-burst—surely no more appreciated now than when it happened —and sighed. Another person I loved and couldn't seem to impress—God, the list was becoming endless! No doubt all three of my sisters were on it, Father, Mother, Ivy (it goes without saying), Pierce (ditto), that goddamn Rex Stone, look-ing down from his flier's paradise . . . Quickly I buried myself under the sheets, artistically twisting the blankets around my ankles to suggest the unrest of total, heat-soaked exhaustion. Mother knocked on the door.

"Sumner, are you asleep?"

"Not really."

"I'd like to talk to you."

"I know what I said was wrong. I shouldn't have said it. I shouldn't have said anything. I'm sorry."

She opened the door, turned on the lamp, and sat down on the edge of my bed.

"I'd like to talk anyway," she said. "But not about dinner.

Though your outburst was understandable. Nobody blames you. Least of all me.''

I listened in doleful silence.

''I know this has been very trying for you,'' Mother continued. ''And I know you're troubled—deeply, terribly troubled —by everything that happened. You will be for a long time. You've had the misfortune, at a young age, to experience something most of us only read about—one of those monumental tragic events, like the eruption of Mount Vesuvius or the Lisbon earthquake. Things that are so terrible, so vast and so dreadful and so arbitrary that it's impossible not to wonder what conceivable purpose a loving God could have had, allowing such pain and woe.''

She hesitated for a few seconds, sighed deeply, and started talking again. ''I can't tell you why the *Titanic* sank and what it all means. I can't tell you if it means anything. I only can tell you what's in my heart. I've never told anyone this, but you need to know, and I should have told you sooner—I should have told you the instant I had you back in my arms.''

''Tell me what? There's nothing you need to have told me. There's nothing I don't already know about what I did.''

''It's not about you,'' she said. ''It's about me. From the very first moment I heard about the collision—from the very first *fraction* of the very first second—I had only one thought. Only one care, only one worry. Not for what 'Women and children first' would do to women's suffrage. Not for the other passengers. My only concern was whether my beloved son would be returned to me. And when I saw your name on the survivors' list . . .''

Mother stopped. She was crying. I had never known her like this—never known her in tears, never known her in pain, never known her in sorrow. After a few moments, she recovered.

''I believe, and will always believe, that women are equal to men in every way," she said. "And I further believe that men who refuse to acknowledge this—men like your grandfather—choose to deny this self-evident truth because they don't wish to be required to share political power with half the population of the planet. However . . ." She sighed, then continued. "However," she said, "it was men just like your grandfather who saved the women and children of the *Titanic*. Men of the opinion that women *are* children saved the *Titanic*'s women and children. I believe that these men were wrong in their views, terribly wrong—and yet, had they not held these views, they may not have so willingly sacrificed themselves; had they not held those views, I might be mourning my only son this very minute. So I'm left thanking men just like your grandfather for what they did, for whatever reason they chose to do it."

She took my hand, squeezed it, and said, "I'm so glad you're with us. I'm so happy you managed to live. Try to be happy yourself. Be thankful for what others did for you, but don't keep wondering whether you should have done it yourself. You shouldn't have. I couldn't have borne it if you had died. You did what was right. For the people who love you, you did what was right."

She lifted my hand, kissed it, and pressed it against her cheek; my fingers could still feel her tears. "Go to sleep now," she whispered. She rose, turned off the light, and quietly left my room. A few moments later, I heard her own door open and close.

I lay in the darkness, staring at the ceiling. I knew Mother's visit was meant to have comforted me, but its effect was the opposite; she had made me feel worse than ever. For she might be able to thank those poor dead heroes for choosing to die and leave it at that, but I couldn't; I knew exactly what it had taken for each of them to have made his choice, because I had faced it myself and had failed to make the correct one. Mother loved me, and so she was able to forgive me anything. But I despised myself, and so could forgive myself nothing.

I shuddered, flushed with a wave of self-loathing as burning as any fever.

Behind my closed door the house settled quietly. A handful of sleeping women: innocent, still. But not silent: no house is completely silent. I heard the stairs, creaking with ancient footsteps, heard the whisper of curtains, the thump of rollers on wooden rods. Bedsprings quivered; the Meeting House bell, down on Charles Street, tolled. I sat up, took off my pajama top, walked to the window, reopened it, walked back to bed. The air was so humid it could not dry even a nighttime sweat. I got back out of bed and lit a cigarette.

Then I lay down on the floor, closed my eyes, and put the Sobranie into my mouth. But at an awkward angle, as though someone were kneeling beside me, holding it for me. I took a drag and made myself cough. Then I gave a soft moan.

"Don't die, Rex," I said out loud.

My voice was too high; I lowered it.

"Don't die, Rex," I repeated. I tried to remember everything I could about Pierce's voice: its range, its softness, its smoker's rasp. Its extension of certain vowels. The patterns of speech: the run-on sentences, the flight metaphors.

"Please don't," I whispered.

"How is he?" I pictured Ivy asking.

"He's dying," Pierce answered. He picked up my right hand. Ivy pressed my left hand to her cheek.

"Don't leave us," she whispered. "We need you. We're nothing without you."

I had been flying Pierce's biplane over the Common, dropping leaflets. "Women of Boston! The men of the *Titanic* died for humanity! Do not let their deaths further your slavery!"

Then I had looped the plane. The small craft quivered, dipping. I had tried to pull out, but I couldn't, I couldn't . . .

"It's all my fault," my Pierce-voice whispered. "You were testing my new design . . ."

My throat felt as though I had swallowed flaming petroleum. But I couldn't die and leave him with that much guilt. "No, it was a good design," I croaked.

"You're dying a martyr to a noble cause," Pierce said. But then I cringed—not even in imagination would Pierce come up with a line like that. "Your death's a bloody, pointless waste," Pierce said instead. "I must be bad luck. All the people I care for keep dropping like flies, while the ones I don't like hang on forever."

I stood up. I had not even gotten to Ivy's farewell, which was, after all, what this whole scene led up to—my telling her how I'd felt from the moment I saw her, her telling me—no! I must stop it this instant! This was pathetic! This was sick! I would *not* mock Rex Stone's memory with my fantasies! Out, out, had to get out. Out where? Anywhere—just out of this room. Quickly I slipped out of my nightclothes and got dressed. I grabbed my Sobranies and tiptoed down the hall and stairs.

At the front door, however, I paused to consider. I had never been on the street this late—what if somebody hurt me? Worse yet, what if somebody *saw* me? Saw me, recognized me, came back home, woke my mother. . . . Doing this was madness. Madness was why I was doing it. I opened the door and breathed in the silence.

God, warm nights in cold climates! The air felt like wet tissue, like warm blood; like the air—or so I imagined—in a Turkish bath. Soft, heavy, thick: it was like trying to breathe through the camphor-soaked washcloths Mother once placed on my face for bronchitis. Only instead of the sting of camphor, this air smelled of gardens; instead of sickness and nursing, this smelled of flowers, and the tang of the river, and the must of three-hundred-year-old trees. The simple fact that I was standing here instead of lying in bed transformed even the heat; instead of an irritation, it was a gift. Seduced by the night's hot sweetness, I stepped outside. It was just after midnight.

Because I had never done, or thought about doing, what I was doing now, I had no idea where I should go. I concocted several possibilities, but each, for some reason, was flawed: it would take me till dawn to get over to Cambridge; strange people slept under Longfellow Bridge; even those tobacconists over by the State House—those catering to the most hardened of addicts—would be closed at this hour. I decided to walk toward the Charles River. I closed the front gate and stepped into the street.

One pace and the whole block exploded. Beacon Hill, all cobblestones, iron, and brick, was constructed by people not given to midnight strolls; it is rife with patches of easily triggered nocturnal echoes. I took a fresh step, this one on tiptoe: stones groaned, gates creaked. An orangey cat, also on tiptoe, sashayed past. The air was as mellow as cooling caramel. I followed the cat into Louisburg Square, that green inlet park set like the tiniest emerald between Pinckney and Mount Vernon streets. The square abounded with kittens and cats.

So this is where cats go at night! They looked as though they'd assembled for some sort of feline convention. I had never seen this many cats in my life. I even saw some I recognized, including a trio who, after a decade of receiving top cream on the back steps, and tummy pats, and neck rubs, deigned to acknowledge me; they purred amiably and noisily from their bivouac at the foot of the Columbus statue. A strange and unusual pleasure, affirmation by cats. Darkness and cats and statues: a good Gothic writer really could cook with this scene. But Louisburg Square was so familiar to me it could never seem threatening, not even now, at this ready-made witching hour. Instead I gloomily thought about all of the innocent hours I'd happily spent here, reading in warm green shade, dozing in autumn shadows. Once I had fallen asleep, short-sleeved and knickered in summer sunshine, and winter had come while I napped: I had awoken covered with leaves, the temperature frigid, all the birds in the city departed till April. All in under an hour. Another time I had tripped over somebody's lilac, playing catch with Marcella and George.

I walked the length of the square, emerging on Mount Vernon Street. In a way I knew Mount Vernon Street better than any other, including my own: it was the first "foreign" street Mother had let me visit, my toddler's hand fearfully clutched into Julia's gloved one. A few years later Cornelia had muddled me totally by telling me this was *the* Mount Vernon, where Washington lived ("The lights of Liberty brightly burnin' / While he sits 'midst the bricks of old Mount Vernon"). I passed my hand along a certain cast-iron gate, rough burrs grazing my open palm. I had touched this gate so often I knew the location of every defect—knew even before it scratched just when it would happen, could brace myself for its metal tickle. Upstairs in one of the houses, behind a pane of the famous Beacon Hill purple glass, a lamp burned and flickered. Violet light splashed onto the sidewalk. I felt like an actor standing just outside the reach of the houselights, awaiting my cue.

I had received my cue by the time I reached Charles Street. I was *not* to go to the river. Instead I turned left, walked down to Beacon Street, crossed the intersection (utterly empty but look both ways anyway), and entered the grassy shadows of Boston Common.

Even in darkness the air appeared green. Trees rustled, and the deserted benches were covered with whispering leaves. I looked at the sky. It was thick with constellations. I thought of

Rex Stone splattering out of that sky, and forced myself to imagine his face—what remained of it, anyway—as anyone else's but mine. I thought of Charles Sumner. I thought of Ivy. I thought of Pierce. The park was crowded with ghosts of people I'd rather be.

God, isn't there such a thing as a second chance?

I moved deeper into the Common, and lit a Sobranie. Up ahead in the darkness, and exposed by the flare of my match, I glimpsed what looked like a small raised stage. Curious—and relieved to discover I could still feel curious about anything—I hurried forward. The object towered above my head, and as I approached, it turned white and bulky, bulging within the darkness like a grand piano covered with sheets. For a horrified instant I thought I was seeing an iceberg.

Then I recognized what it must be. Bundled in yards of fluttering muslin, protected from interested eyes and unlikely rain, this was the *Titanic* memorial statue, delivered by night for next Saturday morning's unveiling.

I edged toward the covered monument. The sheets were draped and extensively tucked, but not tacked down; one good tug and they'd fall. I looked around. The Common was empty. No one but me—me and this statue commemorating the single most notable moment in my existence.

I put out one cigarette and instantly lit another. I tried telling myself this was my monument as much as—if not, indeed, more than—almost anyone else's; certainly it was my privilege to see it whenever I wanted. But I knew this wasn't exactly true, and I definitely had no special right to see it this very second. Still . . .

By now I had made enough feints and shuffles and half steps to be standing directly in front of the statue, so close to the edge of a sheet that I could have ignited it with my Sobranie. I lifted my hand. Let it fall. Lifted again. Lowered again. This was not a good thing to do, I realized; it was also illegal, probably. But legality seemed so trivial, so petty, so minor-league, in the Rex Stone scheme of things. I lifted my hand a third time, and tugged. The sheets fell away in a pile of blue-white cotton.

Unswathed, the monument was smaller than I had expected —seven feet high at the most, plus a narrow slab. There were three human figures, and a lifeboat. The tallest figure was a man. He stood with one foot on the edge of the boat and the other in a crest of raging marble water. His face was calm, beatific, and his attire, an evening jacket much like the one Pierce had worn, was spotless. He was smiling at the woman, who stood in the middle of the lifeboat weeping tears of stone and helpless despair. One arm reached out to the man; the other cradled her swaddled, sleeping baby. That was it.

Except for the slab. Carved into its side were a date, and nine words.

APRIL 15, 1912. OUT OF DEATH, HONOR ETERNAL. WOMEN AND CHILDREN FIRST.

I looked at the statue from all four sides. Observations, objections, and rebuttals bounced at once into consciousness, and I warned myself not to examine any of them, only to look: not to judge, not to think, not to feel, not to remember. But it was a meaningless warning, because I remembered constantly, and I never remembered a scene like this. A man, a woman, a baby, a lifeboat—it didn't even make sense. It was as maudlin and garish and simpleminded and tasteless as it could possibly be.

And yet it was perfectly accurate.

I climbed onto the slab and covered the statue; climbed off the slab and covered it too. I wished I could cry but I felt too exhausted; if I let myself start, I wouldn't have the strength to stop—not tonight, not ever. I turned from the monument and started to walk.

After about three minutes I came to the leaf-covered benches. Ivy was sitting there.

Happiness—that now-so-unfamiliar emotion—collided with utter shock; for a second I thought I had conjured a spirit. Would Pierce appear next? I blinked, almost expecting, when I opened my eyes, to see the bench once again empty. But no, it was Ivy, still dressed as she'd been at the dinner, still wearing that same expression of unfamiliar unease.

"What are you doing here?" I asked her. "I thought you'd gone back to New York! I heard you saying good-bye."

"Changed my mind," she said, and patted the bench. "Sit down."

I sat. "How long have you been here?" I asked.

"A while. I was at the station and just about ready to board when I started thinking . . . maybe someone should take a look. In case there was anything really horrible we needed to know about."

"There isn't," I said. "I mean, it's mawkish and all, but not really awful."

"That's what I thought too."

"You mean you looked?"

"Like you," she said, nodding. "Just a peek."

I crumbled a couple of leaves. "Do you think about it a lot?" I asked. "Not about the statue, but about—about what happened. About that night. Because I think about it all the time."

"Well, that's only natural," she said, her voice coolly brisk. "It was a major event in your life. In all our lives. I'm sure we all think about it a lot."

That's not what I mean, I thought. I mean I think about what happened *with you and me*. How instead of being a hero, I was a greedy and terrified coward. How in one second I lost any chance I might have for your—all right, not love, love was too much to ask, not for your love but for you to respect me, admire me, *notice* me . . .

"That's not what I mean," I said. "It's not just how tragic it was and how scary it felt. I mean I look back at how I acted and I look back at everyone else—I think about you and Pierce coming to my cabin to save me—you and him in the lifeboat . . . Mr. Phillips . . . Jack. . . . Everyone did what was right except me. But I didn't want to die."

"I didn't want to die, either," said Ivy. She leaned back on the bench. Her hair, curly and heavily netted, cushioned her head.

"But I should have," she added.

I was so astonished I leapt off the bench. "Should have died?" I cried. "Why?"

"It's all in that poem," she answered calmly. "They're right. We can't say we want equality and then say we want it at this point but not at that point. Equality means all points. I should have died for what I believe in."

I sat back down. It had never occurred to me that Ivy's behavior that endless night had been anything less than perfect— that she might feel guilt, or remorse, or anything, really, save the grief we all felt for the people who died. And now to discover . . . ! I shuddered. No tragedy is ever worse for the living than for the dead, but this one was coming close. I gazed at her heavy hair. Let me help you with this, I thought, let me save you. I saved nobody then, let me save you now. Ivy—be my second chance.

"You wouldn't have furthered the cause for women," I said, "by dying. You can't think if only you'd given some man your place, it'd have made any difference—Mother's right, that's an insult to everyone. It reduces pure valor to arithmetic.''

"That's not what I'm saying. I'm saying I'm female and if men were dying then women should have been dying too. I'm not saying I had to want to. I'm saying I should have been willing to. That's all. And now it's too late.''

I looked at the draped memorial, pictured its pitching lifeboat. APRIL 15, 1912. HONOR ETERNAL. WOMEN AND CHILDREN FIRST . . . What a cruel forum. What a challenge, what a setting, how unyielding and fierce a crucible to prove yourself in! I looked up at the stars. How could I help her, what solace could I suggest? Every hour, every minute since I had entered that lifeboat I had been trying to comfort myself and had come up with nothing; what could I offer to Ivy that I couldn't even offer myself? If I could go back there, back to the ship, what would I do? Would I still get in line for a lifeboat? I probably would. Would Ivy? I hoped so. Should I tell her that? No . . . what difference would that make, what good would that do her, what help would that possibly be?

But what *would* help? What *would* do her good? What *would* make a possible difference?

Then something happened. Or, rather, *nothing* happened. Nothing *was*. It was like the night that we danced, the night that we sank, lying in bed, noting the engines—noting there *were* no engines, noting the engines had stopped. I felt like that now. For I had just realized, in this silent process of questions, this silent process of trying to conjure up something to ease Ivy's sorrow, that my own sorrow—so constant, so ceaseless, so unrelenting—had ceased and relented. Ceased and departed. Gone.

And would it return? Maybe not if I helped her. I cleared my throat.

"But what happens," I asked, "if dying's not good enough?"

She turned toward me.

"What if it isn't enough?" I said. "What if you die and whatever you died for still needs you?"

She shook her head. "I know what you're trying to do, Sumner," she said, "and it's very sweet. Only it isn't true."

"But it is true," I said. "Being heroic: it's not always lifeboats and icebergs and statues—and Pierces and Charles Sumners. It's little things too. It's kindness. It's goodness. It's everyday effort and everyday sweat. We can't change the fact we didn't die. But you—we—we can keep trying to do the little things right. Over and over and over again. In the everyday world. Where you don't die—you don't even get noticed. Where everyday people live."

She was silent for what seemed centuries. I let myself look at her starlit face. Her expression was vague—not exactly agreeing (I can't honestly say *I* exactly agreed) but, somehow . . . respectful. Like Pierce on the dance floor, observing my choice of partner: respect that this child, whose thoughts and opinions had barely, if ever, impressed her, had managed a sharpness she simply had never expected. Then she smiled. Perhaps, in this second of pure surprise, she too had forgotten her grief.

Though perhaps not. Perhaps she merely was doing a kindness—a little thing right in the everyday world. Perhaps we both were.

When she finally spoke, it was her usual voice. Crisp, self-assured, self-reliant, a little impatient—the way she had spoken in London, spoken to me when we danced. "Interesting," she said. "If you can't make a big difference one day, you're stuck making little ones every day. Well, I don't know. But I'll think it over."

She rose; I did too. "It's late," she said. "You'd better start heading home. And I'd better get back to the station."

"Would you mind if I walked with you?"

She put out her hand; touched mine; squeezed it. "It would give me," she said, "the greatest pleasure."

For the everyday world, it was a triumph. We walked arm in arm through the warm green night, speaking, gratefully, of everyday things.

AFTERWORD

IVE YEARS AFTER THE SINKING OF THE *TITANIC*, THE UNITED States entered the First World War. Sumner enlisted in the Army Air Corps two months later, after graduating from high school. By the time he reached France, however, most of the air war was over. He became a flight instructor and remained in Europe for several years. He then returned home.

When the Second World War broke out in Europe, he went back and tried to enlist in the Royal Air Force. Considered too old—and too American—he again became an instructor. Following the massive losses of the first four weeks of the Battle of Britain, he was temporarily activated and flew combat missions until October of 1940. He served as heroically as everyone else.

When the war ended he went back to Boston to resume everyday life.